HEAVEN SENT

BOOK THREE
VENGEANCE

JL ROTHSTEIN

COPYRIGHT

The characters and events portrayed in this book are fictitious. Any similarity to real persons, living or dead, is coincidental and not intended by the author.

No part of this book may be reproduced, or stored in a retrieval system, or transmitted in any form or by any means, electronic, mechanical, photocopying, recording, or otherwise, without express written permission of the publisher.

Cover design by Jeff Brown

Printed in the United States of America

DEDICATION

I dedicate this book to those I have loved and lost over the past few years. To my mother, Muriel, who was not healthy at the time my first book came out and passed away soon after. I know she would have very much enjoyed it. An avid reader, she would have laughed at her daughter writing a fantasy series with characters named after her nine grandchildren.

To my husband's aunt Gilda. A book lover and enthusiastic supporter of the arts. You made a difference to the lives of the people you touched. Your generous spirit will not soon be forgotten.

What a blessing it was to have them both in our lives and how heartbroken we are to have to say goodbye. We'll steady ourselves with the knowledge we will be with them again one day.

ACKNOWLEDGMENTS

Thank you to Beth Dorward, my Editor and Mentor. I have learned so much on this journey with you.

Many thanks to Jeff Brown who designed the covers for all three of the books in my Heaven Sent series.

As always, special thanks to my husband, Alan. Your love and partnership in this endeavor means the world to me.

To my sister Grace, your unwavering support and abundant guidance is so appreciated.

"Vengeance is in my heart, death in my hand, blood and revenge are hammering in my head."

William Shakespeare, Titus Andronicus

CHAPTER ONE

The metallic aftertaste of blood lingered in Kelly O'Mara's mouth, a crude reminder of an earlier fight that morning. Her arm ached from a deep gash barely sealed and slow to heal. There was a throbbing pain that clobbered both sides of her head. Hunger rolled through her like a windswept ocean tumbling over on itself. The air was crisp, the smell of firewood tinged with death.

She locked eyes with the vampire standing before her. His hair a simple crew cut. His clothing rumpled and stained. His second iris a screaming blood thirsty red. He didn't pause long to take in the magnitude of the dead vampire that lay between them. He swung for Kelly's head and missed. Grabbing his arm Kelly pulled him toward the ground. With his momentum already projecting him forward he fell.

Kelly took the spear and stabbed his right ear.

"No!" The vampire screeched as he swatted wildly at his head.

Panicked, the vampire bucked and grabbed the pipe end of the weapon and yanked it from his ear. He staggered onto his feet and made it a yard or two before collapsing once more. Digging his nails into the ground he crawled away from her. Reaching a nearby tree he managed to painstakingly claw his way back to a standing position. Slowly he turned to face her.

"You think you've accomplished something here today?" Demonic liquid sprang from his eyes and dribbled down his face as he stood breathless. Covered in varying shades of red, he was a grisly hellish rainbow. "It's too late, Guardian. We've already won."

CHAPTER TWO

Five Days Earlier

The pounding headache would not abate no matter how many donuts Kelly consumed. Sitting on the tar covered roof of an old building she gazed over the city. It was peaceful under the moonglow with streaks of iridescent light casting Boston in milky shadows. The view did nothing to mask the smell of fast food and lingering exhaust fumes from cars now long gone.

The city's streets were essentially paved cow paths. During the day the honking of horns was a melodic tune of angst over its narrow streets, difficult navigation, and double-parked cars. Tonight all was quiet as the city slept.

Kelly stared up at the starless sky and sighed. Rumpling an empty bakery bag she formed a make-shift ball and tossed it into the air. It sailed upward and then arced landing in a nearby bucket.

The building she sat atop once housed a local furniture company. After a fire ravaged the interior, the business closed never to reopen its doors. During hot summer days the faint smell of paint fumes and burnt pine hovered in the air. Today was no such day. It was after midnight in September and the nighttime air was cool. Kelly shivered, but not from the descending chill.

Kelly pulled her knees up to her chest and rested against them, contemplating the past. *I was trapped in Hell and tortured by a fallen Arch Angel.*

Closing her eyes, she tried to think back to that time only forty years ago. Not long when compared to the two hundred and twenty-eight years she had been walking this planet guarding humans from demonic intrusion. As much as she tried, no memories of the event came to her.

Damn you, Antonio!

Warmth came from her left signaling her brother Dan's aura. Streaks of yellow light splashed across the blackened rooftop and within seconds Dan stepped out from within them.

"No food?" he asked as Kelly huddled on the ground. "Should I go get some?"

Kelly shook her head. Dan walked over and sat next to her.

"How did you know to find me here?" she asked.

"Kelly, you and I have had more talks on this rooftop than I can count. There's something about this skyline that helps you. You're able to stop and take a breath up here before you force yourself back into the fray."

They sat with that understanding as they gazed out over the glistening landscape.

Dan broke the silence first. "So, how many donuts did you eat?"

Kelly squinted her eyes at her brother. He wore jeans, a black T-shirt and sported a five o'clock shadow.

"What makes you think I ate donuts?" Kelly asked him. "I would have gotten rid of the evidence if I had."

Dan smiled. "Well, that's the thing about honey dipped donuts. The smell kind of lingers." He paused. "That and you have white flakes on your sweatshirt."

Kelly swatted away small shards of crusted sugar. "Ugh, there is no hiding things from you."

"Since when do you want to hide things from me?" Dan's shoulders lifted as his palms turned outward. "I'm your favorite brother."

"True." Kelly smiled. "That means you know the sugar did not make me feel better."

"I do, but I know you have to do it. It's part of how you process things."

Kelly sighed and fidgeted with the ring on her left hand. "I guess it is."

"Still toying with removing that ring Jared put on your finger?"

"I already tried," Kelly confessed. "I knew it was bound, but I did it anyway. I don't know why."

"Because you're as stubborn as a mule."

Kelly elbowed him in the side and chuckled. "Don't start with me."

"Me?" Dan said with a slight lilt to his voice. "I would never."

"Why did you come? Was it to drag me back to the beach house?'

"I'm here because you needed me to be."

Kelly's eyes watered and instead of flippantly answering she simply rested her head on his shoulder. "Yeah, I guess I'll always need my big brother."

"No need to go implying you're that much younger than me."

Kelly smiled. "I didn't mean it that way."

"I know."

"I'm glad you came. Thank you."

"No need. You would have done it for me."

They sat peering out over the cityscape with no words between them, just a momentary pause in an otherwise chaotic world.

Kelly lifted her head off Dan's shoulder. "Antonio's betrayal, it's just so raw. I trusted him and I told everyone else they should too."

"There was no reason for you not to trust him."

"How could he remove memories? How could he do something like that to me, to Deb, to any of us?" Kelly's heart broke a little more with every thought of her friend lying to her all this time. "I have been friends with him for forty years."

No, that's not right. Kelly tried to backtrack in

time and count the years but stopped.

"I don't even know how long we've been friends because he took memories from me!" Kelly rambled on. "On top of that, he knew how hard we were all taking the loss of Gabriel and Jared and still he said nothing, he did nothing! I fought alongside him in battle! He knew me, we were more than allies, we were actual friends!" Kelly took a sharp intake of air and after a moment she confessed. "I don't know what to do with this anger."

"Why do you need to do something with it? Maybe let it run its course, learn to sit with it for a while."

"What, in hopes of letting it go?" Kelly mocked. "Like there is such a thing."

"There is," Dan said flatly. "You'll have to let it go eventually, Kell."

"I don't know if I can do that. I wouldn't even know where to begin."

"I would say one day at a time." Dan smirked. "But I'm sitting too close to you and don't want to get punched."

Kelly's shoulders relaxed and she sat back against the wall staring out at the skyline once more.

"When do you think we need to go back?" Kelly asked.

"We'll know," Dan answered.

***

Gen's brothers tried coaxing her away from Xavier's lifeless body, but she wouldn't budge. Her chin lay against Xavier's forehead as she slowly rocked. Her tear-soaked face stared down at the bloodied sand beneath them.

How could this have happened? I can't do this. Maybe Deb was right, maybe we've been the only ones following all the rules and now look what it's cost.

The flapping of wings from above announced more Arch Angels were arriving. They were here to escort Xavier to Heaven.

I'm not ready to let go,

The angels would perform a ceremonial procession as they did when Antonio retrieved Jacob's body. Their numbers broke the remaining cloaking that had encompassed the beach.

The small cottage was barely recognizable. The windows were shattered, the cornucopia of colorful lounge chairs smashed. Part of the deck railing hung precariously over the side banging against the wooden floorboards every time the bay breeze swooped in.

We lost, Gen thought. *We've never known loss like today.*

"What's going on?!" Kelly's voice rang out over the beach.

Gen locked eyes with her sister. "He's gone." Gen's voice was barely a whisper. "She killed Xavier."

Kelly ran toward Gen and fell to the sand on the other side of Xavier's body. "No. This can't be." Kelly clasped Xavier's hand and wept. "I'm so sorry brother."

Her voice cracked as she spoke. "Who did this?"

Antonio reached down and touched Kelly's shoulder. "Please, let us take him home."

Kelly's head snapped to her left and she slapped Antonio's hand away. "Don't you touch him."

Quick to her feet the mood on the beach became instantly confrontational. Kelly's eyes fell upon her brothers' grief-stricken faces.

"What happened after I left?" Kelly asked through gritted teeth.

Antonio attempted to answer. "The vampires attacked–"

"Shut up!" Kelly yelled. "I don't want to hear anything from you right now."

Gen continued to sob. *I already had to live through the loss of Gabe. That was bad enough. This is beyond painful.*

Michael stepped forward. "Wrath and the vampires attacked from the beach. We tried to hold the high ground, but they kept coming. The beach was overrun. Eventually a portal opened, and Azza came through it. Somehow, we think with the help of Wrath, her wings were restored. Xavier was closest to her and attacked. He sliced her wing and drew blood. As he hoisted his weapon to strike once more, she thrust her wing forward and slashed his chest."

Gen's moans returned. "She killed him, Kelly. Azza murdered Xavier."

"You did this Antonio!" Kelly pointed her finger at the Arch Angel. "This is your fault!"

"She's right," Michael added. "You've been

keeping things from us. How did Azza get that portal open? She was in Hell for forty years. What changed? Was it Jacob's ring? You wouldn't tell us why Wrath took it, but Jacob's ring helped restore Azza's wings, didn't it?"

Antonio's face crumpled in distress. "I did what I was ordered."

"Stop it!" Kelly shouted. "For once, just tell us what's really going on. Tell us the truth."

"I didn't know what Wrath could do with Jacob's ring," Antonio confessed. "I told the magistrate about Jacob's hand being cut off."

"Where is the magistrate?" Tom asked as he walked past Gen to stand alongside Kelly. "Why don't you go get her. I believe our brothers murder qualifies as urgent."

Gen's brothers crept closer to Kelly. *They're getting in defensive formation,* Gen thought as her siblings built a warrior's wall between her and Antonio. *These are fighting lines.*

"I can't," Antonio said emphatically.

"Can't or won't?" Kelly seethed.

"She's gone." Antonio's hands sprung out before him. "We don't know where she is."

"Hell's first army has been unleashed on Earth." Michael's voice grew cold. "Your magistrate is either a victim or an accomplice in Azza's plan, but right now the humans are the priority. We will fight alongside the Arch Angels to defeat Hell. The consequences of your betrayal on this family will have to wait until that's done."

Dan stepped between the two groups. "You should go Antonio. Let another Arch Angel escort our brother."

"I trusted you!" Kelly yelled over Dan's shoulder. "We all did."

Antonio's wings burst forth and he shot up from the beach without another word.

"What do we do now?" Gen asked. "How are we supposed to just go on after this, not to mention Deb."

"What do you mean?" Kelly asked. "Where is Deb? Is she with Dmitri?"

"No," Frankie answered. "Dmitri went looking for Jade. During the battle Deb was on the deck, keeping the demons from entering the house. Then Vermillion showed up."

What?!" Kelly shrieked. "Why would he come back?"

"We don't know," Frankie told her. "But we think it has something to do with Jade. We think Vermillion sent Deb to Hell. If the Accord wasn't already broken, and it should have been when they killed Jacob, it's certainly shattered now."

"No," Kelly said breathlessly. "You actually think Deb's in Hell?"

"Yes." Gen gingerly handed Xavier's body over to a female Arch Angel who had walked up from the shoreline. The Arch Angel nodded at Gen and then slowly stepped backward. A male Arch Angel stepped between them draping Xavier's body in a purple cloak.

The female slowly ascended, her feet pointing toward the sandy shoreline she left behind. The other Arch Angels followed in formation, their lit torches guiding them toward Heaven.

The O'Mara siblings lined up with their arms wrapped around each other as they peered upward. Praying and saying goodbye to their fallen brother. When the firelight in the sky dwindled to a mere speck, they let their arms fall free to leave the beach.

"We're heading to Michael's," Dan announced. "Come when you're ready."

Gen nodded as her brothers disappeared into varying shades of their colorful auras.

Kelly walked over and grabbed Gen's hand. "I'm sorry."

"For what?" Gen asked her.

"I should have been here."

"Don't do that to yourself. Blame and guilt will get us nowhere as Harry would say."

"Where is Harry?" Kelly asked. "And what happened to Jade?"

"Harry took Gerry, Lacey, and Gardenia to another safe house, if there is such a thing nowadays," Gen told her. "No idea where Jade is. Vermillion took her from the deck, Dmitri soon followed, probably trying to trace their movements."

"How do we get Deb back?" Kelly asked.

"We don't. We have to have faith she can get herself out," Gen answered. "Hell's first army is restored and roaming Earth. Saving humanity is our mission."

"We're going to hunt down the vampires." Kelly commented.

"Yeah," Gen said. "Because that's why we're here."

CHAPTER THREE

A rancid odor assaulted Deb's nose as the roamer demon looming over her inched closer.

Deb's heart hammered inside her chest. She didn't know if it was hot where she landed or if the searing heat was coming from the massive burns that covered her body.

"Cat got your tongue, Guardian." Schlosser coughed and then continued. "I have to admit, I didn't think you would come alone." The demon pointed at her face. "I thought you would bring that crazy one with the long dark hair. She must want revenge on Azza."

"Kelly?" Her sister's name fell from her lips.

"Yeah, that one." Schlosser nodded. "You seem a little frail, but hey, you are the one sleeping with Marcus, so I guess the solo act fits."

"What are you doing here?" Deb refused to take the bait.

"I'm supposed to be here." Schlosser derided as

wheeziness plagued him. "You must have had one heck of a head scramble if you don't know where you are."

"Hell." The word snapped Deb back to the reality of her circumstance. "I'm here for Marcus. Where is he?"

"Really! You don't say." Schlosser scoffed. "I thought you were here for the ambiance."

Ignoring his sarcasm, Deb walked around the demon. She made her way toward an opening on the far wall that was illuminated thanks to the fire Schlosser had ignited upon her entry.

"I wouldn't walk out there if I were you." The demon nearly cooed the words.

"I didn't come all this way to be stuck with you." Deb limped forward. "Besides, aren't you a pariah down here after your betrayal and subsequent marking?"

Everything hurts, she thought in a haze. *My skin is ravaged, my leg is messed up, and I have no idea where I'm going.*

"None of that matters. What matters is that I can find him. Maybe, if you ask nicely, I might even be able to find some salve to put on those wounds. Some of them look pretty nasty."

"Now you're the friendly demon?" Deb continued toward the doorway but stopped when a noise came from beyond the cell like space.

"Oh!" Schlosser mocked. "Don't mind the pitter patter of feet, that's just the hellhounds coming to rip you to shreds."

She stared at the demon not sure what to make of that statement. He returned her stare. His ghoulish smile revealed crooked teeth and a decaying gumline. As she paused to think about how much to trust his comment the thumping grew louder. Whatever was coming was fast approaching.

"Tick tock, Guardian." Schlosser mimed pointing at a watch he wasn't wearing. "No time to waste."

"How do you propose we get away from them?" Deb asked.

"Good choice. I was beginning to think you were going to try and navigate Hell on your own and that would be a disaster, albeit an amusing one."

"Spit it out demon." Deb turned her wrist in a circular motion for the demon to speed things up.

"Break my prison cuffs and I can teleport us out of here and away from the hounds."

As the pounding became a roar Deb instinctively projected her shield.

"Stop!" he yelled. "What are you trying to do, get us killed? Using your powers down here is like putting a light on in a dark room. You might as well be broadcasting your exact location to every enemy you have down here."

I can't trust him. I should just run out of this room right now.

She shuffled back over to his position and paused. After a moment of inner turmoil, she took a chance and dropped her shield. The thunderous running from beyond the room slowed.

Schlosser held his shackled wrists up for Deb to shatter the cuffs that imprisoned him.

"How do I know you won't just leave me here?" Deb asked.

"You don't." He smiled and her head jerked back from the stench.

Deb reached down and pulled the chain apart snapping it in half in her hands. The pounding in the hallway started again. Deb yanked the chain of chaos free from Schlosser's leg. The demon let out a curse as he grabbed the jagged piece from her hand and threw it across the room.

Deb tried not to focus on the monstrous panting sounds of the beasts that were coming for her. Before she could yell at Schlosser to teleport, he grabbed her forcefully by the upper arm and they left the room in a haze of smoke.

The two of them landed in a hallway, the running no longer audible. The walls were made of jagged rock with cold, dirt-covered brick beneath their feet. Old style wrought iron torches dotted one wall. Schlosser seemed to slither away, and Deb followed slowly behind him.

"Where are we going?" she asked.

"Shhh," he demanded. "We don't want to announce ourselves."

When he got to the end of the hallway he turned right and disappeared. As she reached the corner and made the turn, she half expected him to be gone. He wasn't. The large space opened and in the center of it was an enormous trench of molten lava. Off to the right Schlosser was bent over picking through something on the floor.

As she neared his position the burned parts of her skin screamed in pained protest. *Like taking a hot shower after a sunburn.* She moved to her right to get away from the moat of liquid fire.

The demon pulled a pair of ripped jeans free from the pile and tossed them at her. Before bending over to pick them up a pair of black sneakers followed, along with a muscle T-shirt, oversized denim jersey, and several worn out socks.

Schlosser pulled off the bloodied oversized cotton shirt that hung loosely around his frame and tossed it into the pile. His back and shoulders were covered in red welts and partially healed wounds. He grabbed a dark green shirt and a pair of heavy boots and put them on.

He pointed at the floor. "Beggars can't be choosers, Guardian."

"What is this place?" Deb asked. "Why are there random pieces of clothing on the floor."

"Don't ask questions you don't want the answers to, Guardian."

"I won't. Now tell me whose clothes these are?"

"Isn't it obvious? This is a Hell Fire pit," Schlosser snapped. "These are the clothes of the damned. They're stripped naked before being thrown in."

Deb tried to push the ghoulish image of human souls being tossed into Hell Fire out of her mind. She reached down and put the clothes on that Schlosser had tossed at her. The sneakers were too big, she assumed that's what the extra socks were for, to help anchor them to her feet.

"Do you know where Marcus is or was that just a ruse to get me to free you?"

"Of course I know where he is, we shared the same cell."

"He was in that room we just came from?" Deb wailed. "You liar, take me back to him."

"Did you see him in the room?!" Schlosser barked. "They took him away before you got here."

"Do you know where he is or not?" Deb went to cross her arms in protest, but the burns hurt too much to make the aggravated pose.

"He's most likely on the torture table." Schlosser turned and walked away.

"Why don't we just teleport again?"

"You want me to teleport us inside the persecution room?" Schlosser stopped and turned back to face her. "You're not the bright one, are you?"

"I assume we can get close enough to sneak in." Deb brushed off the insult.

"That's the plan. First, we need weapons and rations if we can find them."

"Weapons are all we need."

"Speak for yourself, Guardian. You may not eat–" Schlosser looked her up and down. "*ever* from the looks of it, but I plan on saving my strength for the trek."

"Wait," she insisted. "You mean you can't teleport out of here?"

Schlosser choked on a laugh. "There are only three ways out of Hell. I would have assumed you did some research before coming here."

"Yes, of course," Deb said sarcastically. "I read all the brochures."

Schlosser huffed and stopped to stare into her eyes. His beady black pupils seemingly boring into her very soul making her skin crawl. The mark around his neck that she and her sisters had branded him with before the Horsemen took him away was damaged. Thick scars covered large parts of his neck where wounds were closed but not completely healed.

He looks like he's no stranger to the torture table himself. I pray he's wrong and hope Marcus is not suffering, but I fear he may be facing a similar fate as Schlosser.

"Well, you're as unprepared as you are ugly." he sneered.

"I didn't know you had such discerning taste, demon."

"You're disgusting, all skin and bones." Schlosser's body shook in exaggerated fashion. "All humans and human forms repulse me."

Deb's anger flared. She hit him square in the chest with her shield knocking him back several feet.

"Alright, alright. Don't get yourself all worked up. I already told you it's not a good idea to use your powers down here. Stop advertising where we are.

You're going to get us caught."

"Just get to the point. How do we get out of Hell once we get Marcus?"

"I already told you, there are only three ways out." Schlosser held up his forefinger indicating he was going to count as he spoke. "One, you make a trade to get pulled out."

"No one is going to make a deal that helps someone from Heaven get out of Hell."

"Correct!" Schlosser agreed in earnest. "Maybe you're not as dumb as I thought you were, Guardian. Second, you sneak out through one of the gates in purgatory." Schlosser paused. "But we both know that won't work after your bitch sister ratted me out to the horsemen. Thanks to Genevieve O'Mara purgatory has additional security now."

"You deserved it. What's the last option?"

"You fight your way out."

"Fight our way out?" Deb asked confused.

"Yeah, right onto the floor of the Pit and up the cliffside to freedom."

"*The* Pit?" Deb asked accentuating the first word.

"There is only one Pit, Guardian. Surely, you remember where your precious brother in-law and friends have been all this time."

"What do you need me for?" Deb stood her ground refusing to follow him any further until he answered. "You know the way, but yet you're helping me which means you need something. What is it?"

"You're catching on pretty quick, Guardian. Maybe there's hope for you yet."

"Well, what is it?" Deb asked. "I'm not taking one more step until you tell me."

"I will help you get Marcus, no guarantees about his condition, in exchange for your help with the key."

"I'm almost afraid to ask." Deb paused.

"Don't bother, I already know you have no idea what I'm talking about. If we're to get out of here, we need one of only nine available keys. A Hellcrux. And only someone from Heaven can wield one."

CHAPTER FOUR

"**Y**ou still haven't answered me." Deb began pacing. "How could someone from Heaven wield a weapon forged in Hell?"

"Who said it was forged in Hell?" Schlosser scoffed as he rose from his crouched position picking through a pile of rubble.

"What?" Deb asked. "Are you saying Hell has a Heavenly weapon?"

Schlosser grumbled something incoherent and left the pool of Hell Fire and wandered in and out of empty rooms searching for supplies. Along the way they managed to find a small cord of rope, a makeshift knife, a dented can of brown beans, and a ripped carton of condensed milk.

So much for gathering supplies. More like trash.

"Are you done picking through junk?" Deb deadpanned.

"You'll be happy about my findings later when you're hungry and there's food to fill your empty stomach." Schlosser walked out of the cavernous space they were standing in. He continued the hunt for supplies and food for several hours. Deb found a ripped backpack and handed it to Schlosser.

"For you to carry all your treasure in." She smirked and he grabbed the bag.

"It's about time you did something useful."

"You mean like breaking your prison cuffs."

"If it weren't for me, you'd be dog meat by now."

He turned right at the next fork and stopped.

"Do you smell that?" he asked.

"No. I think I have adjusted to the stench down here."

"You're not as observant as I thought you'd be." He began moving again.

"What's that supposed to mean?"

Walking along the torch lit path the worn brick below their feet turned to tar. The caves became more uniform in shape and color, each one adorned with a thick wooden door.

"Is this the ritzy section?" Deb sardonically asked.

Schlosser pushed open the first door and entered. Deb walked in behind him but stopped short at the smell. It was as if she had just walked into a spring garden in full bloom. The floral perfume hung heavy in the air.

Deb walked toward the glimmer of light. She

stepped into a large living space. The room was awash with the glow of daylight lamps strewn about. Vines with yellow and white flowers grew wildly along wooden lattice attached to the far wall.

"Honeysuckle." Deb sighed. "How?"

"Shh." Schlosser hushed from behind her. "Do you have to announce yourself everywhere?"

"Hello!" Deb yelled. "That's announcing, just so you know the difference."

Schlosser groaned as Deb walked further inward. The botanical scent was soon replaced by the aroma of garlic and fresh herbs. Standing over a makeshift grill was a male figure sprinkling seasoning onto something he was cooking.

He didn't turn upon their entry instead choosing to continue to dote on his meal and hum along as he went about cooking. The scene contradicted everything about their circumstance.

"We don't want any trouble," Schlosser announced.

"No," the male replied. "Trouble is bad, you know that more than most don't you Schlosser?"

This is strange. If Schlosser knows this being why the song and dance looking for dented up cans of food when he could have just come here to eat?

"It seems you're getting better at hiding, Lenny." Schlosser walked past Deb to place the beans and milk on the table, which was setup opposite the cooking area.

The male inhaled deeply and then eyed the items placed on his table. The left side of Lenny's face came into view. Burns marred his skin, his salt and pepper hair covered only half his scalp.

"An offering in exchange for something hot and a jar of Meena's salve."

Deb took in the scene playing out in front of her. *How could Schlosser eat right now?*

"It's going to take a lot more than that to get Meena's salve," Lenny commented.

"It's all we've got, and she needs the salve." Schlosser pointed at Deb.

No need to go telling him I'm slow to heal. He might as well be announcing that I'm vulnerable or worse, letting the demon know I don't belong here. Although, on that last part I wholeheartedly agree. I don't belong here!

"Oh, but it's not all you've got, is it?" Lenny cooed. "She's a healer. I can feel it even in this dungeon. I can feel the warmth of her essence."

Deb took a half step back toward the door and nearly fell over someone standing behind her.

"Now, now missy." An older woman with weathered hands and chipped nails reached out and steadied Deb. "No need to go rushing off, you just got here."

Deb presumed the female was Meena. Her dress was faded to a washed-out gray, any semblance of color worn away to the point it was nearly see through. Her feet were dirty and cracked from walking barefoot on rough and rocky terrain. Her mud-colored hair was pulled back into a tight braid which made her bulging eyes and crooked nose more pronounced.

Like a television version of a witch.

"She can't heal you even if she wanted to," Schlosser told Lenny.

"That's the price!" Lenny yelled to Schlosser.

"She came all the way to Hell. Yelling isn't going to sway her. She needs the salve, and we have items to trade for it."

"Don't talk about me as if I'm not in the room," Deb snapped. "I can speak for myself. I would heal you Lenny, or at least try, but according to Schlosser that sends a signal of my location when I do."

"Liar!" Lenny screamed at Schlosser.

"It wasn't a lie when I said it," Schlosser rebutted.

"You got caught, didn't you?" Meena asked as she crossed the room to stand next to Lenny. "The only realm that would give off her signal is the Hell Fire sphere. You were in a cell because you got caught trying to leave."

"Something like that, yeah." Schlosser took back the items he had foraged and turned to walk away.

"Wait!" Lenny yelled after him. "Why didn't you just tell us that you failed. We've been wondering why you never came back for us. We helped you escape, we expected you to return the favor."

Schlosser closed his eyes and took a calming breath, a feigned attempt at patience. "Are we making a trade for food and salve or not?"

Meena and Lenny gave each other a knowing glance. Lenny nodded. "Leave the beans and milk. Sit, seems you have impeccable timing as always. It's ready."

Schlosser placed the items back down on the table. Sliding a chair out he sat at the end facing Lenny. Deb followed cautiously, pulling a chair out on the opposite side, her back was to the exit. The uneven legs of the chair shifted quickly and thrust her back in her seat. She leaned forward placing her elbows on the table for stability.

Lenny brought over two large terra cotta plates. The forks he dropped on the table were missing tines, one handle was broken, the other bent to the left making it awkward to use either one. Meena filled cups with water and sloppily placed them on the table. Deb picked up the cup and smelled it before taking a sip. Lenny pulled the food off the grill and placed it all on a platter that he then left between her and Schlosser.

"Eat," Lenny ordered. "Then we negotiate for the salve."

Meena and Lenny left the room while Schlosser doled out food onto each of their plates. "Eat quickly."

"Why are we eating at all?" Deb asked.

"Trust me." He never took his eyes off the doorway. "You're going to need your strength."

Trust. Seriously, maybe I should just leave and try to find Marcus on my own. This is not getting me anywhere. The aroma of garlic and oil made her stomach growl. It was loud enough that Schlosser rolled his eyes at her.

"Eat, even though you don't want to," he urged.

"Who are these two?" Deb asked.

"That's not a conversation for here."

"Okay." Deb sighed. "So what is a conversation for here?"

"Why would you come here?" he asked. "What's the real reason that you've put yourself in mortal danger?"

"I'm not talking to you about Marcus."

"See." He smiled. "We each have things we're unwilling to talk about."

Deb brought a forkful of food to her mouth. *Here goes nothing. Hope it tastes like chicken.*

The food hit her mouth and she nearly moaned it tasted so good. "This is amazing, now as long as we don't keel over and die this will have been worth all the trash picking."

"And exactly what did you contribute to that effort?" Schlosser scoffed in between bites.

"Hello, the bag to carry it all in."

"Does that kind of effort count in Heaven?" Schlosser flippantly responded.

"I don't actually have to talk to you." Deb shoveled in a few more bites.

"Thank the gods you finally came to a reasonable conclusion." Schlosser took several more bites of food and then dropped his fork onto the empty plate. He then began rummaging around the space. Meena and Lenny had yet to return.

"Finish up," Schlosser told her. "We have about five more minutes before whoever they went and ratted us out to shows up."

Deb nearly choked on her food. "We should go then." She shoveled a few more forkfuls of steaming hot food into her mouth.

"Check that cabinet." Schlosser got up to rummage through the few drawers in the room. Finding a pair of scissors, he stuffed them into his pants pocket.

Deb quickly made her way to the curio cabinet. She opened the one functioning door and pulled out a plastic travel mug, running back to fill it with water.

"We're out of time, we need to leave, now." Schlosser threw the beans and milk back into the backpack and hastily walked back out the way they entered.

Great. Going back out the way we came means there is only one way in and out.

When they got to the wall of honeysuckle, Schlosser retrieved the scissors and cut several snippets off the vine.

"Put this in your pockets." Schlosser proceeded to fill the bag with several large trimmings. "There's only one thing this is good for."

"What could that possibly be?" Deb asked.

"It keeps away the hellhounds. They hate the smell of this stuff. They'll run miles out of their way just to avoid the scent. This wall is a botanical gold mine for those in Hell."

Deb ripped a piece of the vine loose and rubbed it all over her arms and neck. Normally, she would have laced a piece through her hair, but there's no way to attach a flower to your scalp.

They pulled the heavy wooden door open and turned right just as Meena screamed.

"There they are!" The woman's voice echoed down the hall after them.

"Run!" Schlosser ordered. "Don't turn back."

Deb took off alongside Schlosser, a few yards in and the road curved with an incline set ahead of them. Her muscles burned as she struggled to keep stride with the nearly seven-foot demon. At the top Schlosser turned left and Deb followed close behind. About ten yards in front of them was a large hole in the ground, there was no avoiding it as there were walls on either side. Her mind couldn't process where to go, but instinctively she slowed.

Schlosser grabbed her hand and pulled her back up alongside him.

"Faster!" he yelled.

We're jumping, Deb agonized.

Her feet hit the pavement hard, she pumped her forearms back and forth for additional speed. Her feet left the ground, arms swinging wildly as if she were able to make them into propellers and fly. Deb judged the distance to the other side. She wasn't going to make it. Beneath the opening was the molten lava from the Hell Fire pit. She closed her eyes and prepared for the worst.

Her body started the descent but then Schlosser's hand grabbed hers. He landed on the edge as her body hung precariously below him. She opened her eyes and was surrounded by steam. Pain rode up her already burned legs and her body coughed involuntarily from the wretched odor of death as it enveloped her.

The being chasing them missed the jump as well. The male demon plunged to his death. The lava sputtered and bubbled up upon impact then swallowed him whole.

Schlosser yanked Deb up and onto the outer edge of the crater. Breathless, she sat on her knees and concentrated on not puking as he got to his feet.

"Tell me you didn't know that was there?" she demanded.

"It was the only real escape route." He held his hand out offering to help her up. She slapped it away and got to her feet.

"You could have killed me. You could have killed us both."

"Newsflash, we're in Hell. Death defying antics is all we have."

"Take me to Marcus right now or so help me God, I will leave you right where you stand."

"Alright, alright, calm down. You want to go rescue Marcus with a shiv and a pair of dull scissors, fine. I'll bring you to the torture caverns."

"Caverns," Deb said without thinking.

"Yeah, you didn't think there was just one room, did you?" Schlosser shook his head. "You're most likely going to die down here, Guardian."

Deb blasted Schlosser with her shield, the demon flew backward through the air and hit the wall with force. He bellowed in pain and slunk to the ground momentarily winded.

"I've been underestimated my entire existence." She sneered at him from above. "I have no intention of dying down here. You are either taking me to Marcus or you're in my way. You decide which and make it quick."

Schlosser put his arms up palms facing out as if in surrender. He slowly got to his feet and pointed left. "I believe he's down here. Before you go all crazy on me, there is no way to know which room. We're going to have to search."

"God help you if you're screwing with me." Deb walked away from him.

God help me if I'm wrong for coming here.

CHAPTER FIVE

"It's been several days, and nothing has happened." Kelly was pacing on Michael's vast front porch. He made his home in a large log cabin with giant windows that overlooked a small lake. The property was surrounded by sprawling acres of ponderosa pine trees. They were in Montana, but to Kelly it might as well be in the middle of nowhere. Her fuzzy socks masked her footfalls as she treaded back and forth on the front deck.

The Accord's broken. Hell is literally on Earth. Kelly could not wrap her mind around the magnitude of it against the peacefulness of her current surroundings. *No vampire attacks, no demon attacks, nothing. What are Azza and Wrath up to?*

Grabbing the zipper on her navy-blue sweatshirt she pulled the metal clasp up tightening the garment around her. Despite the sun having risen, it was a crisp September morning that wouldn't warm until later in the day.

Big Sky, they call it. It certainly is. Plenty of space with beautiful mountain ranges and lots of fresh air, yet I can't sleep.

Kelly had been awake for several hours before movement came from the kitchen below and she got dressed to come talk to whoever was wandering about at this early hour.

"If I had to guess," Dan commented between sips of coffee, "they're infighting about what to do next."

"Maybe. Just frustrating waiting around for something to happen, or more aptly for them to attack."

"I have a bad feeling we won't be waiting long," Dan remarked.

"You're probably right."

Rushing water echoed from underneath the house. Someone else was up. She and her siblings had been staying together at the cabin filling the time with training and readying themselves for battle, but where and how it would come, no one knew.

"Where's Michael?" Kelly asked as she stopped at the door. "I would have thought he'd be rounding us up for training already."

"He'll be back soon, he's off on his morning run. The guy barely sleeps." Dan put his mug down on a small table next to his chair. He reclined a bit and took a deep breath. "Isn't it great out here? Nothing but trees as far as the eye can see."

"Hmm, yeah." Kelly peered through the front door to the inside of the house.

"I know you like the city better. But a change of scenery can be good. You should take a walk today. I remember a time when you hiked a great deal."

Kelly sighed and turned back toward the view. The sun had risen just over the mountain range in the distance, the bright orange hues giving way to streaks of yellow cascading down through the pine trees. Fall had arrived across this landscape with the leaves of aspens, larch, and cottonwoods turning golden. The past three nights Kelly needed a sweatshirt to fight off the chill in the air. They usually ended their long days sitting together around the outdoor fire pit in the back, the black of nightfall enveloping them on all sides. There wasn't another house for miles, no tall streetlamps to cast shadows, nothing but darkness surrounded them under a starry night's sky.

"Yes," Kelly finally answered. "It's been a while since I went for a long walk like that. I don't remember why I stopped."

Kelly stared out into the dense treelined forest surrounding the property. *A hike might be nice. Maybe it will get rid of the vibrating tension in my stomach.*

"You should take Gen." Dan's comment drew Kelly back to the conversation. "I don't know that she's sleeping either. Two city girls stuck in the wilderness."

"Ha ha," Kelly snorted. "I'm going to make more coffee. I think the others are finally waking up."

"You're going to need to figure out how to rest out here Kell," Dan hollered as she made her way through the door and into the house. "You're no good to anyone if you're not a hundred percent."

Kelly didn't respond. She busied herself with the coffee grinder when Gen and Greg came into the room behind her.

"Hey, you're up early," Gen commented. "Or did you not go to bed?"

Greg chuckled and opened the fridge grabbing a container of orange juice from the top shelf. "It's not easy coming from the lights and noise of the city and adjusting to the quiet out here."

"That's an understatement."

"Ditto." Kelly put the coffee machine back on and turned to face her siblings.

"I promise, if you give it time," Greg told them, "you'll end up loving it. I never sleep as good as I do out here. There is something about being out in the fresh air all day that leads to the best night's sleep. In summer, I like leaving the windows open, no matter what the weather is during the day, the nights out here are refreshingly cool and dry."

"I don't think we'll be waiting around here for summer," Kelly commented. "The vampires are probably as restless as I am."

"That's most likely true," Greg agreed. "It's funny, now that I think about it Xavier never really got used to it out here either. He loved to swim and go for a morning jog, but he would have rather done that somewhere by the ocean, not way out here."

"How are you doing, Greg?" Gen asked. "You lived with Xavier. It must be difficult adjusting."

"It's hard on all of us," Greg answered. "But, yeah when you live with someone it hits a little closer to home, you know."

"Yeah," Kelly commented. "It feels like you lost a piece of yourself, doesn't it?"

Greg nodded. "It's weird how the things that used to bring joy now hurt."

"What do you mean?" Gen asked.

Greg poured a glass of juice and sat down at the table across from the two of them. "Like last night for instance. There was a soccer game on. It was a good match too. One I know Xavier would have made me stay up to watch. I put it on, but–"

Silence fell between them. The palpable sadness stretched out across the room like toxic fumes swallowing them whole.

"You couldn't get through it," Gen finally answered. "I know what you mean. Everywhere I look I see something that reminds me of him, a rocking chair, a baseball, a light blue sweatshirt. It's everywhere, like his favorite things are ghostly remnants strewn about for me to find."

The screen door creaked open and then snapped closed. Michael walked in with Dan closely behind him. Michael's tall frame was draped in sweat. He wore a long-sleeved white T-shirt underneath a thin outdoor vest, gray cargo pants, and hiking sneakers stained green and brown from the natural terrain that surrounded the house.

"Looks like I don't need to wake anyone this morning," Michael commented. "Anyone hungry?"

"I'm always hungry," Kelly answered. "I half expected Tom to be with you. Where are he and Frankie?"

"Tom doesn't run, he walks." Michael navigated around Gen and over to the sink to wash his hands. "He'll be back shortly. He's usually about fifteen minutes behind me."

"And Frankie?" Kelly repeated.

"He's at Harry's." Dan made his way past Kelly toward the coffee pot.

A soft glow formed to Kelly's left and she turned as Tom arrived. Her brother's hair was windswept, his cheeks flush from being out in the chilly morning air.

"There is a small group of vampires about four klicks southeast from the house."

"What are they doing?" Kelly asked ready to bolt after them.

"They appear to be camping, but that's not all," Tom answered.

"Were you seen?" Greg asked.

"No, I'm pretty sure I got my shield up before they could feel anything."

"What else?" Michael asked as he methodically walked to the closet and began pulling out weapons for all of them.

"There were multiple carcasses surrounding the encampment. At first, I was relieved they were just animal, but then–"

"Humans?" Gen asked. "They murdered a human?"

"I'm not sure." Tom's face grew somber from seemingly recalling the discovery. "I saw two bodies, they were bloody and strung up a few feet off the ground, maybe to drain?"

"Everyone, grab a weapon," Michael ordered. "Greg, tell Frankie what's happened, get him back here now."

The room seemed to awaken from its morning slumber as they began moving quickly throughout the open space.

"Tom, can you get us close?" Michael asked.

Tom nodded and took the long spear Greg held out for him. Kelly wrestled with her boots while Gen pulled a jacket off a nearby hook and put it on.

Frankie arrived behind them in the living room. "Harry got us more Holy Oil." He passed around small amulets to each of them. "How many vampires?"

"I saw two awake—a male and a female—and another lying in a sleeping bag by a campfire."

Kelly walked to an open chest in the living room and retrieved thick metal cuffs. The wrought iron shackles could hold a vampire prisoner and keep them from teleporting, but she didn't know for how long. She put the cuffs in a small backpack and slung it across her back.

"How many are we going to attempt to take prisoner?" Kelly asked.

"One or two at most," Dan answered. "Any more than that and it might give off too much energy. Remember the cuffs will keep them from leaving, but not from movement. It they're soldiers they will be able to fight, cuffs and all."

"That's the thing, I'm not sure they are soldiers," Tom told them. "But, if the one in the sleeping bag is still asleep, I would target that one for the cuffs."

"We're going in a bit blind, but we're ready," Michael told them. "Stay close and be as quiet as possible. The element of surprise will be our biggest advantage."

***

Tom brought them to a small clearing. Given the early morning hour the shaded area provided minimal cover. The smell of fire was strong as billowing smoke snaked through the tree lined canopy to greet them. Anyone hiking in the area would have known someone was camped nearby.

The vampires are just down the hillside from here, through those trees. Tom pointed past Kelly who was facing him. *Once we enter the trees I don't know if we'll be able to speak to one another telepathically. I wasn't able to call out to any of you when I first came across them. They were cloaked but it's a small area. I was easily able to walk clear of it and teleport out.*

Tom and Gen, spread out and take the high ground. Michael told them. *Signal us if anything else enters from outside the perimeter. Greg and Frankie take the one in the sleeping bag.*

Kelly pulled the backpack that contained the cuffs off her shoulder and passed it to Greg,

Kelly, you and I can take the two that are awake, Michael continued. *Dan, check behind that large rocky formation to make sure there are no others.*

Kelly turned first and walked slowly into the thick layer of pine forest. She peered down to the bottom of the embankment. Just as Tom had described, one body appeared to be encased in a dark colored sleeping bag near the campfire. The bag covered the body completely, no telling who or what was in it. The other two were turned away busy with the rope they were using to hoist two figures, presumably humans, off the ground.

Michael walked off to the right and Kelly followed. Her brother used the thick branches of the pine trees as partial cover as they descended. It was a small hillside, and they reached the bottom quickly. As they neared the vampires position the pine was replaced by the rank odor of something rotting. The first dead animal they passed was fresh, Kelly didn't think it had been there long.

Michael grabbed Kelly's arm and nodded

toward bloody impressions leading away from the campsite. Her eyes followed the footprints which stopped about twenty yards away from their position. Under the cover of a hollowed-out tree was a male figure. He was on the ground with his arms enveloping either side of his small frame as he rocked back and forth moaning.

Kelly pulled at her own sweatshirt. This signaled to Michael to examine their clothing. They were not wearing the long thick coats of armor that Garrick and the other soldiers wore. They were in jeans and sweatshirts, hardly the typical attire of hells first army.

Michael backed up a few paces and caught the attention of their siblings. He signaled one more to their right and Dan who had already checked around the rock wall came forward to join them.

A broken plea rang out behind them.

"Stop, please!" A male voice yelled out. "You're killing us! Please just let us go."

The bodies hoisted up in the trees were alive.

This makes no sense. Kelly's mind was racing. *No vampire would leave a human alive after feeding. They're too efficient. It's drink, kill, move on.*

Losing all patience Kelly walked out of the cover of the tree branches and spoke. "Stop. Step away from the humans."

Michael and Dan burst forth behind her.

"This was not the plan," Michael said quietly as his head spun right to left.

The two figures on the ground seemed stunned.

They relinquished their hold on the rope sending the human bodies hoisted in the air careening toward the ground. The male who had pleaded to be set free let out a scream, the two landed with a thud.

"So much for the element of surprise," Dan said to Kelly. "Now what?"

"Somethings not right." Kelly turned back toward the young man behind her. He stilled, no longer rocking, his pale face bruised and bloodied. His eyes wet with tears, he must have been no older than fifteen.

"It's okay," Kelly told the young man. "We're not here to hurt you, any of you."

"The one in the sleeping bag is dead," Greg announced.

Gen had made her way down from above and was standing over the sleeping bag with Greg and Frankie.

"What happened here?" Kelly asked the two standing over the humans scrambling to free themselves.

"Please don't hurt us!" the female yelled. "We're trying, but it's not working. The blood it's just making us sick. We can't bring ourselves to do it."

"What can't you do?" Kelly asked.

"We were told only blood would keep us alive," the male answered. "We tried animals first, but–" He stopped short and didn't finish his sentence.

The woman shook her head and began to cry. "We couldn't kill them. I think you need to drink so much it would kill the person and we couldn't do it.

Please, if you're here to kill us, just do it quickly, but spare our son."

The human captives rolled over and got to their feet, only their hands were still bound to the rope. They were helping each other untie the knots when Gen reached them.

"The two imprisoned can't see me," Gen announced. She raised her hands over the two victims and healed them enough to hasten their retreat away from the scene. They took off running and quickly disappeared into the thickness of the surrounding forest.

"It makes sense they can't see us if all these two were doing was feeding and not turning them," Kelly surmised.

"What happened to the one in the sleeping bag?" Michael asked.

"It's my brother," the male answered. "He refused to drink any of the blood, animal or otherwise. No matter how much water we gave him, he just got sicker, until he finally passed out. We thought he was sleeping, but then I couldn't wake him."

"How long have you been out here?" Dan inquired.

"A few days maybe," the woman answered. "What are you going to do to us?"

Kelly caught Gen's eye. "We can attempt to heal them, but I don't know if it will work."

"Please, I don't know who you are, but if you can heal, start with our son."

Behind her, the young man was now on all fours throwing up. He had his head down and his back seemed to arch in an unnatural position as his body heaved.

Kelly and Gen walked to the boy. Holding their hands above his head they used their power to bathe the boy in healing light. The hurling stopped soon after. The boy sat back and rested his head against a tree as they continued to work.

"What are you?" the Male asked. "Are you angels?"

"Not exactly," Frankie answered. "Let's start with your names?"

"I'm Bob," the male answered. "This is my wife Clara and that's our son Joey."

They began to walk toward their son, but Michael stepped out to impede them. "We need to know who did this to you?"

"We don't know." Bob shook his head emphatically.

"We have a way of seeing, but it's not going to be easy." Michael motioned to Greg.

"What does that mean?" Clara asked.

"Will you help us?" Michael continued. "We need the information you have in your memories."

"If you save our son, we will help you," Bob answered.

"Good," Michael said simply. "It will take them a bit to heal all of you, then you'll need shelter, food, and rest. There are no guarantees, but if you feel the hunger return, and drink blood to abate it, you will either fully transform or die in the process. Understand?"

"Transform into what?" Clara asked shakily.

"Into what did this to you." Michael deliberately left out the word vampire.

Bob's eyes darted toward his wife and then back to Michael. "Why would you help us after what you saw us doing?"

"We know you were just trying to survive," Dan told them. "We really are here to help. Do you believe that?"

"I think I believe in just about everything now," Clara stated.

Bob stared over at Gen and Kelly. "I never thought I would encounter evil, not in its truest form. Those things that showed up at our ranch, they weren't human. They were unnaturally strong and no matter how much I fought back they were unfazed. Like some zombie monster movie."

"They weren't human," Dan told them. "Neither are we."

"You aren't evil though," Bob retorted. "What I felt when I stood across from those things, it was the opposite of what I feel now."

"What are you feeling now?" Greg asked.

"Hope," Clara said flatly. "I feel hopeful, even when there is no reason to be."

"Look, I'm not going to sugar coat this," Michael told them. "I am cautiously optimistic. My sisters, they are the best at healing and you two, you didn't kill anyone, but there are no guarantees any of you will make it."

"We'll take our chances," Clara told him. "Anything is better than the hell we've been living through these last few days."

CHAPTER SIX

Genevieve stood at the back of St. Ann's church positioned at the main entrance. Despite the chill in the air the double doors were pushed wide open. Throngs of people made their way into what used to be considered quiet hour. The hum of whispering voices collided with creaking wood as people slid down the ends of the pews to fill every available seat.

Behind her, several news vans clogged the parking lot clamoring to record images for their nightly newscast. The headline, *Vampiric Virus Spreads Across the US and Europe.* It was the latest in a series of news segments where governments attempted to clarify the unexplainable. The media an all too willing participant to capitalize on a crisis.

The vampires were turning humans by the thousands. Pulling demons from hell to increase the speed and force of the spread. The O'Mara's were running on empty as were most of the Guardians they knew. At this point they had to separate, each having to cover a town or a section of a large city. In a matter of days they went from waiting around to find out what the vampires were going to do to, to a near end-of-days scenario.

A virus, Gen thought. *Though incorrect, the analogy is apt. The pace with which hell is turning people and the number of humans dying during the transition is very much like a contagion.*

Gen paused to examine her injured body. Her palm covered a stab wound on the left side of her abdomen. She had just killed two vampires at the back of the rectory. Out of breath and laboring, she witnessed a sea of people making their way into the church and lumbered along to join them.

She could not join them in human form, it was too dangerous, and she was a mess. Her jeans were ripped, face bruised, blouse splattered in horror-movie red.

Genevieve couldn't bring herself to leave the spot where she was standing. Outside of weddings and funerals there hadn't been this many people gathered in a church in decades. An organist began preparing for the service by striking multiple keys in short rhythms and then stopping.

Father Donovan will be out soon, Gen surmised. *He's got a full house today. Deb would be happy. I pray you're safe Deb. I hope you get to Marcus and get out of there quickly. You need to come home. I can't lose another sibling.*

The gentle chime of bells rang out from the altar and people stood. Father Donovan came out of the sacristy in a black cope, a signal this wasn't a mass, but a prayer service. He waited while the organist played an opening hymn. People in attendance sang along.

Genevieve pulled her hand away from her stomach, the bleeding had stopped. *Amazing. I'm healing at an incredible pace.*

A soft glow rippled across the dark wooden pew to her left. Tom stepped out from his aura and walked over to her.

"Are you alright, Gen?"

Her brother's forehead was split open, blood trickled down the right side of his face. Flush from a recent encounter his left eye was puffy, the injury too new to have blackened yet. The front pocket of his sweatshirt was torn and hung by a mere thread.

"I'm about as good as you are Tom."

"I can see that," he answered with a slight smile.

"I could feel you again," she told him. "I called you here for this." Gen nodded in the direction of the churchgoers in front of them. The music stopped. People sat down as the priest explained the prayer service about to take place and how they could follow along.

"Hard to believe just a week ago he might have had a dozen people here," Gen commented. "I imagine it's like this all across the country."

"Not just this country. The world. Do you think it's enough to tilt the odds in our favor?"

"I can feel the effects already and I've only been in here a minute." He reached for his forehead. "My cut is already healing."

"I know. I was stabbed and it's already sealed. That's why I called you here. We need to tell the others. Tell them to find the closest gathering, where humans are collectively meeting, singing, praying. Whatever the building, this may be the result."

"Incredible." Tom's eyes spanned the pews. "There isn't a seat to be had and they're still coming."

People were filling in the back area between the last pew and the exits. The mood was somber, some were even crying. Several people held pictures of loved ones presumed lost to this war. Sunlight streamed through the stained-glass windows and the scent of incense drifted through the air. It was a beautiful fall day outside but the fear and sorrow in the church overwhelmed any semblance of normalcy.

"I think they know it's not a virus," Gen told him. "I think they sense it on an entirely different level."

"Maybe. There are videos out there now. Pictures of people being attacked. Small towns and villages annihilated. It's getting harder to argue it's not hell on Earth."

"I haven't seen Michael in two days. The last time I called his phone, he said his battery was dying. The myriad of vampiric cloaking is interfering with our telepathy, and I don't know how much longer today's technology will help us," Gen told him. "Have you spoken to Michael? Does he have any idea how to get in front of this?"

"No. I think he's just as busy as the rest of us, running from encounter to encounter. It's dizzying."

"Maybe that's the game plan," Gen thought aloud. "To have us running around so much we can't think our way to an advantage. Tom, we're running from fight to fight, getting seriously injured and worn down in the process. What if that's the real intent of all this? To keep us distracted and fatigued so we aren't strong enough to stop what Wrath and Azza do next."

"You might be right," Tom answered. "I haven't rested more than two, maybe three hours in several days. Even so, every minute we spend in here, means people are dying out there."

"I can feel Greg and Frankie," Gen said. "I just told them to come here. Fill them in, will you. I'm going to find Harry. I might have an idea."

Tom reached out and squeezed her arm. "Be careful Gen."

"You too, Tom." She smiled as she placed her hand over his. "I'll see you soon."

Gen wrapped herself in her aura and teleported from the church to the last known safe house Harry was in.

***

Gen arrived behind the small wooden cottage. All seemed quiet. The surface of the lake was still, the clouds above reflected a near perfect mirror image off its surface. Birdsong rang out across the trees. Hummingbirds fluttered back and forth between the red oak trees and a feeder attached to a nearby shed. The nectar faced away from the sun, but its colorful glass shined through the dappled shade.

Harry stepped out onto the back porch peering right to left with a large wrought iron fireplace poker.

I must have set off some sort of alarm system.

"Hey Harry," Gen called out. "Are you okay?"

"Oh Genevieve!" Harry's lilted voice carried more relief than fear.

"Sorry, didn't mean to scare you." Gen walked toward the back steps. "I wasn't sure you were still here."

"It's alright. We are still here and could use your help."

We. Gardenia must still be with him.

Gen walked up the back steps and went inside. Not expecting more than Gardenia she stopped short when she entered the small living room in the center of the house.

Gerry was leaning over a person lying down on the sofa. Lacey was standing behind him, her eyes were dry but puffy and red like she had been crying.

"What's happened?" Gen asked.

"He happened." Gerry pointed at the dead vampire whose legs were sticking out from behind the sofa.

Gen walked around the sofa to check on the vampire first. His skin was already gray, the blood around his head evaporating as she was examining him. Back in the living room, Gardenia lay on the sofa. The young girl's eyes were darting back and forth between Harry and Genevieve.

"Was she hurt?" Gen asked.

Harry didn't answer. Lacey didn't either.

"Was she bit?" Gen followed up knowing the answer before it came.

"Yes," Harry told her.

"How long ago?" Gen said as she made her way over to the young girl who sat up and cowered away from Gen's approach.

"Hours," Harry admitted. "She's already hallucinating. Gerry just got here, he's the only one that she's allowing near her."

"Anyone else bit?" Gen asked as she calmly walked around to stand next to Gerry.

"No," Lacey answered. "Gerry and I were pulled away to different battles."

"Harry?" Gen needed confirmation.

"No," Harry answered. "I saw one outside, but we couldn't teleport. I told her to stay inside and away from the windows. When I got back inside the vampire was already–"

I have to get her out of here, Gen thought. *Kelly will*

never forgive me if I don't try to heal her.

"We need to go," Gen said. She reached down to grab hold of Gardenia and the girl recoiled and swiped at her hand. "I don't know where Kelly is, but I know where Frankie is."

"Where?" Harry asked.

"St. Ann's," Gen told them. "Let's get you all out of here and regroup."

Gen arrived with Gardenia. Her brothers were not there. Panic ripped through her. *They must have healed quickly and left to rejoin the fight.*

Gardenia screamed and all eyes at the church turned toward them.

What's happening? Gen's mind raced. *Are they seeing her? How?*

"Harry!" Gen yelled. "Get in human form and tell me what they are seeing."

Harry closed his eyes, but before he had a chance to tell her what was going on the church erupted.

"She's infected," someone yelled.

"Vampire," a chorus of voices screeched.

People began running, screams echoed off the high ceiling of the spacious church. Gardenia started screaming too, a high-pitched tone that seemed to send her body into convulsions. She collapsed to the floor and began rocking back and forth coughing and spitting up blood as she did. A few people took their phones out and started filming.

"Harry," Gen ordered. "Influence everyone out of here, now."

"There's too many Genevieve," Gerry told her.

"Just do what you can," Gen told them.

Lacey joined Harry but she would be little more than moral support as Watchers had no sway over humans.

"What can I do?" Gerry asked her.

"Just try and keep her calm." Gen closed her eyes and tried to feel for a sibling. "I can't feel my siblings. I'm sorry Gerry. I will try and heal her, but I don't think it will be enough."

"I have faith in you Genevieve," Gerry told her. "It *will* be enough. It has to be." His voice trailing off to a mere whisper.

What am I going to do? Gen's head hurt, it seemed to be more painful the harder she tried to find her siblings.

The police showed up and dragged the rest of the onlookers out of the church. As Father Donovan was escorted from the church Harry whispered to him on his way by. As the priest reached the end, he spoke to Gardenia.

"I will pray for you child." The priest scurried along and out the front doors just before they closed.

Sirens were getting closer. The camera crews outside would be clamoring to get footage and may even attempt entry from the side or back door.

"Keep an eye out Harry," Gen told him. "Anyone else enters, get them out of here. We don't want any more footage than what is already out there."

Gardenia was moaning as Gen did her best to

heal her. After a few minutes Gardenia quieted, and her body stilled.

It's not enough. Gen knew the girl was nearing the end. *Even with Frankie's help I don't know if I can save her.*

"Gardenia hasn't picked a side, that's why they refer to her as one of the lost," Gen mumbled aloud. "I don't know what happens to a neutral soul that's been bitten."

Time slowed. Gen's chest tightened as she tried to beat the clock and heal Gardenia enough to keep her heart from stopping. If the young girl stopped breathing, only blood could bring her back.

Who knows if it would work, or what we would be bringing back if we did that? Gen's mind reeled. Gerry got up from the floor where he was kneeling next to her. He was crying. Lacey came over and wrapped an arm around him.

Gen slammed her fist against the wall behind her in anger. Holy water spilled from the font above her head and splashed across both Gen and Gardenia. The Hellish liquid essence that had seeped from Gardenia's mouth immediately turned to steam and evaporated.

"What was that?" Gen asked without thinking. "It didn't catch fire. Harry, is the Holy water in the fonts real?"

"Yes." Harry remained at the front to influence people to stay outside.

"How?" Gen asked as she reached up and removed the plastic liner inside the font bringing the water down to Gardenia's lips.

"Antonio brought me gallons of it," Harry answered. "I put it in a bunch of churches after he told me that it didn't burn or harm any of the demons the vampires had turned. I thought, maybe it could help people in some way, it is from Heaven after all."

"Holy water is only a weapon against hell's first army." Gen gently lifted Gardenia's head to allow for the cool liquid to slide down the girl's throat. "It doesn't harm any of the demons the soldiers turn. However, assuming Antonio got this from a purity pool, it should be able to heal Gardenia."

Gerry and Lacy stepped closer.

"Is it working?" Lacy asked.

"I don't know," Gen answered.

Gen raised her hands once more in the air to heal Gardenia. She silently called for her brothers once more and Frankie arrived.

"What happened?" Her brother made his way to Gen.

"Thank God you're here, Frankie."

Frankie put his hand on her shoulder. When their powers entwined, the warm light that fell across Gardenia's chest expanded and encompassed her entire body.

Come on, Gen urged silently. *Gardenia please come back to us.*

After several agonizing minutes the girl coughed and opened her eyes. Gen dropped her hands and there was a palpable sigh of relief as Gardenia attempted to sit up.

"What's going on?" Gardenia asked her voice rough from coughing. "Gerry, what happened?"

"Here." Gen held up the cup of holy water. "Drink some more of this."

Gardenia took the water. With a slight hesitation she brought the cup to her lips and drank.

"She's going to be alright." Gen got back to her feet. "You should get her out of here before the emergency personnel re-enter this building."

"Can they still see her?" Gerry asked.

"I don't know, but we don't want to take a chance," Gen answered. "She could probably use rest and some food. Where are you taking her to now, Harry?"

"I only have one safe house left." He grabbed Gardenia's hand. "Vinalhaven Island in Maine. If the vampires go there, they'll have to take a boat to get to us."

"I'll get there as soon as I can," Gen told them.

Harry nodded and the four of them left Frankie and Gen standing at the back of the church. Emergency personnel entered and were confused to find no one inside.

"Later they'll talk about how all the exits were covered," Gen told her brother. "They'll want to know how she got out."

"I think we have more pressing things to discuss," Frankie told her.

"What do you mean?" Gen told him. "I take it

Tom told you about people coming to church and their praying healing us faster than anything I've ever experienced."

"Yes. That's great, but what's more important than us healing?"

"Healing them." Gen followed his train of thought.

"Yes. If that holy water healed Gardenia, maybe it could work on humans."

"We have to find out. Antonio gave it to Harry, but let's take a bit of it now before we leave, maybe we can go back to that family near Michael's house."

"I think that's a great idea. We may want to leave the Antonio part out when we tell Kelly."

Gen smiled. "I get the reasoning there Frankie, but we committed to tell each other everything."

Gen carefully pulled the plastic liner from the font preparing to take it with her.

"True enough," her brother admitted. "Let's get back to Michael's and regroup. I don't know that Michael will be there, but we can leave a good old-fashioned note in code." Wrapped in his aura Frankie teleported from the church.

At the altar, several police and firemen were searching for the infected girl that caused a scene.

"If we can heal people on a large scale," Gen thought out loud. "That might be the advantage we need. Now I just need to get us all in one room at the same time, which might be harder than it sounds."

Gen left the church just as a news camera

popped in from the side entrance.

Good luck trying to reason away this mystery. Gen headed to Michael's. *Some things just can't be explained.*

CHAPTER SEVEN

Kelly was tucked down behind a barn as two vampires approached from the opposite end on her right side. Since saving the family in the woods near Michael's house, she and her siblings had been in multiple encounters every day. Kelly was alone at this point. At first, Michael mandated pairing. Then even he had to admit they could cover more ground and save more people if they separated.

Now her siblings were seldom together and only to cover for one another as they slept, which was never more than an hour or two. Kelly's stomach rumbled. She couldn't remember the last time she ate. Her left arm was still sore from this morning's fight. The vampire had dislocated her shoulder. The pop it made would haunt her. Once she managed to kill that vampire, she found this barn.

Slamming herself into one of the wooden pilings, she reset her shoulder and then passed out. She had no idea how long she was unconscious, but when she woke, she knew she wasn't alone. Keeping low she managed to get outside and spotted two vampires watching the barn from the front. They must have tracked her but hadn't gone inside for some reason. Like so many others she had recently encountered, they were not part of hell's first army. These demons were pulled from hell and turned by the soldiers.

The odds are in my favor, Kelly thought. *But it does beg the question, where is hell's first army and what are they doing?*

The abandoned building smelled of hay with an occasional whiff of manure. The barn's red paint had peeled over time. The natural wood weathered to a washed-out gray with only streaks of reddish-brown remaining. The grass that ran along the far side of the building was almost as tall as she was, a good place to hide if she needed the cover.

These guys are like ants. You kill one and the rest scatter and then return in a new group. You just can't get enough of them at a time to make a dent.

Kelly wore jeans, a brown sweatshirt, and combat boots. She reached in the front pocket of her sweatshirt and pulled out a hunting knife. The wind picked up and the breeze tousled the leaves already straining to stay tethered to their branches. The sun was high in the sky, she guessed it was early afternoon, which meant she had been sleeping for at least two hours.

It could have been worse. I could have woken up with the two of them standing over me.

She was about to confront the pair when Gerry arrived just behind the tree line.

Oh come on. This new Watcher thing he's got going on is distracting me. Now, I have to worry about him when I should be focused on the fight.

Gerry scanned the landscape and stopped upon spotting her. Her former Charge now turned historian waved and pointed at the vampires to his right.

We are all kinds of violating things here. I am pretty sure you are not supposed to be helping me, Gerry.

Kelly nodded at Gerry in acknowledgement, and he took a few steps back into thick cover.

Smart. Now if he'd only just stay there, I might be able to get through this quickly.

The two vampires separated when they reached the front. The door of the barn squealed in resistance as it opened. Peeking through some of the broken boards she studied the male vampire walking along the outside of the barn toward her position. He was skinny, no more than five foot nine, and wore a gray T-shirt, jeans, and sneakers. The baseball cap crushed down on top of his head completed his All-American boy next door look. The faded blue hat had seen better days, and it accentuated his rather large ears as it pushed them forward.

Guess I'll wait for them to come to me, Kelly took a deep breath and readied herself for a fight.

The male vampire's footfalls trampled through grass, stopping periodically as he surveyed the area. Kelly peered into the barn through the broken wooden slats and confirmed the female was gingerly climbing into the loft. She was quiet, only light creaking escaped the worn staircase.

Nice. Kelly silently applauded. *Taking on one at a time will most definitely help. Now, if I can just kill him quietly, I might be able to get the drop on her as well.*

As the male neared the corner Kelly crouched down in preparation for her jump. He reached the end of the building and Kelly lunged at him. She took him down to the ground swiftly.

She punched him several times in the nose drawing a fair amount of blood. He put his hands up in a defensive posture, not swinging back at her.

Kelly brought her right arm outward, then swung it down upon him aiming for the side of his head. The blood made the handle slippery, and the knife slid forward slicing her hand open. She dropped the weapon and slammed both fists onto his ears simultaneously.

The demon grunted and then yelled out as he tried to buck her off him. He raised his own hands and used them to cover both ears. Since his face was left undefended, she threw several punches until he finally jabbed back at her, landing a punch. Kelly's head snapped back. The male vampire thrust up and managed to roll over and crawl out from underneath her.

Kelly retrieved the knife from the grass and stabbed at his neck. His movement caused her to miss the intended target and the sharp tip of the blade punctured his ear. The vampire's head thrust upward, and he let out a piercingly loud scream. Red liquid gushed from his wound. Kelly reached over and pulled the knife from his ear. His face slammed into the dirt below them. The quiet that followed was earie. The male didn't move again, he was dead.

What just happened? Kelly whispered.

Kelly lost track of where the female was. She got to her feet quickly spinning around just in time to get slammed in the face by a two by four ripped from the barn. As she sailed backward toward the side of the barn, Kelly caught a glimpse of Gerry and knew he had moved closer.

No, Kelly silently pleaded. *Stay back, Gerry.*

Kelly's back made an unnatural cracking sound as she landed on the ground. Pain ripped through her. Kelly struggled to catch her breath.

An uncontrollable moan escaped her lips. She tilted her head upward, but the female wasn't readying for another attack. Instead, the vampire was on her knees trying to wake the male. She nudged him several times and then started shaking him harder.

"No," the female yelled. "How can this be? This can't be, he can't be dead."

Kelly rolled over and got to her feet slowly.

"He is most definitely dead. You should go, before you end up lying next to him."

False bravado. Sometimes, the bluff is all you have left.

"You bitch!" The vampire got up and ran toward Kelly.

With no weapon Kelly grabbed the latch on the side door and timed her swing to collide with the vampire. The vampire barreled through the door and rolled away from the opening coming to rest several feet inside the abandoned building.

The female's black leggings shredded during the collision. Her dirty blonde hair blending into the hay strewn floor of the barn.

Kelly grabbed a loose board and entered the barn. As the female was working to get back up, Kelly swung the board at the side of her head. The female yelled out and rolled further away.

Kelly followed taking swing after painful swing. Each twist sent a sharp pain through her lower back, but she couldn't stop. If the vampire got ahold of her again, Kelly feared she may lose the fight. Bent forward, Kelly was unable to stand straight. Tears streamed down her sweat-soaked face as she tried to work through the spasming ache.

The vampire grabbed something on the floor and threw it at Kelly's head. Too injured to twist out of the way the object grazed Kelly's cheek, splitting it open.

Kelly glanced at the object. It had a bright yellow handle and was some sort of power tool. The metal bit on the end popped off upon impact with the ground.

Kelly held her breath as she leaned forward to retrieve the metal part. The piece was long and narrow with a hard metal cap on the end.

Kelly stood over the female, her feet straddling either side of the vampire's body as she peered down. The vampire was face down as she dug her nails into the ground attempting to get back to her knees.

"You can't kill me," the vampire mumbled.

"I can and I will," Kelly uttered near breathless. "If you see Azza, tell her Kelly O'Mara is coming for her."

With a deep breath Kelly forcefully stabbed the vampire in the ear with the metal object. The female bellowed in pain before collapsing into a fit of convulsions. Kelly stumbled backward and stopped when she hit the doorway. She turned her head slightly to the left. Gerry was about five feet outside the barn.

"This isn't going to work if you take sides, Gerry."

"I'm dead. Ain't nobody gonna tell me who to root for."

Couldn't have said it better myself, my friend. Kelly fought against the pain-induced haze enveloping her.

"What can I do?" Gerry asked.

"You got any pizza bagels?" she asked him as she tasted blood on her lips. "I love those damn things."

"For the love of Pe–"

"No!" Kelly managed to interrupt him. "Don't you say that name! You know Wrath has ruined that name."

Gerry sighed. "For the love of chips and cheeseburgers." He grabbed hold of her falling body helping her settle onto the ground.

"That's more like it. Any chance you have a phone? I can't hear the fam, which means they can't hear me. Looking for you to phone a friend here, Gerry."

Lacy appeared next to Gerry and Kelly squinted at her. The watcher did not seem pleased as she folded her arms across her chest in silent protest. Kelly didn't know if Lacey's obvious disapproval was caused by her current condition or something else.

"We should get back to Gardenia," Lacey said in a huff.

"It's not like I can control where I get pulled," Gerry responded.

"What's wrong?" Kelly's voice was fading. "Is Gardenia in trouble?"

"I am not leaving her here like this," Gerry said to Lacey.

"We might need to work on this calling for help thing for the future, Gerry," Kelly teased.

Lacey disappeared and after a few moments she returned with Michael. Her brother viewed the situation and nodded at Lacey.

"Thank you, I've got this." Michael leaned down and slid both arms underneath Kelly. She winced as he picked her up off the ground.

"How did Lacey know where you were?" Kelly asked as Michael avoided Lacey's gaze.

Lacey blushed, her high cheekbones a glossy shade of pink.

"Are you two dating?" Kelly blurted out.

Michael cleared his throat. "Let's get you back to the house before you pass out."

"You're going to be alright, Kelly." Gerry reassured.

"That's not a denial," Kelly whispered to Michael as her head became foggy. "Just to be clear tacos would have really added to the rescue." The words were jumbled as her head fell against Michael's shoulder and she gave in to the enveloping darkness of unconsciousness.

***

Chilly air assaulted Kelly's face and she struggled to open her eyes. The blanket was warm across her body, but the cool breeze made her shiver. Kelly sat up and Dan was squatting next to her.

"You're awake!" Dan announced. "How are you feeling?"

"Surprisingly, I feel great." She sat up. "Where the heck are we?"

The dark red carpet she was lying on smelled musty. There were several humans standing around and singing was coming from somewhere behind her.

"We're in a church about fifty miles from Michael's house," Dan told her. "People are continuing to come in, but I'm influencing them away from our position. Even though they can't see us, I didn't want you to feel the sensation of people standing over you. Sorry for the chilly air, it's from the doors opening and closing. This is the best spot, we're at least somewhat out of the way. Now that you're awake, we can head back to the house."

"I am assuming there is a story behind why we are in a church," Kelly told him. "But the hunger pangs I'm experiencing are keeping me from caring about it."

Dan chuckled. "Yeah, I told them to have food ready, that we'd be there soon. Gen is anxious to chat about something she and Frankie came across today."

"Great," Kelly answered. "I love listening to stories while I eat."

Dan grabbed Kelly's hand and helped pull her back to her feet.

"This church is huge, and it looks completely full," Kelly commented.

"Yup," Dan answered. "That's why you healed so fast. You've only been out for about forty minutes."

"Wow!" Kelly said. "That's incredible on multiple levels. I will assume this is part of Gen's story."

"Yes," Dan answered. "As is Gardenia."

"Is she alright?" Kelly's mind raced as she remembered Gerry and Lacey talking about the young woman just before Michael arrived in the barn.

"She's healed," Dan told her. "Gen healed

Gardenia in a church, much like this one."

Kelly was relieved that Gardenia was healed, but there was an edge to Dan's voice that made her uneasy.

"We should get going," Dan told her. "Gen is eager to explain."

Kelly nodded and the scent of candles followed them as they were wrapped in their auras and teleported away.

CHAPTER EIGHT

T he aroma of garlic and warm bread filled Michael's house. Steam drifted from the boiling pot on the stove in thin billowing strips, its humidity fogging the windows and dampening the air. Gen stood in the living room waiting on her siblings. She stared out at the big open space that lay beyond Michael's front doors.

Not all my siblings. I envisioned this day a hundred times. That eventually one or more of us would lose our life in this seemingly endless conflict. I understood and yet, knowing brought me no comfort when the day came. The loss flooded her. It was a ruthless unceasing pain. An emotional assault the likes of which she knew would haunt her.

"They're coming." Michael's voice snapped her back to the present.

"I'll help Tom finish up." Gen walked into the kitchen. Pulling mismatched plates from the cabinet she placed them on the counter next to falling stacks of silverware.

It's not a dinner party. Kelly needs to eat, we all do. This is a necessity.

Gen surveyed the table. Frankie sat with his head resting against the wall, his blue T-shirt smeared with dirt and blood. His eyes were closed as he held an ice pack against his right eye. Greg had sunken into the living room sofa with ripped jeans revealing a bloodied leg. He pulled out a kitchen chair and propped his wounded leg upon it. Greg's wavy hair was pulled back into a slick ponytail, his piercing blue eyes red rimmed and bloodshot. Michael's war-torn face set serious and ragged with fatigue, his normal crisp white T-shirt worn and wrinkled. Tom, who typically hummed as he cooked, moved about the kitchen slowly. They were battered and bruised, but there was more to come.

The front door creaked open and then snapped shut. The chilly air swept in, the window blinds rattling in protest.

Dan walked into the kitchen and nodded at Greg. "You should take that leg to a nearby church when we're done. It's miraculous how quickly you heal. Standing there watching over Kell, all the human's prayers healed things in me I didn't even know were hurt."

"Yeah," Greg answered. "I might nap while I'm at it."

"I experienced it a bit when I met up with Gen at St. Ann's," Frankie added. "It was startling how quickly it happened."

"Speaking of St. Ann's," Kelly interrupted. "What happened to Gardenia?"

"I will get to that," Gen told her. "Let's carb up here, might as well eat while you listen. We need the sustenance before heading out again."

Kelly nodded and made her way to the stove where Tom had drained the pasta and put it back in the pot with some butter. A small saucepan on the adjacent burner brimmed with tomato sauce. It was a simple meal, but more than adequate for their needs.

"There is bread on the counter." Tom pointed to his right where a wooden cutting board held sliced bread ready for the taking.

Plates were filled and carried to the table. Michael placed water bottles in the center for all to reach, then sat himself.

Gen ate, trying to be grateful for this moment of comfort that she was able to share with her family, but it was difficult. The ravages of war left their marks both inside and out. As plates were emptied and bottles drained, the heaviness of Xavier's loss and Deb's absence encroached.

It's not the same without them. But we must move forward.

"I encountered a few vampires just behind St. Ann's today," Gen told them. "I was badly injured, my stomach nearly sliced open. My right leg punctured. I was lucky to have gotten out of there."

Tom grabbed Gen's right shoulder. "We're glad you're okay."

"Thank you." Gen's smile waned at the sight of her brother's bruised and burned face. "I walked alongside the church, making my way toward the street when I noticed all these people waiting to get inside the church. I don't know why, but I followed them inside."

"Pull of Heaven maybe?" Tom theorized.

"Could be," Kelly added. "What happened at the church?"

"All these people were praying and waiting for Father Donovan. It was some sort of prayer service. With what's been going on, they're happening all over. There were several news crews in the parking lot filming it."

"Isn't that odd?" Greg stated. "Why would they film that?"

"I don't know," Gen answered. "I heard one of them talking about a vampiric virus, a contagion."

"Great," Kelly huffed. "Just what we need, the media calling this a virus, spreading panic."

"This stuff is all over the news," Dan commented. "I don't think they're saying anything people haven't already experienced on some level."

"They have to call it something," Michael added.

"Agreed." Gen continued. "While I was inside my wounds starting healing."

"I felt the power of it," Kelly attested. "Since waking up, I feel more than healed. I feel almost restored, well except hunger, but the pasta fixed that. Thank you, Tom."

"You're welcome," Tom answered. "I think we all needed it."

"We did," Gen agreed. "Somehow the people praying healed me in a way I have never experienced. It was more than physical, it was a sort of complete healing, inside and out."

"Maybe we should be having this meeting in a church," Greg quipped. "I could use a little help with this leg."

"I thought of that," Gen told him. "I changed my mind because I wasn't sure if they would see us."

"Who?" The lilt in Michael's voice revealing his piqued interest.

"The humans," Gen told them.

"Why would you think that?" Dan asked. "We just came from a church. It was packed and I don't remember anyone even looking in our direction."

"Let me start over," Gen told them. "I went inside the church and within minutes my stomach sealed over, I could feel myself healing. I stood at the back of the church within feet of all these people squeezing into every available seat."

"That must have been something," Michael commented.

"It was. As soon as I felt Tom, I called him there."

"I felt what Gen is referring to." Tom nodded. "I told Greg and Frank about it, we stayed long enough to heal and then went back on patrol. All of us immediately encountered vampires."

"I assumed that's what happened," Gen said. "I went to Harry's to ask him about it, only to find that he and Gardenia were attacked by a vampire."

"Oh no!" Kelly leaned forward, elbows on the thick oak table. "That must have been awful, are you sure they're alright?"

"Yes." Gen wanted to alleviate Kelly's fears. "I don't know all the details, just that Gardenia had been bitten."

Gen sat back, the slats of the chair digging into her spine. "I took Gardenia back to the church. I couldn't be sure it would help, but I hoped between the people praying and Frankie boosting my powers that we might be able to heal her."

"I'm sorry we didn't stay longer." Frankie squeezed the melted icepack he was using, droplets of water beaded on the table.

"You came back." Gen's eyes met her brothers. "That's what matters."

"Dan said she's alright, so the healing worked," Kelly surmised.

"No," Gen answered. "I tried, but it didn't work and the people at the church, they saw and heard Gardenia howling in pain."

"How is that possible?" Michael asked.

"I don't know," Gen told him. "Gardenia screamed out and people turned and looked right at her. Then someone in the crowd yelled *she's infected, she has the virus,* and everyone started running. Everyone panicked, it was chaos."

"The veil." Kelly's voice was barely a whisper. "It must be tearing."

"I hadn't thought about that." Gen paused.

"I guess that was bound to happen," Tom said with a sigh. "The sheer number of vampires and now demons roaming Earth, it must be too much."

The veil was a nickname for the power that kept the supernatural from being revealed to humanity. It wasn't perfect but it had been in place for thousands of years.

I guess it's not the first time the veil was weakened, Gen thought. *There have been other conflicts during which the strain on the veil nearly brought it down.*

"I guess I never thought I'd be here to see the day it gave way, you know?" Gen asked.

"The longer this war stretches on, the weaker it will get," Kelly said. "Eventually, humans will see all of it, both Heaven and Hell. Right now, it's probably only people touched by Hell that are seeing through it."

"I doubt everyone in that church was touched by Hell," Tom added. "I think it may be geographical too. Areas that have seen very little activity, may not be affected as much as those who have seen heavy conflict."

"I think this is a worry for another day," Michael commented. "What happened next, Gen?"

"I tried to heal Gardenia, but it didn't work. I was so mad I banged my fist against the wall. Water from the font splashed on me and Gardenia. I don't know exactly what it did. It was as if the water cleansed the demonic fluid that had seeped from Gardenia's body. It turned the muddy liquid into steam and then it evaporated."

"It healed her?" Michael asked. "How?"

"Harry told me it was holy water, that he got it from Antonio." Gen paused knowing the Arch Angel's name alone was still a source of stress for Kelly.

Kelly shifted uncomfortably in her chair but said nothing. Her thick black hair was braided and fell to the middle of her back. Her raincoat bulged on the side, the glimmer of a weapon peeking out through the opening.

"Harry said when the holy water didn't work as a weapon against the demons the vampires were turning, he started putting it in churches and hospital chapels," Gen told them.

"You think it came from a purity pool?" Kelly asked.

"I think it may have," Gen said. "I poured it down Gardenia's throat. I began to heal her, then Frankie showed up. Together we brought her back, but that holy water was the difference. Gardenia would be dead if it weren't for that. I'm sure of it."

"If that's true, how are we getting this out to everyone?" Dan asked.

"First," Gen answered. "I want to see if we can heal someone else. To be sure it's not an outlier."

"Who did you have in mind?" Tom asked.

"The family we came across not too far from here."

"We did tell the parents we'd be back to check on them." Greg labored back up to his feet. "No time like the present."

"Actually," Gen interrupted. "Anyone hurt should head to the closest religious gathering and heal. If the holy water works on their son, Joey, we'll need to get that information out to all the other Guardians. Which means we need everyone healthy."

"Agreed," Michael added. "We don't all need to visit the boy. Dan and Kelly since you're healed, why don't you go with Gen over to the ranch. I'll write down the address. The rest of us will stop by the nearest house of worship. Once we're healed, we'll come back and wait for you here."

Dan stood up. "Sounds like a plan."

"Be safe," Frankie offered before heading out.

"You too." Gen tried to muster confidence. "See you soon."

Michael handed Gen a piece of paper. "Be careful, we have no idea what's happened to them in the last several days."

"We will."

Michael left the kitchen enveloped in his aura. Gen asked Kelly. "Are you truly better?"

Kelly nodded. "I feel better than I have in several days."

"Good," Gen said. "If this works, it might be enough to shift things back in our favor."

"We need a win," Kelly added.

***

The property was about twelve miles south of Michael's house. In addition to the main house, there was a fenced off riding area, a barn, and a large shed. It was eerily quiet. There wasn't a person in sight. The home's curtains were drawn, windows and doors closed.

The sun was setting and wind rustled through the trees, knocking around some wooden buckets left by the barn door.

"Looks abandoned," Dan commented. "They may not have stuck around."

"Can't blame them if they couldn't bring themselves to come back here," Kelly added. "It's not like they could return to normal life."

"No," Gen agreed. "It is home though, and people do have a tendency to return home."

The thought of coming home made Gen think of Gabriel. How she yearned to be home with him once again. Not that they still had a home to return to. Garrick and Keeva attacked her and Kelly in the home she had shared with her husband. Now it was burned to the ground, nothing but a pile of rubble, a bitter reminder of how fleeting this life is.

Gen walked toward the front porch. *Someone is watching. I can feel eyes following us.*

The house needed a new coat of paint and the

floorboards creaked in protest as she made her way forward. The door swung open. The smell of a hot meal wafted out to meet them.

"Why are you here?" a woman asked. "You should go, it's not safe here."

Gen didn't recognize the older woman. Her gray hair fell in waves down to her shoulder. She smelled of onion and rosemary and wore a stained white apron that read *Got Soup* on it. Her blue eyes peered out under heavy lids, like sleep eluded her.

Before Gen could speak the door was pulled back further. A man stood tall behind the older woman wielding a handgun.

"It's you." The man lowered his weapon. "You came back."

The older woman asked the man. "These the angels you talked about?"

"We aren't angels," Kelly grumbled. "We don't have a lot of time and we need to come inside."

The two stepped back away from the door and Kelly led them into the house. The floor plan was open, the hardwood floors gleamed throughout the massive space. The ceiling was vaulted with wooden beams that ran the length of the house.

"Apologies, I never did get your names," the man said. "I'm Bob, this is my mother, Dorothy."

"I'm Gen and these are my siblings, Dan and Kelly."

"Are your wife and son here?" Dan asked following deeper into the interior of the home.

"Yes," Bob told them as they walked. "They aren't well."

Gen stole a glance over at Kelly who arched an eyebrow in return.

"We'd like to see them," Gen told them.

"We just finished making them some soup," Bob answered with a slight quiver to his voice.

"They aren't eating?" Gen asked.

"Some," Bob answered.

"Not a lick," Dorothy corrected. "Clara is on death's doorstep if you ask me."

"Don't say that," Bob snapped.

"It's okay." Kelly held her hands up as if in surrender. "We're here to help, bring us to them."

"They're each in their rooms," Bob told them. "It's down the hall, I don't know that my son will let you near him."

"Angel or not, I doubt they'll want to step anywhere near Joey," Dorothy added.

"What do you mean?" Gen asked.

"Devils got ahold of my grandson." Dorothy shook her head. "Ain't no amount of praying going to bring him back."

"Dan and I will start with the boy," Kelly told Gen. "You see if Clara's up for a drink of water."

Kelly pointed down the hall. "Which door is Joey's room?"

"Last door on the left," Bob answered. "My wife is in the second door on the right, after the hall bathroom."

Kelly walked off closely followed by Dan.

"We'll do what we can," Gen told them. "I know you and your wife were bitten, but how about you, Dorothy. When were you attacked?"

"I haven't been. I came out to the ranch and found it empty," she answered. "The animals in the barn were slaughtered, at first I thought maybe wolves had gotten in there, but then I found Jack."

The older woman grabbed the top of a kitchen chair and wrapped her knuckles tightly around it. The memory clearly rattling her.

"Jack worked for me," Bob answered. "He stayed in a small house about five hundred yards beyond the shed."

"When I didn't find anyone home, I went to the barn," Clara continued. "When I saw the carnage, I went to Jack's. There were red stains all over the house, like someone had been throwing his blood all around. Furniture was smashed, cabinet doors ripped off the hinges. There was splatter on every wall, stains on the carpet. Such a mess, whoever it was had to have spent a good amount of time in there. That was nothing compared to finding poor Jack nearly severed in two."

Dorothy shook her head and turned away from them.

"I'm sorry," Gen answered. "I needed to know if you were infected."

Since Dorothy can see us, the veil must be thin here. Gen thought. *Tom was right, humans don't have to be directly touched by Hell to see the supernatural. They just have to be an area where the veil is weak.*

"My wife." Bob's voice cracked as his eyes filled with tears. "She tried holding Joey down during one of his violent spells. He clawed at her like a wild animal."

"I can't imagine how tough this has been on all of you." Gen's heart broke a little at the thought of what this family has been living through.

The pot on the stove boiled over. The soup splashed over the side, the flame underneath flared and hissed. Dorothy walked to the stove and turned off the gas.

"Give us a few minutes." Gen told them as she walked toward the hallway. "We'll let you know how it goes."

The hallway was dimly lit and when Gen turned the knob to the bedroom door, she half expected to encounter something ripped from a horror movie. Instead, Clara was lying face up on the bed tucked under several blankets. There was a low moan that escaped Clara's lips, the cadence lilted up and down with no discernable pattern.

Blue drapes were drawn shut, light sparsely seeping through the thin gap between them. Clara's chest heaved as she struggled to breathe. Gen reached the end table next to the bed and turned on the lamp. The woman's gaunt face barely flinched at the sudden illumination. Clara's eyes were closed, but her pupils rolled back and forth continuously.

Nightmares. If she's in a coma-like state now, she's trapped in her own horrific memories.

Clara's face was ghostly white, and her cheeks were sunken in. The area under the eyes was dark and discolored. A stark contrast to the room's décor. The walls were painted in an off-white color. The comforter was yellow with navy blue flowers. Next to the lamp was a basket of blue and purple ageratum. The head of the flower was like a small fuzzy mum. The air smelled of fresh laundry and fresh cut flowers.

Dorothy was right, Clara wasn't sick, she was dying.

Retrieving an amulet of holy water Gen lifted the woman's head and slipped the water over her lips and into her mouth. Once the water was safely down Clara's throat, Gen gently placed the woman's head back down on the pillow. Raising her hands above the woman's chest, Gen prayed as she attempted to heal her. Within minutes the woman's eyes blinked open and her body convulsed. Gasping, she coughed trying to clear the demonic liquid from her chest. Pillows fell from the bed as fluid sprang from her eyes and dribbled down her nose. As if in the throes of a great fever her face turned a ruddy shade of pink and her forehead beaded with sweat.

Gen closed her eyes and continued to pray, focusing all her energy down upon the woman. She could sense a push and pull happening within Clara's body. It was several minutes before Clara stilled and her breathing steadied. Slowly the woman pushed her hands down on the bed and managed to get herself into a partially upright position. Her small frame was nearly lost in the large bed. Clara's shirt was stained, she pulled one of the blankets up to her chest and peered at Gen seemingly trying to make sense of why Gen was in her bedroom. Her stained lips quivered, but she didn't speak.

"Clara?" Bob asked softly from the bedroom doorway. Tears streaked Bob's face. "You're awake!"

"Bob." The woman's eyes fell upon her husband. Her coloring continuing to return to her face.

Bob rushed past Gen and collapsed onto the bed enveloping Clara in an embrace.

After several moments, Clara mumbled into her husband's shoulder, "How's Joey?"

A thud came from down the hall. Crashing glass shattered the quiet of the house.

"I'm going to check on them," Gen told Bob. "Stay here, Clara needs more rest."

As Gen pivoted toward the door, she found a tearful Dorothy in the entryway. The woman's hands were covering her mouth as she struggled to make sense of her daughter-in-law's sudden recovery.

"I didn't think anything could save her." Dorothy whispered to Gen as she stepped clear of the doorway. "Please, save my grandson. I know he don't look human anymore, but please, save that child."

"We'll do everything we can."

Not human anymore, Gen thought in horror. *If he's already turned, we may be too late.*

CHAPTER NINE

Kelly turned the knob to Joey's room and pushed it open. She was taken aback by the scent of pine cleaner barely masking the pungent odor of urine. The window openings were covered with cardboard crudely taped to the wall in haphazard fashion. The click of the door behind her dimmed the room further.

Panting was coming from her right. When her eyes adjusted, there was a figure crouched at the end of the bed. Joey was awake and staring over at her.

We should get some sunlight in here, Kelly said telepathically.

When Dan didn't move, nor answer, Kelly knew the room was cloaked.

"We can't talk privately, Dan."

"Yeah. I realized that when you said nothing about the ambiance."

"Joey," Kelly announced. "We met in the forest when we helped you and your parents. Do you remember us?"

"Go away." The whisper carried the stench of bad breath and decaying flesh.

Dan walked behind Kelly toward the windows. Yanking the curtains open, Joey screamed.

"No light!" The boy scrambled away from the edge and back toward the headboard.

Joey was half naked, he wore some sort of vest with a gray T-shirt underneath. His white underwear was stained and threadbare. His hair was slick and matted against the sides of his head. Joey's eyes were bloodshot, lips cracked with the corners bleeding. Joey was bruised from head to toe as if he had been beaten.

"Calm down, Joey." Kelly held her hands, palms facing out. "We're not going to hurt you.

The boy swatted at the air, his body jerked, and he made animalistic noises and grunts. The rattling of metal on metal drew Kelly's eyes to the mattress. Someone had mounted a chain to the wall just above the headboard. Joey was harnessed. He was effectively pinned to the confines of the queen size bed.

Oh my. This is no vampire.

The navy blue sheets were torn. What was left of them hung over the left side of the bed, the exposed mattress was covered in yellow and brown stains. Someone had attempted to clean up the mess, but Joey was essentially living in the remnants of his own feces.

Aside from the bed, the room was ordinary. Painted in a neutral pale gray, the hardwood floors were stained a deep chocolate brown. One lone framed photograph of a snow covered Wilson's Peak hung on the wall behind where they were standing. The end tables had been moved to the other side of the room, no longer within range of the bed.

The setting sun washed the room in a gloomy yellow. Joey backed away from the streaks of light that cascaded through the now cleared windows.

"This is not what I expected," Dan stated.

"Tell me about it," Kelly retorted.

"Hey Joey." Dan turned back to the teenager. "We want to help you buddy. Get you back up on your feet, and out of this room. Do you want that?"

"Yes." Joey sang the words. "Let me out."

"We're going to give you something to drink, okay?" Dan asked without waiting for an answer. "It's best if you lay down on your back, Joey. Your head closest to us."

"No." Joey answered with a small giggle. "I'm not going to do that."

"You're going to leave this boy's body." Kelly's tone was firm. "We're not leaving this room until you do."

Joey leapt to his feet and ran for the edge of the bed closest to them. He flung his arms above his head and yanked the ceiling light free from its brackets and threw it at them. Kelly ducked and the glass shade smashed to the floor behind them.

"You sure about this tactic?" Dan asked as the teenager clawed at his own flesh while leering at them. "I'm not sure we're actually talking to Joey."

"Agreed, but Joey is still in there," Kelly answered. "We need to get that demon out of him. Harry can call an Arch Angel. We'll need help with the exorcism, and they know the ritual."

The door to the bedroom opened. Light from the hallway came into the room. Joey screeched and once again scurried back toward the far end of the mattress away from it.

"What's happened?" Gen asked. "Everyone alright?"

Shards of glass crunched under the weight of Gen's shoes as she walked further into the room.

"Yes," Dan answered. "Joey threw the ceiling light at us when we suggested he take a sip of something we brought with us."

"What's wrong with him?" Gen asked. "Why is he chained to the bed?"

"In Joey's weakened physical condition, he's been taken over," Kelly answered. "This was not on our radar. Now, we have something new to watch out for."

"How far along?" Gen asked as her eyes took in the entirety of the situation.

"Joey's dead," the teenager cooed from his crouched position in the corner of the bed. "He's not coming back."

"Have you started?" Gen asked Kelly.

"No." Kelly pulled a small bottle of holy water

from her inside jacket pocket. "I think one of us should go tell his family to prepare."

"The mother's awake and asking for him," Gen answered.

Joey's head snapped to his left and he stared at Gen. "Mommy's awake?" The teenager's tone turned sinister. "I want to see mommy, let me see mommy!"

With the help of her husband, Clara had fumbled down the hall toward the bedroom. When she got to the doorway her eyes fell on Joey, her bruised and battered son, and she screamed.

"Dear God!" Clara cried. "What's happened to my son?"

Bob turned his wife away shielding her from Joey. "We had to tie him down Clara. He hurt Mom and then he started hurting himself. We couldn't control him any longer."

"Mommy?" Joey's voice lilted upward suddenly resembling a toddler.

Clara pushed back against her husband. She braced her hands on either side of the door frame for stability.

"You." Clara pointed at Kelly. "Get that thing out of my son!"

Clara swayed and fell back into Bob's arms as Gen walked toward the two of them. "I'll explain what's about to happen." Gen turned back toward Kelly. "Are you doing this alone?"

"No," Kelly answered. "I'm calling Antonio."

Dan placed his hand on Kelly's shoulder. "Why

him? We can tell Harry to call someone else."

"Antonio and I have worked these together before," Kelly answered. "We could call someone else, but we'd have to waste time learning how the other operates. This will be faster."

"It's your call," Dan commented.

"It's the only call," Kelly retorted. "At this advanced stage, we need to act fast. It's not about me right now, it's about Joey."

Gen nodded from the hallway, then turned right toward the kitchen.

"I'll call Harry," Dan said walking toward the door. "I'll give him the location so he can relay it. He should be here within a few minutes. If not–"

Joey was sitting cross legged with his back to them. The teenager was banging his forehead against the headboard. Urine splattered the wood and trickled to the floor under the bed.

"Antonio will come," Kelly answered.

"Are you sure?" Dan asked. "Antonio might know of someone else he's worked these cases with that can help."

"I can do it," Kelly answered. "I think you should call and tell the others what we're doing."

"I will," Dan told her. "What else will you need?"

"Candles and something that can handle fire," Kelly told him. "I think I saw an old burned out barrel by the barn."

"I'm on it," Dan answered before exiting the

room.

"You can't have him," Joey warned Dan. "You need more than an angel to get me out."

"I know exactly what I need to get you out, demon." Kelly's voice was barely a whisper.

Joey's body fell backward onto the mattress. He wrapped his bare knuckles around a long piece of the metal chain and swung it toward his arms and legs. He repeated this motion until the teenager's skin split open. Blood sprayed from the wounds and added yet another stain to the ruined mattress.

Kelly removed the stopper on a bottle of holy water and stepped closer to the bed. She shook the bottle toward Joey and holy water splashed across his body seeping into his open wounds.

Joey screamed, his back arched upward, and the chain dropped back onto the bed.

"Thanks for letting me know you've never done this before, demon."

Breathless, Joey rolled over and crawled toward her. The wounds on his chest were already sealing.

"Please," Joey said in a normal tone of voice. "Don't do that again, it hurts."

"It's going to hurt a lot more when I get my hands on you, demon."

Kelly took another vile and dosed him with more holy water before he could scurry away from her. She began praying in Latin while she waited. The sky cracked with the roar of thunder and lighting. Flapping noises came from above.

"No!" Joey yelled. "You can't have him. He's mine!"

Gen came back into the room. "He's here and he's not alone."

Dan appeared in the doorway with the barrel. "Where do you want it?"

"Here." Kelly moved to her left and pointed to the floor. "Center it at the bottom of the bed, but several feet back out of his reach."

Dan rolled the barrel into place, Gen lit candles and left them on the end tables on the far side of the room away from Joey.

"What else?" Gen asked.

"Firewood." Kelly answered.

"No need." Antonio answered from the doorway. "I have some."

Entering the room, the Arch Angel dumped two pieces of wood in the barrel. His handsome face was covered in a beard several days in the making. His boots were muddy and the black mid-length raincoat he wore was torn at the elbow.

"Make sure none of them come down here," Kelly told her siblings. "No matter what they hear."

"I think they understand that, but we'll be there with them," Gen answered before making her way out of the room with Dan.

Kelly stood alone with the Arch Angel, every bit of the tension between them palpable.

I can't think of him as Antonio. He's just another Arch Angel here to help me pull a demon out of a fifteen-year-

old.

"Who else did you bring?" Kelly asked.

"I brought Samantha and May. I didn't know how old it was, Harry didn't say."

"You brought the heavy hitters," Kelly said. "That's good, but this demon didn't seem to understand the ramifications of splitting open Joey's skin in front of me."

"That is good." Antonio walked closer to the bed peering at the child cowering away from him.

Joey spit at Antonio, but the Arch Angel was quick enough to move out of the way. The teenager laughed and went about picking at his short nails. Some were already bitten to the quick. He gnawed at his fingers causing them to bleed, the blood trickled down his hands and he laughed.

The teenager held his hand out toward Kelly. "You are going to lose this war. We're already crawling all over Earth. We're coming to get you, to kill all of you."

Kelly sprayed the teenager with the last of the holy water she had. The child yelled in protest and started speaking in a foreign tongue, one she couldn't understand.

"I hope you brought replenishments," Kelly stated.

Antonio took off his jacket. Across his shoulder was the strap of a brown leather satchel that hung over his hip. He took the bag off and opened it. Inside were several vials of holy water and holy oil. He handed several to Kelly.

"Are you ready?" he asked.

"Hell's not getting this child," Kelly seethed.

Joey began jumping up and down on the bed whipping the chain as he went. The clanging of metal reverberated off the empty walls. Screeching at the top of his lungs, Kelly winced at the piercing pitch of Joey's voice.

Antonio leaned toward Kelly. "He thinks he can keep us from communicating this way."

Kelly nodded in understanding. "Let's do this."

Antonio went to the barrel, doused the firewood with holy oil and lit it using one of the nearby candles. Despite the length of the barrel, and only igniting two logs, the holy flame was tall. It blazed several inches above the rim, but in no danger of reaching the ceiling.

Joey quieted, got on all fours, and crawled to the edge of the bed as if drawn to the flickering flame.

"That's good, Joey," Antonio soothed. "You like fire, don't you?"

Kelly began praying once more. Joey was panting, he kept staring at the barrel.

Antonio joined in prayer and the teenager began crying but kept to his position on the bed.

After several minutes, the teenager laid on his side, facing the fire. He seemed mesmerized by the glorious glow.

Kelly locked eyes with Antonio and he nodded slightly giving her the go ahead. She uncapped the holy oil and soaked her right hand. Kelly placed one knee on the bed, reached across and placed her hand on the back of Joey's head.

The teenager rolled quickly toward her. He used the chain to harness her right hand as it fell away from his head. He pulled and Kelly's feet left the floor. The smell of fire, candle wax, and sweat filled the air.

Kelly got to her knees and punched Joey with her left hand. The teenager's head snapped back, and he let go of the chain long enough for her hand to slip free. She didn't back off, instead Kelly climbed onto the teenager's chest. Forcing Joey's hands down onto the mattress took a great deal of effort. The teenager writhed up and down on the bed. Antonio grabbed more holy oil and made the sign of the cross on Joey's forehead several times as he prayed.

The teenager bucked, took a deep breath in, and then a blast of energy left his body. Kelly flew several feet in the air slamming against the wall to the right of the bed. She hit the floor face down and blood trickled from her nose. When she lifted her head Joey was leaning over the bed.

"You lose, bitch." He reached for her, but Kelly recoiled.

"Not likely," she replied through gritted teeth.

Antonio jumped on the bed, grabbed Joey from behind, and lifted him onto his feet. The Arch Angel pulled Joey's arms behind his back to keep him in place. This gave Kelly another opening, and she seized it.

Leaping onto the bed, she placed her hands above his head and focused her heavenly energy down upon the possessed boy. Joey was sucking in air, yelling, and spitting. He pulled so hard to get away from Antonio that he dislocated his shoulder and fell to his knees.

It went on like this for quite some time. The back-and-forth dance between Antonio and Kelly seemed effortless, each anticipating what the other would do and when. Without words they moved around each other as they grappled with the possessed teenager.

The battle for Joey's soul was just beginning.

CHAPTER TEN

Gloominess lay ahead, it was getting darker the farther down the path Deb walked.

"Up ahead the area will open up and be lit with torches again." Schlosser whispered from beside her. "Keep an eye out. There aren't many places to hide in the vast openness of the space we're about to walk into."

Inching her way along the path cold air wrapped around her ankles. At the next turn, the flickering of light bounced off a stalactite on the cave ceiling. The space was a relief from the enclosed darkness they had been walking in. The cries of tortured voices sent chills down Deb's spine, a sick reminder of her present circumstance.

There is no solace to be had here.

Deb paused letting her eyes adjust to the light. Schlosser's hand nudged her lower back prodding her to move along.

"They're further away than they sound, Guardian." His husky voice was barely audible over the rolling tide of moaning that seemed to come and go from multiple directions. "Don't lose your nerve now."

Deb shook off his touch and moved forward taking longer strides toward the far side of the space. A reddish-yellow glow came from the opening at the opposite end of where they stood, she followed it. As they came to the end of that path, the area opened to a large, cavernous space. Shadows seemed to dance in every corner. Numerous openings leading off to various paths inward lay in front of them.

How in the world am I going to find him? Any of these will lead me further in and potentially further away from Marcus.

Schlosser walked past her retrieving the carton of condensed milk from the torn backpack she had given him. He opened the container and walked to her right stopping to pour milk at one of the openings. He then continued until he was lined up directly across from her and leaned down to pour another. Coming back around he poured a third amount on her left forming a near perfect triangle. As he finished a vibration rumbled like a wave under her feet. Schlosser took off running toward her position, motioning for her to move back as he did so.

Spinning around she found a large boulder she could stand behind. Once there she crouched down. The demon hastily made his way to join her. As Schlosser bent down next to her, she mouthed *what now?*

"We wait."

"For what?" she whispered.

Before he could answer, claws scraped against rock. Something was running toward them. The shrill that followed raised the hair on Deb's arms.

Whatever it is, it sounds monstrous.

The space became overrun by small-winged creatures. Their long reptilian heads dove for the small pools of milk Schlosser had laid out for them. Each one had a scale covered tail that stood straight into the air. As they jockeyed for position their tails grew spikes and they began swiping at each other. Something akin to blood splattered the gray stone around them.

How is this helping?

Deb began to stand but Schlosser grabbed her arm and pulled her back down to her knees.

"Wait," he demanded. "He'll be here soon."

Deb stared at the scene playing out in front of them. The smell of sour milk mixed with soot and blood. The small creatures tore and ripped at each other trying to reach what little remained of the liquid Schlosser had drawn them out with. With a flash the cavern burst into chaos as streaks of fire sailed through the air. As the flames landed on the horde of animals their tails ignited with the fury of kindling. The cacophony of screeching erupted as the animals grew fearful. The small creatures scratched and clawed their way toward escape.

As a second blast of what Deb assumed to be Hell Fire soared above them and a demon appeared at the base of one of the openings. Brandishing a battle-axe in his left hand the demon surveyed the animals scrambling for cover with disdain.

"Get out of here!" he yelled as he kicked the creatures still vying for the last remnants of milk. "Useless scavengers."

The demon stood seven feet tall, his square chest and large frame obliterated the opening from which he had come. He wore a blood stained gray T-shirt, black fatigues, and steel toed boots. His thick black hair was pulled into a tight ponytail, which made visible a thick rubbery scar that stretched from his scalp down across his forehead. As he scanned the area for the source of the disturbance his dark brown eyes cast downward at the milky white substance below. His arms were covered in tattoos of demonic writing, each line separated by symbols cast in red ink. He leaned down and swiped at what was left of the milk rubbing it between his two fingers. He took a quick sniff of the liquid then wiped the remnants on his pants.

The intricately carved blade of the axe glistened as it swung through the air toward a few straggling creatures at his feet. He caught two of the animals with the blade but missed a third which wasted no time in making a hasty retreat. He slammed the axe against the rock wall to clean the blade. The creatures slid off, but their blood remained.

A plume of smoke formed in the middle of the cave-like space and Azza stepped out from within. "Still chasing hellcats, Robino?"

"What do you want?" he asked without turning toward her.

"For each one you kill, ten more are created. I don't see why you waste your time on such trivial matters."

"I'm not asking twice Azza," Robino scoffed.

"You know what I want," the female snapped. "I know that Guardian is here, and I want her head on a spike."

"Do it yourself, angel," Robino growled. "I won't do your bidding bitch."

Angel? Deb's mind raced. *How could Azza have found us? Unless someone told her I was here. Jade? No, she wouldn't, would she? Maybe, Jade's husband Vermillion sent her. He is one of the horsemen of the apocalypse after all.*

The female's wings burst forth from her back, their once beautiful wine color transformed into a midnight black. The edges of her wings were sharp like the rocky ceiling threatening from above.

How? Deb's mind went back to the night she was last with her family. The night the vampires attacked them on the beach. *Antonio told us Jared had sliced her wings off when he rescued Kelly. How does Azza have her wings back?*

"You will if I open those gates, Robino." She snarled at the demon.

"You think because Wrath got you your wings back and stole a Hellcrux that somehow that makes you powerful?" Robino took several menacing steps toward Azza. "It doesn't. It makes you a target."

Azza turned left, and Deb was yanked back away from the edge of the rockface by Schlosser. The two of them held flat against the bolder they were hiding behind. Deb closed her eyes and calmed her racing heart. One wrong move and she would be face to face with the murderous fallen angel who killed Christian and dragged Kelly to Hell.

"I am not the enemy," Azza told the demon.

"You sure about that?" Robino taunted. "You come down here, sell a heavenly soul so you can get juiced up with hell fighter venom, then kill a bunch of a demons and think you're worthy of something."

"Fighting is pointless," Azza stated. "When I open the gates–"

"When you open them!" Robino bellowed. "You're some piece of work. Your own kind sliced off your wings and escaped with your prisoner. Why in the world would anyone turn their back on Lucifer and follow you?"

"You have no idea what I'm capable of," Azza threatened. "I have let loose hell's first army on Earth. Wrath is close to collecting all his siblings' powers, and I have a Hellcrux. You should reconsider your position."

"You forget," Robino snarled. "You aren't the first to unleash the vampires. They've been waiting for any excuse to ravage. They have no allegiance to you, and you have no control over them."

"That's not true. We formed an alliance. It's not too late for you join us."

Deb peaked around their hiding spot once more. Azza was standing with her back to Deb, directly across from Robino. The fallen angel's wings were once more folded inside her body.

"You know what I heard," Robino mocked. "I heard the Guardians are killing vampires by the dozens, hunting them down and slaying them like the rats that they are."

Killing vampires. Deb was confused. *How did they figure out how to kill so many vampires?*

"I don't care." Azza shook her head. "The vampires will hold the line. They know what's important. The Guardians are running around trying to keep humanity safe, while we consolidate power. By the time the Guardians figure out what we're really doing, it will be too late. I will have what I need from Wrath. I will open the gates to all seven realms and unleash hell on Earth."

"You should care," Robino laughed. "The demons tell me this one Guardian in particular is a killing machine."

Silence fell across the space. Robino's boots scraped against the stone floor as he made his way closer to Azza's position.

"A female demon just returned, said she was beaten and stabbed through the ear." Robino paused, clearly enjoying the suspense. "Her skull penetrated, but not before she was given a message."

"I don't have time for games," Azza snapped.

"Oh, it's no game." Robino leaned in close invading Azza's space. "The Guardian that killed my demon told her, *if you see Azza, tell her Kelly O'Mara is coming for her.*"

Kelly! Deb's mind squealed. *Kelly's hunting down Azza!*

"Now." Robino walked back toward the opening he had come through. Before exiting he turned back to face Azza once more. "If you get past Vermillion and get to Jade. If you outrun and out maneuver both those in Heaven and those in Hell who stand against you. If you make it through the Pit and open the gates to the seven realms, then we can talk. Until then, enjoy being hunted. I can't think of anyone who deserves it more."

With a whistle Robino turned, threw his battle-axe onto his right shoulder, and left in a dusty haze of smoke.

Azza's wings burst forth and she left in a huff. After several moments Deb stood and walked out from behind the large column of rock.

"Azza stole a hellcrux," Deb stated.

"Apparently so, though it's more likely she struck a deal."

"How do you know she didn't kill for it?" Deb peered around the space ensuring they were once again alone.

"Did it look like she could have killed Robino?" Schlosser peered at Deb.

"He didn't seem to be a fan," Deb commented. "Maybe she's overestimated her influence around here."

"One can hope." Schlosser sneered. "Now you know there are seven realms in hell. Each one has a hellcrux, a weapon, but also a key, a way to get out."

"Wrath figured out how to restore Azza's wings." Deb was perplexed. "Do you know anything about that?"

"I know they wanted to kill an Arch Angel, something about a ring."

Jacob, Deb remembered. *That's why Wrath killed Jacob.*

"How are we going to get a hellcrux?"

"We're going to steal it." Schlosser gave her a sly smile.

"How do you know where they are?" Deb asked him.

"Each realm is ruled by one of the seven gods of darkness." Schlosser paused waiting for the information to settle in. "Each god has a hellcrux."

"Oh is that all." Deb mocked as she fisted her hands on each hip. "Steal a hellcrux from a ruler in hell. How do you suppose we do that? Assuming we can even find one of these so-called gods." Deb said the last word using air quotes.

"We just did," Schlosser told her.

"Robino?" Deb asked turning back to the spot the demon had been standing in.

"Yes," Schlosser confirmed. "Robino is one of the seven gods of darkness. He has a particular disdain for hellcats and apparently fallen angels."

"My head hurts." Deb huffed.

"Here." Schlosser removed the jug of water from the backpack and handed it to her. "Drink."

"Are we following Robino down that path?" Deb pointed out across the cavern.

"Later," Schlosser answered. "I know where he is, we'll go get the hellcrux after."

"After what?" Deb wiped her mouth with the back of her hand.

"After we rescue your boyfriend," Schlosser told her. "Let's go get Marcus and then get out of here."

"Are we close?" Deb asked.

"Yes." Schlosser nodded. "I just needed to know which path we were taking once we got back here. Azza dropping in was unexpected. She seemed a little desperate if you ask me."

"Yeah," Deb agreed. "She stood her own against Robino, though."

"She was shaking in her boots." Schlosser laughed. "He's not even the worst of them. I would love to be a fly on the wall for some of her other proposals."

"Let's get out here," Deb said. "I need to get to my siblings sooner rather than later."

"Seems if you wait long enough, one of them may be coming to you."

"You did seem to think Kelly would be with me," Deb said flippantly.

"Oh believe me," Schlosser smiled. "I want Kelly to find Azza. I like a good vengeance storyline."

CHAPTER ELEVEN

Deb followed Schlosser down a sloping path. The rock walls were warm to the touch. The air was musty and drier than the other dungeon-like spaces they had been walking in.

"There's warmth coming through the walls. Where's it coming from?"

"A searing hot desert," Schlosser answered. "We'll be at the opening in just a sec."

Desert, like with an actual sun? The idea that something as natural and warm as the sun existed in hell seemed impossible. It must be a nickname.

The trail ended at a large metal door. Light seeped through the creases of the encasement. Every few seconds the door rattled as if something on the other side were attempting to open it. Deb took an involuntary step back. Schlosser reached inside his pants pocket and retrieved the pair of scissors he found earlier.

The door was tied shut with a rope. Schlosser

went to work on loosening the knot.

"This is a short cut," he told her. "Hope you're a good runner."

"I take it there's something out there we don't want to encounter."

"There are many somethings. But it's the wind that will get you."

Deb paused. There was no noise except for the door. It continued to bang as he worked through the rope. It was unsettling to think about where she was, the great unknown held no alure for her. She would much rather be safe on Earth, surrounded by her siblings and everything she held dear. More than once she had to remind herself this wasn't about her own security. It never was.

This is about helping Marcus. I will not let him rot in hell, discarded, like the relic of an old war, forgotten.

Schlosser put the scissors back in his pocket. "Keep your head down. Take this end of the rope and don't let go. We're running straight across to the other side."

Grasping the frayed rope she stepped closer to Schlosser. He pulled the door open, and light streamed in from beyond the doorway. The temperature was excessively hot, an oppressive assault on her not yet fully healed wounds. The dry climate evaporated all moisture, immediately drying her mouth and throat. The red orange glow in the atmosphere reminded her of Venus, so hot that steam drifted continuously off the surface.

Stepping up to the doorway, Schlosser peeked right and then left before he started running. Deb nearly lost her end of the short rope as he pulled it ahead of her. Her sneakers were no match for the scorching grains of sand that enveloped her feet and whiplashed her legs as she ran. The burns on her scalp tingled as she was subjected to the blazing heat. Her lungs burned as if the area were comprised of gas and not oxygen. Pain rippled through her. Tears escaped her eyes but evaporated before they could dribble down her cheeks.

Within moments they were huddled at the opening to a cave. The rocky overhang granting shelter from the searing heat. The cave was unlit. Her eyes still adjusting from the desert made it impossible to determine what was inside. Schlosser walked in, still holding the rope. Deb followed when the rope pulled her forward.

Once inside the dim space she let go of the rope and took a moment to catch her breath.

"That saved us several hours of walking below," he told her as he coughed. Removing the travel mug, he took a swig of water and handed it to her. "Drink."

Deb took the mug and drank the liquid. Schlosser coiled the rope and threw it in the satchel he carried. The water was cold, but everything Schlosser touched was tainted by his wretched stink. She held her breath and took another sip before handing it back to him.

"That felt like walking on another planet," Deb said.

"I told you it was hot."

"That was beyond hot."

"We had a short distance to go, and the timing was right. A few more minutes and the tornadoes would have returned."

"I hear wind now. I didn't before."

"The wind is a precursor to the storms."

"If the wind hadn't come yet, why was the door rattling?"

"No idea. It's probably some sort of warning not to open it." Schlosser chuckled. "Storms almost here, there will be plenty of lightning based on how fast it's approaching."

"Just like Venus," Deb mumbled.

"There's a set of stairs at the back of this cave. The territory up here belongs to the gutter demons. They catch us here, and we're toast."

"The gutter demons go out in that heat?" Deb asked.

"They live and roam out there. Their blood is as cold as ice. It's part of what makes them immune."

Deb remembered back to the courtyard at Saint Anne's. The day Michael was nearly killed. They were attacked by gutter demons. It was Deb's first encounter with the demonic scavengers.

Their blood was blue. It was cool and slick to the touch. That day seems like a lifetime ago, but it wasn't. It was the precursor to a battle led by Schlosser, the demon guiding me through hell.

Deb gazed back toward the entryway. The wind

whipped against the exterior walls, tufts of sand drifted in and out of the space. The light from outside extended only a few feet into the interior cave as if it ran into a wall and stopped.

"Are we any closer to Marcus?" Deb asked. It seemed like she had asked this question a hundred times already.

"The torture room is one level below us." He walked toward the far wall. "I'm hoping he's in a prison cell just outside the main room."

"Are we coming back up this way?"

"Yeah. No one would suspect we'd be crazy enough to escape across the desert."

They descended the stairs slowly. The cement steps spiraled to the left. The walls of the stairwell were covered in crude depictions of torture, each one more violent than the next. At the bottom, demonic symbols were painted in red and dotted the walls on all four sides of the room. There were five doorways, all of them open. Each cell had a lit torch by the entrance.

"No security?" Deb whispered.

"To what?" Schlosser asked. "Keep Guardians from breaking and entering?"

"Very funny."

Schlosser walked to the first door and peered inside but did not enter. At the next entry, he threw his palm backward to halt her movement. Deb froze. The smell of campfire drifted out of the cramped space.

Schlosser moved onward, but the scraping of chains slowed his approach to the next door. Peering around the corner of the cell entrance Schlosser seemed hesitant to enter, but eventually did. Deb followed leaving several feet between them.

The room was colder than the hallway. The air smelled of urine and mold. At the far end of the room a body lay on the ground, crumpled in the fetal position. The male faced them, but his eyes were far away. His body trembled from head to toe. Prison cuffs bound his hands and ankles. The chains rustled across the muddy Earth with his jerking movements.

Schlosser coughed and the prisoner narrowed his focus and appeared to gaze upon them for the first time. As Schlosser approached, the male crawled away until his back hit the wall and he could move no further.

"No, no," the male whimpered.

Schlosser held his hands in the air to signal he wasn't a threat. The prisoner focused past Schlosser to Deb who stood just a foot from the door.

"We're looking for someone. A sentinel, do you know him?"

The man eye's darted between them. His fair skin was split open in several places, his brown eyes red rimmed and raw. He simply shook his head in response.

Come on Marcus. Where are you?

Before Schlosser had a chance to turn back, the man yelled out.

"No!" The prisoner thrust his hands in front of his face as if holding something back.

Deb turned toward the doorway, but it was too late. A hard object smashed the left side of her face.

Thrown across the room, Deb's body slammed against the knobby wall of the cell, and she fell to the floor with a thud. Blood gushed from the wound on her head. Her hands flew to her face, but the warm salty liquid had already seeped into her eyes. Her vision blurred and there were two of everything in front of her.

Schlosser was fighting off a large male demon, easily five inches taller and quite a bit heavier than him. The demon's muscles flexed as he threw blow after blow targeting Schlosser's side. He collapsed to one knee.

Shackles rattled on Deb's right. A female towered over her. She wore tight black pants and brown leather boots. Her tank top showcased the sleeves of demonic tattoos that covered her arms. Before Deb could process what was happening the female demon cuffed and dragged Deb out of the room.

"I didn't help them!" the prisoner pleaded.

The female tightly grabbed Deb by the collar of the denim jersey she wore. Two rooms over, the demon pulled Deb inside and fastened the chain of the prison cuffs to a clasp bolted to the wall. She shoved Deb down, kicking her before walking away. Deb kept her head down. She didn't want the demon to so much as sniff that she wasn't supposed to be here. Deb buried her head in her hands as the female lit a torch inside the cell.

Schlosser was tossed next to her. Deb peaked to her right. He was lying on the floor facing away from her. Guttural moans accompanied the blood pooling around Schlosser's lower back. Rolling onto his back exposed a large knife protruding from Schlosser's stomach.

"You so much as think of escaping," the male demon sneered from above. "I'll serve you to the hounds."

The two demons left the room but marked the floor of the entryway with Schlosser's blood. Deb crawled toward Schlosser but couldn't reach him, the chain restrained her just inches from his position. Her head swam as her heart hammered. She was now cuffed inside a cell near the torture room. She was a prisoner.

Stay calm. We're close to Marcus. I can feel it. We'll think of something, we'll get out of here. We have to get out of here.

"How long until they come back?" Deb asked.

Schlosser coughed and struggled to get his bearings. "No idea."

"I didn't hear them approach," Deb said.

"We probably tripped an alarm of some kind."

"I can break these shackles, just as I did yours," Deb said waiting for that to sink in.

"I know." Schlosser's body stilled. "But you need to wait."

"How long?" Deb asked. "That looks pretty deep, not sure how much time we really have here."

"Keep it together. They were low level sentries. They don't know who they have."

"Something else is coming by to take inventory," Deb whispered. "I can feel him."

"You need to make yourself small." Schlosser coughed, liquid escaped his trembling lips. "Get to the back corner of the cell. Turn away and face the wall. Do not look in the demon's eyes."

Deb paused, not wanting to wait around for something else to join them in the room. Schlosser pulled the scissors from his pocket and slid them over to her. Deb picked up the only weapon they possessed.

"Go." Schlosser hacked and rolled side to side.

Following Schlosser's instructions Deb moved to the furthest point away from him. She placed the scissors on the ground next to her and sat with her head against her knees just inches from the thick rock wall.

Deb said the rosary, when she reached the last prayer, she began again. Schlosser's wheezing quieted, several times she paused to make sure he was still breathing.

The cold seemed to settle on top of her like an ice blanket. The bloody wound sealed but pain throbbed the sides of her head and made her neck ache.

Where are you, Marcus? Deb fought the fatigue settling in. *Does he even know I'm here?*

Deb swayed and her right shoulder came to rest against the wall. The next thing she remembered was being startled by her own soft snoring. She failed to shake herself awake, too weak from the blood loss. Deb had no idea how long she had been awake at this point. Had she been in hell several hours or had it been days now? Wrapping her arms tightly around her sides, her entire body slumped, and she nestled into the corner unconscious.

Deb knew she was dreaming. The beach she was

standing on was comforting, her bare feet cocooned in warm sand. The sun was high in the sky, puffy white clouds drifted slowly above her. The ocean lapped softly against the shoreline while seagulls soared in the sky. The bay breeze rustled her floral sundress and the air smelled like a mix of suntan lotion and fresh cut grass. Her hair fell in soft waves to her shoulders. Several feet behind her sat an oversized beach bag on top of a light blue blanket, the corners held down with rocks and seashells.

Deb walked toward the water's edge. Her feet touched the wet sand and she stopped. She peered down at the sparkling pebbles. The pebbles suddenly became shards of glass. She bent to pick one up and it melted in her hand, it wasn't glass it was ice. The water wasn't simply cold, it was frigid. The view didn't match the temperature of the ocean. Deb understood these were the confusions and illusions of dreamland. Turning around she walked back toward the blanket. She could tell someone was coming before they manifested.

A dark aura swirled in the air on her right. Stepping out of it was Schlosser. "What have you done, Guardian?"

"I think I fell asleep."

"More like that smack to the head rendered you unconscious."

"Why are you here?" Deb asked more to herself than to Schlosser.

"You pulled me here somehow. I'm grateful to

be unconscious myself now that I'm on the slab."

"What are you talking about? You're passed out also? I or we must be dreaming."

"I would not dream of this." Schlosser walked closer to her. "This is definitely your mind we're in."

"Where is Marcus? Why is it taking so long to find him?"

"Well if you hadn't passed out you might have heard me telling you he's straight across from us."

"He is?" Deb's heart raced. "I need to wake up."

"I don't think concussions work like that."

"Are we close to getting out?" Deb asked.

"Hell is a vast place. Seven realms, seven gods of darkness, we're many miles from getting out."

The smell of smoke and burning wood drew her eyes back toward the area where the blanket once sat. It was gone. An involuntary gasp escaped Deb's lips. She was no longer on a beach. Standing atop a cliffside she peered down at a wide valley below. The land was covered in dead grass, trampled by heavy footfalls, and ravaged by war. Fire surrounded the edge of the landscape. Smoke twisted its way skyward dulling everything in gray smog. Locked in combat were demons and Guardians as far as her view would go.

Gargoyles sailed through the sky screeching and darting toward Arch Angels. The heavenly warriors wore gray fatigues and wielded their swords and metal shields.

"The Accord's been broken." Schlosser came to stand next to her. "You did that."

"No. Hell did that when they murdered innocent historians like Sebastian. Don't forget Wrath killing an Arch Angel. Jacob never saw Wrath coming. It wasn't fair."

"Fair, what does that word even mean in our world? What about what you did? Selling your blood to Torin. You must know that it was used to restore the vampires. You had to know coming to hell to rescue Marcus was wrong."

"Wrong? You have some nerve."

Schlosser grabbed her shoulder and spun Deb around to face him. "Nothing is ever as it seems."

Deb peered into his eyes. "What is that supposed to mean?"

"You're spinning your wheels. Even if you get to Marcus and get out, you don't know what's waiting for you on Earth, do you?"

"My family–" Deb began before he interrupted her.

"It's war!"

"You're lying." Deb shook her head.

"Stop calling me a liar!"

"You're offended by that?" Deb mocked.

"Yes. I told you it's not my sin."

Deb couldn't understand this riddle of a conversation. Her attention went to her right at a gargoyle swooping close to their position.

"You have no idea." Schlosser took a few steps back away from her and started laughing. "You're here on blind faith."

"Faith isn't blind. It's enlightening."

"Here I was thinking you were crazy or maybe reckless for coming here alone. But no, you're bloody clueless."

"This can't be my dream. I wouldn't have called you here to insult me."

"Ignorance is bliss." Schlosser huffed.

"Are you done?" Deb crossed her arms and leveled a cold stare in his direction.

"Haven't you ever wondered where you come from, where I come from?"

"I know where I come from."

"You do?" Schlosser's voice rose. "Oh please, spit it out."

"I don't need to answer to you. This is getting us nowhere." Deb's arms fell back down at her sides. "If I am asleep, I need to wake up."

"You need to wake up alright. You were once human. I take it you don't remember that. Or maybe they don't let you remember. Only humans get free will after all."

What is he talking about? Why would he think I used to be human?

"I suppose you were human once also?" Deb chuckled. "These dreamland ideas are quite inventive."

"I was created in a fiery lake of human sin." Schlosser stated simply. "I was manifested the day a man killed his wife and unborn child. That's why I roam the Earth lured to every violent situation facing a pregnant woman."

"That can't be true! I would know if it were."

Schlosser chuckled. "Why do you think there are so many more vampires than Arch Angels? Legions of demons compared to the few hundred clans of Guardians."

"You're trying to get under my skin by lying!"

"I told you, lying is not my sin. If mankind wants to be free of the creatures from hell, all they have to do is stop sinning, stop killing, stop hurting one another."

Deb's head spun, the sound of war raged up the cliffside and drowned out her thoughts.

"The war that's coming isn't about your family. It's about theirs." Schlosser pointed at the Arch Angels entwined with the vampires.

"Nothing you are saying is making sense." Deb yelled over the roaring battle echoing up from below. "I'm dreaming. I've fallen asleep after being captured. We're in a prison cell."

"I found Marcus. I guess now we'll see if you keep up your end of the bargain."

"I can't trust you."

"You shouldn't trust anyone." Schlosser said as he shoved her.

Deb's feet went out from under her, and she fell backward over the cliff. Screaming her arms flailed as if she could keep from tumbling to her death. She should teleport, but her mind was a torrent of scrambled thoughts, and she couldn't concentrate.

Schlosser became but a mere speck in the great distance above, but the demon spoke as clearly as if she were still standing next to him.

"Wake up. We can't die here."

Deb startled awake. Her right shoulder was numb. Her body trembled in the frigid air of the prison cell she was tethered to. Slowly she sat up and took stock of her injuries. The blood had dried on her face, she rubbed her eyes and the crumbles of sleep fell down her cheeks.

The pungent odor of death irritated her nostrils. She snapped her head to the left. Schlosser was gone.

Deb broke her own prison shackles and got to her feet. She walked every corner of the cell as if she may have missed the six-foot demon.

They took him. Was my dream real? Is Marcus just across the hallway?

Deb walked closer to the doorway mustering the bravery to walk over the mark embedded in dried blood below her feet.

Would walking over the rune trigger an alarm? Or was it merely a mark describing the number of prisoners?

"Deborah." A man weakly called from the cell directly across from her.

Deb's hands flew to her mouth to cover the scream that wanted to escape.

Schlosser was right, Marcus is here. Relief was abated by anxiety. *Schlosser is on the torture table.*

CHAPTER TWELVE

An hour into the exorcism Samantha and May entered the room to take over and give them a break. Kelly stepped away from the bed. Samantha's blonde hair was pulled up into a tight bun that Kelly assumed must have been pinned as it never loosened. Samantha, or Sam as Kelly always called her, had beautiful green eyes that glistened like diamonds. The two Arch Angels wore gray fatigues, thick soled boots, and short sleeved blue T-shirts.

May was taller than Sam by several inches and her bulging muscles were a testament to how hard she trained. Her light brown eyes had a twinkle in them. When she was in battle she was in her element. Her hair hung in several thin braids that she pulled into a singular ponytail. Her ebony skin was perfect, with the exception of one scar above her right eye.

Sam and May worked seamlessly. Anticipating each other's maneuvers they went right to work. Sam stood close to the right side of the bed and Joey flung himself toward her. May leapt onto the bed and wrapped her arms around the teenager lifting him off the mattress. Joey squirmed and kicked but May held onto the boy.

Kelly opened the windows, lit new candles, and added firewood before making her way out of the room and down into the kitchen. She found Dorothy in the kitchen drinking coffee.

"You got anything stronger than coffee?" Kelly asked.

Dorothy reached into the cabinet and pulled out a bottle. The red label simply read *whiskey* with the picture of an elk just above the words.

"This do?" Dorothy asked.

"Yes." Kelly took the small round glass Dorothy had pulled out for her.

"Help yourself."

Kelly poured a small amount in the glass and threw it back. The liquid burned and left a caramel finish on her tongue.

"How's he holding up?" Dorothy asked.

"He's strong. You must have faith he'll hang on."

"'He's such a good kid. Helped everyone, never in trouble, just pure joy. To think of what's happened to him—"

Dorothy didn't finish. Instead she grabbed the bottle and poured some into her own cup.

"Thanks for this." Kelly pointed at the bottle. "How's Clara doing?"

"She's worn out. She and my son are in their room consoling one another over Joey. They can't be in the room with all of you, but they wanted to be close."

"I understand."

"Your siblings are out on the porch. Your brother's walked the ranch a few times, patrolling. Your sisters been counseling Bob and Clara."

Kelly smiled. "Sounds about right. They're not good at sitting around."

"Me neither."

"Well, I appreciate the drink and the chat." Kelly glanced toward the front door. "I'm going to head outside for a few." Kelly took the glass to the sink.

"Leave that. It'll give me something to do."

Kelly walked out the front door. Dan came around the back of the house and strode toward her.

"How's it going?" Her brother's brow had a slight sheen of sweat. Clearly, he hadn't rested while Kelly and Antonio worked.

"Exhausting." Kelly sighed. "He's hanging on, strong kid."

"That's good." Dan wiped his forehead with the back of his hand.

"Why don't you sit with me for a few?" Kelly said as she took a seat on one of the rocking chairs on the porch.

"Do you want to talk about it?" Dan asked.

"Not now," Kelly answered. "I'd like to just clear my head."

Dan nodded his eyes spanning the sprawling ranch. The wind pushed the dirt around in the riding area. Kelly took a few cleansing breaths to bat down the thumping ache on each temple. She rocked and the chair groaned in response. They sat in amicable silence as the minutes ticked away. The early evening air was cool.

"I should head back in." Kelly stood and stretched her sore muscles. "Thanks for sitting with me and for not prodding."

Dan smiled. "Be careful and let me know if you need anything."

"I will."

Kelly walked back into the house and found Antonio standing outside Joey's bedroom.

"Ready to get to it?" the Arch Angel asked.

"Yeah. It shouldn't be much longer."

Sam and May finished a round of prayers and stepped away from the bed so Kelly and Antonio could start again. Sam put another log on the fire before she and May left the room.

The air was chilly but at least it did a better job of hiding the acrid smell of urine. Joey was on his knees rocking back and forth on the bed. Kelly went to the left side, he turned his head and leered at her.

"I will kill him before you can get to me." The sinister nature of the threat hung heavy in the air.

Antonio's long arms reached across the bed and pulled the teenager onto his back, he held him there while Kelly climbed on top of him to pray. The boy didn't fight back as much. He twisted and turned his head away from her, but Joey was weakening. His small frame wouldn't hold out much longer.

When the flame of the log dwindled. Joey finally passed out. Kelly and Antonio went out to the back porch to cool down and drink something cold. Sam and May stood watch.

"He's close." Antonio told her as he wiped his brow with a towel. He tossed her a clean cloth. "You're bleeding on the right side of your head. Will you be okay to continue?"

Now you care about me, Kelly silently sniped at the Arch Angel and ignored the question.

After several minutes of quiet, Antonio broke the silence.

"I know what I did was wrong."

"Now is not the time." Kelly said adamantly.

Antonio ignored her tone. "I won't ask for forgiveness, that must be earned. I do hope one day you believe me when I say *I'm sorry.*"

The back door swung open interrupting the conversation.

"May is hurt." Gen told them as she held the door open for them. "Dan is in there holding him down."

Antonio ran back into the house. Kelly was on his heels.

May was standing in the hallway, her hand up against the side of her face. "I'll be okay." May told them as they approached. "I'll go back in as soon as I stop seeing double."

Antonio placed a hand over the wound and healed her. Kelly went past him into the bedroom. Joey was face down screaming into the mattress. Dan was sitting on Joey's back, holding the boy's wrists down by his sides. Sam had her hand on his head praying. Dan's muscles flexed under the strain of holding the teenager in place.

"Dan, he's close, jump off!" Kelly yelled.

Sam stepped back away from the bed. Dan vaulted himself up and off the boy. Losing his footing he fell to the floor just inches from where Joey could reach him. Kelly reached out and grabbed her brother, yanking him further away from the boy, whose eyes were now black as night with no decipherable pupils.

Sam helped Dan to his feet and the two of them went into the hallway.

Kelly grabbed the holy water and splashed Joey with it.

"Let him go, demon. I compel you to release him."

Joey's tongue licked his lips, he was back to panting like a wild animal. "You can't have him."

Antonio motioned to Kelly. "This is it. It needs to be now."

Kelly nodded as she stepped toward the bed. Behind her, Antonio unfurled his wings. Shadows danced across the ceiling. The teenager leapt at the Arch Angel. Even though the demon understood he was harnessed, he kept trying to reach him.

The chain was clanging and the plaster from the wall started to crack.

Kelly took several steps to her left, Antonio went a few to his right. The sparkling flame from the barrel roared between them. Joey kept thrusting himself toward Antonio. After the fifth or sixth time the demon's head and right shoulder came through Joey's body. The demon was reaching for Antonio while trying to stay tethered to the boy at the same time.

The demon was made of Hell Fire, and he dripped venom down onto the mattress as he tried to seize the Arch Angel's wing. If the mattress hadn't been soaked in holy water, it would have ignited.

Antonio stepped backward and tucked his wings back inside his body, he was now at the door. The demon was faced with a choice, leave the boy's body entirely, or retreat inside.

"Hey," Kelly yelled at the demon. "You forget about me?"

The demon swiveled hard right, his foot detaching from Joey's. The demon took another step toward Kelly and left Joey's body completely. The teenagers limp body fell backward onto the bed, he was free.

The demon swung for Kelly's head, and she blocked it with ease. Grabbing the demon's arm Kelly yanked him off the bed. The demon swatted at her chest, but she pulled back before he could make contact.

Sam entered the room. She and Antonio tore the chain free from the crumbling wall and took Joey out.

Kelly swung her fist and landed a blow to the head. The demon stumbled against the wall and fell to one knee causing one of the drapes to ignite.

The demon charged her. Kelly side stepped the demon and wrapped her arm around the demon's head dragging him over to the fire. She heaved his writhing body onto the barrel. The holy fire ignited his form. He squealed in terror.

The room was filling up with smoke. The curtains were gone, the fire now spread up the walls and across the ceiling. Dan stood helpless in the hallway not able to enter as the fumes were infused with Hell Fire venom and poisonous to all but Kelly.

Kelly reached out and pushed the demon further into the barrel and held him there. His body collapsed in on itself as he fell further into the barrel. His screams dwindled and his body burned.

"Get out of there!" Dan yelled. "We'll get everyone out of the house and meet you outside."

Fire exploded from the barrel. Kelly turned toward the open window, that side of the room was nearly engulfed. The open window was obscured through the haze of black smoke.

Her left hand was on fire. She swatted and put the fire out with what was left of the holy water. The holy flame didn't hurt, nor did it burn her clothes.

How did the venom not burn my clothes? Kelly's mind failed to make sense of it, but she needed to move on.

Kelly walked out of the bedroom toward the back door. She jogged around the side of the house toward the front. The fire hadn't spread to the front yet. Everyone was huddled around Joey as he lay motionless on the ground.

"Is he okay?" Kelly asked.

Gen was kneeling next to Joey. She placed her hands on his head as she worked to heal him. Frankie arrived and placed a hand on Gen's shoulder. Kelly joined them.

"His shoulder was hurt," Kelly told them. "We should focus on that area as well."

Joey opened his eyes. "Mum."

Clara collapsed to the ground, cradling her son, and wept.

Kelly sighed. "He made it."

The rest of her brothers arrived. Tom and Greg asked about hoses. Bob pointed toward the shed and the two ran in that direction.

We should move back away from the house, there's no telling if Tom and Greg can put the fire out. The group moved several yards away from the building. The sound of rushing water was followed by footfalls in the grass as her brothers worked to tame the blaze.

The air was crisp, and Kelly shivered in the evening air.

"We need to get them somewhere safe," Kelly said to Dan.

"I've been on the phone with Harry working that out," Dan commented.

"We should all get out of here," Sam told them. "This fire is hazardous to you. I can't imagine it's good for humans to inhale these toxins either."

"Thank you for helping." Kelly said to Sam and May. "I'm grateful you came."

"We can help you with the relocation as well," Antonio told them.

"No!" Kelly said firmly. "You can go now."

"I thought we were on speaking terms." Antonio commented.

"Barely." Kelly retorted.

"Whoa, I knew something was up. I could sense the tension between the two of you." May said. "What's going on?"

"Nothing." Antonio shook his head.

"Nothing!" Kelly bellowed as she got to her feet. "You call suppressing my memories and lying about it for forty years, nothing?"

Michael stepped between Antonio and Kelly. "Dan, why don't you escort these people to where they will be staying."

Clara and Bob helped Joey to his feet.

"We have a car in the barn," Bob said. "It's got a couple of suitcases full of clothes and some provisions. We didn't know when we might need to get on the road with no notice."

"Smart," Michael said simply.

"I'll walk you to the car." Dan told him. "I can give you the address of a safe house and my phone number."

"Thank you," Bob said. "I know that doesn't cover it but thank you for helping us."

Dorothy pointed at Kelly. "You're one strong son of a bitch." The woman placed the whiskey bottle in Kelly's hand and followed her family into the barn.

"Tell me it isn't true?" Sam asked Antonio.

"He wouldn't do something like that to Kelly." May interrupted. "She's practically one of us."

"Tell them!" Kelly insisted. "Go on, tell them or are you going to lie to them too?"

"There is more to the story." Antonio began but couldn't finish.

"Why would you do something like that?" Sam pleaded.

"The magistrate," Antonio said simply.

"Still haven't found her?" Michael asked coolly. "Maybe you should put together a search party for her."

"The magistrate is missing?" Sam asked. "Since when?"

"And why haven't we been told?" May added.

"Seems I'm not the only one Antonio is keeping secrets from." Kelly seethed. "You're nothing but a liar, Antonio. I don't know why I called you. I won't make that mistake again."

Nothing like turning what should be a victorious moment into another heartache. He asked for forgiveness but hasn't changed. He continues to lie, even to his closest comrades. I don't think I ever really knew him.

CHAPTER THIRTEEN

Kelly stepped out of the shower and wrapped herself in the softness of a large blue towel. The vanilla scent of the shower gel followed her around the spacious bathroom. Steam fogged the room and coated everything in a thin layer of condensation. She dug a paper towel out from under the sink and used it to wipe the mirror clean. She bushed her hair back away from her face and it parted naturally just off center.

There were no visible bruises, cuts, or wounds of any kind on her body. The short trip to a nearby peace gathering before returning to Michael's home was the reason. Instead of turning on the noisy air vent, she cracked a window and the rush of cool air wrapped around her. Within minutes the steam had vanished, dissipated by the chilly September morning air.

After returning from the ranch the night before, Kelly collapsed onto a bed and fell asleep, but it was anything but restful. She kept replaying the argument with Antonio. Her mind twisted her memories as she tossed and turned throughout the night. She dreamt of losing her battle against the demon that had possessed Joey. The image of the teenager succumbing to the physical weight of it all stuck with her even after waking. She envisioned trying to explain to Antonio why she was so hurt, but each time he ignored her pleas. The nightmare ended with her standing on the precipice of a full-on war against all of hell's army, flanked on either side by a field full of demons.

Antonio saying the tension between us was nothing paled in comparison to the vision of someone opening the gates of Hell. Kelly shivered.

She dried off and got dressed, hanging the damp towel on a rack by the door before exiting. The smell of bacon drifted up the stairs. She had slept through most of the night, but it was still early.

Trotting down the stairs she was met with a surprise. Dmitri was standing by the coffee pot.

"Hello," Kelly said. Aside from Dmitri the kitchen was empty.

"Hey. I think I finally figured out this coffee machine."

"Where have you been?" Kelly asked as the floor above creaked.

"Chasing Jade." Dmitri poured a cup of coffee. "Haven't caught up to her yet, but I've been close."

"How is a demon out pacing you?"

"It's not like she's an ordinary demon. Jade is Envy, the physical embodiment of a deadly sin." Dmitri placed a mug of steaming coffee on the edge of the counter. "Do you take it black or loaded?"

"I can do either, but I prefer a little cream and sugar. Thanks."

"I am growing fond of taking it that way too."

"So you're just not going back to The Pit? How does that work exactly?"

Footsteps came from the second floor, then the bathroom door clicked shut.

"I think you're cooking bacon this early has woken up the rest of the house."

"Bacon is the best part of breakfast." Dmitri opened the oven door and retrieved the sizzling cookie sheet.

Dan entered the room followed closely by Gen.

"This is unexpected." Gen went right to the stove to put on the tea kettle.

Dan silently maneuvered around the group, poured coffee, and took the cup to sit next to Kelly.

"Who's home?" Kelly asked.

"Tom and Greg," Dan answered. "Michael and Frankie went out a few hours ago to check on a local church. There was a news story about it being under attack."

"To think that not too long ago, that would have caused the entire family to join forces and head out together," Kelly commented. "Now it's just par for the course that we're all split up."

"I don't like it either," Gen agreed. "I can feel them though, they'll be back soon."

"Another meal together," Kelly added. "Feels like a luxury."

"You got to hold onto the wins," Dmitri said. "Harry told me you saved that young kid."

"Kelly did," Gen corrected. "I just paced around stressing."

"That's not true," Kelly remarked. "I couldn't have done it without both your and Dan's support."

Dan gently elbowed Kelly and smiled.

"You look tired, Dan," Kelly told him. "Pull an all-nighter?"

"After Tom and Greg got the fire out, I gathered some things together and took them to the safe house where the family is staying. I brought them some food, water, firewood. I know they had provisions, but I wanted to make sure they were settled in. I knew you would have wanted someone to check on them."

"Thanks Dan." Kelly leaned into her brother's side. His body heat came through the thick gray sweatshirt. "I appreciate it."

"I ended up staying for a few hours to keep an eye on them. They went to bed, all was quiet, so I headed back here."

The clanging of dishes drew Kelly's attention back to Dmitri, who was making eggs. Gen joined him by the stove and threw several pieces of toast onto a cookie sheet and placed it in the oven.

"I'm sure someone has already asked, but why are you here, Dmitri?" Gen inquired. "Shouldn't you have returned and joined Gabriel and Jared in the Pit?"

Dmitri's black T-shirt was snug around his thick frame. His bulging muscles seemed to flex even when he wasn't moving. His short black hair a contrast to his three-day old beard riddled with gray.

"I'm not going back until Deb is safe," he said simply. "I got some leads on Jade, but she's been elusive. She's still being helped by the horseman."

"What do you plan on doing when you catch up to her?" The question came from Kelly's left. Tom stood in the doorway. His jeans were wrinkled like he slept in them. His concert T-shirt was so worn you couldn't read the band's name anymore.

"I want them to tell me where he sent her." Dmitri didn't turn around.

Frankie and Michael arrived just as Kelly was about to ask more questions.

"Did you find Jade?" Michael asked bluntly.

Michael never gets caught off guard, Kelly thought. *It's like his mind deems all the interesting questions irrelevant and goes right to the point, every time.*

"Not yet," Dmitri answered. "I have some new leads, but it might be faster if I can get some help."

"We can't spare anyone," Michael told him. "We're barely keeping up with what's going on here."

The coolness of the statement, though true, seemed harsh.

"I don't agree." Frankie's words snapped the room to attention. "We aren't giving up on Deb."

"That's not what I'm doing," Michael countered. "She made the decision to go into Hell, despite all our best efforts to talk her out of it."

"So what?" Frankie argued. "You're writing her off because she didn't follow orders?"

"What are you talking about, Frankie?" Michael snapped. "You're the one who said you could get through to her, that she wouldn't actually do it!"

"How was I supposed to know she'd go this far for Marcus?" Frankie blurted. "All this for a sentinel she'd only known a few months."

"Hey, let's calm down." Tom walked between his two brothers. "There are no bad guys here, they're all out there." Tom pointed at the front door.

Dmitri forcefully put his mug in the sink. The clanging turned all eyes to him. He didn't return their attention, he just stared at the backsplash behind the faucet.

"I don't need your help." Dmitri finally spoke. "I'll find her, I'll bring her back myself."

Committing to rescuing Deb when she is committed to rescuing Marcus. It's enough to make your head spin.

"I will help you, Dmitri," Frankie told him. "I'm sorry about the Marcus thing, I wasn't thinking."

"It's okay," Dmitri responded. "It's the truth, all of it."

"I'll help you look for Jade too, Dmitri." Gen paused before continuing. "But first, we need to go to the Vatican."

All turned to Gen. She moved back to the stove and retrieved the cooked toast and placed all the eggs on one plate and bacon on another. She brought the food to the table along with some plates and utensils.

"Now," Gen announced. "Let's take this opportunity to eat, as a family." Gen's eyes fell to Dmitri, who nodded.

Despite the early hour, they all opted to fill up while they had the chance.

"What could the Vatican possibly help us with?" Kelly asked.

"The holy water," Gen told her. "It worked, it healed Joey's mother, Clara. We were so worn out with the possession we didn't regroup. We need to get the holy water out there and the church is a great place to start. They have a massive distribution channel and they're worldwide. After that, we keep going. We talk to the head of every church, synagogue, and mosque. We get it out to as many people as possible through as many sources as possible."

"I don't think holy water means the same thing to every religious group," Frankie stated. "And what about the people who are agnostic?"

"We have to try," Gen answered. "We saw what it can do. Let's start with this and then spread it through public waterways as much as we can."

"Harry told me about Gen healing Gardenia," Dmitri commented. "Healing people who have been attacked by a vampire could be a game changer."

"True," Tom agreed. "We should get Harry to help us spread the word to all the Guardians and angels, so they know to keep well stocked and help us get it out to people."

"This is our chance to swing things." Gen told them. "Shift the war back in our favor. If humans can be healed from a vampire bite, if it's no longer fatal, that's big."

"We should teach the humans how to kill them," Kelly announced.

The tension in the room rose, it was clear no one liked that idea.

"I don't think you want people confronting vampires," Dmitri commented. "Seems a recipe for disaster."

"Why not?" Kelly asked. "People have been trying to fight them off when attacked. It hasn't worked. We know how to fight vampires, how to kill them. We should share that."

"Let's just start with the holy water," Tom suggested.

"Whatever." Kelly sniped. "Thanks for the food, Dmitri. I'm going to head outside for some fresh air."

Kelly left the kitchen and went into the living room. Grabbing her jacket, the unlit fireplace caught her attention. The hearth was covered in boxes filled with holy oil and small weapons. The wood floor was worn. The fireplace tool set had been dragged across the floor, leaving streaks of white in its wake.

We should teach the humans to make weapons from things they already have.

"I'm going to go wake up Greg and take a quick shower," Tom said from the kitchen. "We should probably get ready. We'll want to get to the Vatican and get back to patrolling as soon as possible."

"I'm heading out," Dmitri added. "I'll keep you posted, good luck in Italy. They aren't exactly known for being cooperative, despite all they know."

"Dmitri, I'll call you when we get back," Gen told him. "If you haven't found Jade by then, Frankie and I will figure out how to help you. If we catch a lull in the action, we'll skip the luxuries of eating and sleeping to join you."

Dmitri nodded at Gen before teleporting from the house. Gen came into the living room.

"You alright?" Gen asked Kelly. "You seemed a little cranky at the end of breakfast. Bacon usually makes you happy."

"Donuts makes me happier." Kelly knew the joke fell short.

"Anything you want to chat about?" Gen nudged. "I could hear your dreams were unpleasant."

"Sorry, if I kept you up. It was bits and pieces of last night mixed with the craziness of everything going on."

"No need to apologize. I've certainly had my fair share of nightmares, and I'm not quiet about it."

Kelly smiled at her sister. "I remember the night Gabriel pulled you into a different realm, thought we had a house full of demons."

"That feels like it happened years ago, not weeks. I already miss him. You must miss Jared too."

"I do. Feels like we'll never be back to normal."

The weight of that sat between them. Kelly's

thoughts went back to homemade weapons. She picked up the fireplace poker and examined it more closely. This one didn't have the dart at the bottom. It was a straight rod with a curved end.

"What are you doing?" Gen asked her.

"It's too long," Kelly said. "But, if we cut this down, it could be perfect."

"Not for poking logs," Gen deadpanned.

"No. For killing vampires."

Kelly took the fireplace poker back into the kitchen. Michael was standing at the counter drinking coffee and flipping through a newspaper as if he hadn't just come to near blows with Frankie. He put down the newspaper as she re-entered.

"You have anything that can cut this down?"

"Yes. In the garage, why? Are you making that into a weapon?"

"Yup," Kelly walked to the door. "Gen, you're going to drive yourself mad chasing the Church for help. I'm going to make a weapon that is lightweight but powerful enough to penetrate a vampire's ear. That will give humanity a fighting chance. I'm going to make sure people know how to kill a vampire." Kelly stormed out the door before Gen could respond.

CHAPTER FOURTEEN

Gen dressed in the most formal thing she had at Michael's house. Gray pants and a royal blue cotton blouse with three quarter length sleeves. She didn't have any dress shoes. Her black combat boots would have to do.

At least I wiped them clean with a damp cloth. She faced her reflection in the mirror. *This is as professional attire as I can muster right now. I want to be respectful to the venue we are entering, but there's no time to fuss.*

The door down the hall opened and closed, heavy footsteps followed. She knew that was the last of her brothers making their way downstairs to head out. They were going to the Vatican. They needed help getting the holy water out in large quantities and to convince people it was safe to consume.

Genevieve left the room and made her way to the stairs. The importance of the moment weighed on her. Would the hierarchy of the church cooperate with them?

They must help us. How else will we reach people in mass numbers in a place they feel safe?

Gen reached the kitchen to find Frankie and Dan in dark gray suits with white shirts, no ties.

"Where's Kelly?" Gen asked.

"She's still in the garage." Frankie answered.

"I just told her we're ready," Dan added. "She's on her way back in."

Kelly was carrying multiple long pipes under her arm. When she reached the front door, Dan opened it for her.

"Thanks. I just finished making these. Let me know what you think."

Kelly handed each of them a black rod, the thickness and shape of the fireplace poker. She had cut the bottom off and welded a small metal arrowhead to the end of it.

"This is to use against the vampires?" Frankie asked.

"You want to aim for the ear." Kelly wiped sweat from her forehead. Black smudge marks from her hands mixed with the perspiration and streaked across her brow. "Once you've hit the ear, use a hammer or something hard to push it in deeper. When the rod pierces the brain, the vampires die."

"This is lightweight," Dan commented. "Easy to wield."

"That's the idea. Don't bother trying to use it to penetrate any other part of the vampire's body, you'll just waste energy. It's difficult to puncture a vampire's strong skin, but the ear and nose are vulnerable."

"This is great and all, but we need to get going," Gen interrupted. "Kell, you might want to clean up a bit."

"Yes, I'll wash up. Where are the others?"

"They went ahead," Dan answered. "Michael reached out to the Orsini family in Rome to let them know we were coming. He took Tom and Greg with him. Michael is hoping they have advice to share. He also wanted to give them the information about the holy water healing people."

The Orsini family was one of the Guardian families Michael trusted. He had worked with them before, fighting alongside them in Italy.

"He should have shared information about killing vampires too," Kelly remarked.

"I'm sure he will," Frankie added. "When we get back, we should spread the word about this weapon. It might be another shift in our favor."

"Dan, why don't you text Michael?" Gen asked. "Tell him we're nearly ready to go."

"I'll be right back." Kelly walked off toward the bathroom to clean up.

"This is pretty badass," Dan said to Frankie and Gen. "Look at the movement you get with it." Dan walked into the living room and swung the pipe around. "If you're lunging at them with some force, you might not even need another weapon to ram it with."

"I think you're too focused on killing," Gen commented. "I think we need to invest our time into healing humanity."

"We can do both." Frankie answered.

"We need all the help we can get, in all areas," Dan said.

"That we can agree on," Gen said.

Kelly came back into the kitchen wearing black jeans and a white long-sleeved blouse. Her combat boots were smeared with mud, but the grease stains on her hands and face were gone. She grabbed a shoulder harness off a nearby hook and put it on. She wrapped another one around her thigh and loaded it with throwing stars. In the shoulder harness she slid a dagger in one sleeve and a hunting knife into the other. She took one of the pipes she had just made and slid it down her back and into the sleeve that a sword would normally sit.

"Who are you expecting to encounter at the Vatican?" Gen asked.

"I think we should expect the unexpected. How could the Vatican not be a target, and the Swiss Guard is not going to do much good against vampires."

"We should take these with us." Frankie placed a rod Kelly had made into a makeshift sheath inside the lining of his jacket. Dan nodded in agreement.

Kelly grabbed a black raincoat from the closet and put it on, covering most of the weapons she was carrying.

"Let's get this over with," Kelly huffed.

"Did Michael answer where to meet?" Gen asked.

"His contact suggested arriving in Saint Peter's Square," Dan answered.

"What about the general public?" Frankie asked.

"Michael said it's quiet, that most of the square is off limits due to the virus. We can decide what to do and where to go once we meet up," Dan answered. "They are there now, waiting on us."

Colorful beams of light smashed against one another as their aurora's enveloped them for the journey.

***

It was late afternoon local time. The sun was shining, the warmth of their surroundings a surprise.

They were standing at the entrance to the square. With few people, you could take in the vastness of the space that lay before them. It was an impressive piece of architecture, art really. The entire square, from its cobblestone floor, twin fountains, and large basilica, awestruck many a person who visited.

The rows of colonnades on either side of the square were topped with one hundred and forty statues of various saints, martyrs, and popes.

"Michael says they're in the center," Dan

commented.

As they entered, the marble columns on either side enveloped Gen. The square stones underfoot were ground in from the many years of pilgrimages by people from all over the world.

"I see them." Frankie nodded toward the Egyptian obelisk in the center of the square.

Michael held his phone up to his ear. When they reached their brothers, Michael hung up and placed his phone inside his jacket pocket.

"The Orsini brothers are stationed at all the entrances and exits," Michael told them. "They'll keep watch and call if anything from hell shows up."

"Royalty is here. Amazing how you convinced the famous Orsini brothers to help," Kelly cooed. "Let's hope they see the bad guys coming with enough time to warn us."

Ignoring Kelly's sarcasm Michael continued. "Vincenzo said we do not have to be in human view. That most of those in the church hierarchy could see through the veil before this event."

"How long has that been the case?" Gen asked.

"He didn't say. To be fair, I didn't ask."

"Vincenzo's not exactly chatty," Tom added.

"A conversation between him and Michael must be riveting," Kelly snarked.

"It was direct." Greg smirked at Kelly.

"Let's head inside," Michael ordered. "Every minute we're here is a minute a human is without our protection."

Turning, Michael headed toward the basilica with haste. Gen and the rest of her siblings walked quickly to catch up. As they approached the ornate building, the row of statues above them seemed to peer down. It was impressive but slightly intimidating too.

The entire place seems to overwhelm the senses. The size of the space, the number of statues, the perfect alignment of marble columns. It screams, 'God reigns here, humanity is small.'

As they neared the entrance, the holy door, framed in iron with bronze depictions swung open. They were met by two members of the Swiss Guard.

In Italian the guard to the left spoke to them, his arms motioning for them to leave.

"This is not the friendly welcome I was hoping for," Gen said aloud.

Kelly stepped forward and spoke to the guards in Italian. After she spoke Kelly translated to the others.

"I am telling them we need to speak with Cardinal McCormick. He's the camerlengo, the second in command to the Pope," Kelly said.

"I roughly understood what they said," Gen remarked realizing how rusty her Italian had gotten. "They said we need to leave."

The door opened wider and a man in a three-piece navy blue suit moved in front of the guards to speak to them.

"Excuse me, please, why are you here?" His English was laced with a European accent.

"We're here to see the camerlengo," Kelly

repeated. "Please bring us to him, it's urgent. We're the O'Mara family."

A small gasp came from the right. One of the guards seemed bothered by the revelation of who they were.

"I take it they've heard of us."

"One moment please." The man in the suit let go of the door to turn back and speak to the guards. The door creaked as it moved in the direction of closing.

Kelly pushed the door open and walked into the church. The soldiers took large steps backward. The man in the suit put his hands up defensively.

"Where is Cardinal McCormack?" Kelly asked. "If he's roaming the Vatican gardens then we can find our own way."

"Please," the man in the suit pleaded. "Stop!"

With his arms raised, it was visible that he was equipped with a gun, a taser, and a baton.

"None of your weapons will work on us," Gen urged. "Please, we don't want any of you to get hurt. We work with the church in Boston, we're here asking for your help with the current crisis. We just want to talk."

"Forget this," Kelly sighed. "I'll go find the Cardinal myself." With that Kelly was wrapped in the bright light of her aura. The men shielded their eyes as she teleported away.

The Swiss Guards backed away from them and began praying aloud. Their voices lilting up and down in clear distress at Kelly's actions.

"I'm sorry about that," Gen began again. "Our sister is impatient. Surely, there is a waiting area inside the building where we can wait for someone who can help us."

"Yes," the man in the blue suit replied. "I am commander Grafton. Follow me, please."

The commander walked off to the left, and the O'Mara siblings followed. The Swiss Guard trailed a good distance behind them.

Telepathically Michael spoke to them. *"I'm worried Kelly teleported off like that. She should be communicating with us first."*

I think she's just frustrated, Gen replied. *And it did seem to work, they're bringing us inside.*

They exited the basilica, walked across a small courtyard, and entered another building. From there they were escorted to a second floor waiting area. One wall was adorned with a tapestry depicting the Vatican lit up at night. The marble floors were covered with a deep red carpet. A dark brown leather sofa sat along the far wall with a coffee table covered in marketing material about donating to various church organizations.

The two guards stationed themselves at the exits, turning their backs to the O'Mara family. They were blocking anyone else from coming into the space.

A conference room lay just beyond the waiting area. The room had a glass wall to a hallway just beyond where one of the guards was standing. Anyone walking in the hallway would know who was inside the room.

"Wait here, please," the commander said. "I will let the cardinals know you are here."

The commander walked to the door of the conference room and knocked lightly before entering. Several at the table were already facing forward as their attention was on the person seated at the head of the table, his back to the door. The commander leaned down and spoke to the cardinal.

"Your Eminence," the commander said. "The O'Mara family is here."

"Which ones?" Cardinal McCormack asked.

"From the looks of it," the commander paused, "all of them."

The room fell into a fury of chatter as all eyes went to the O'Maras standing in the waiting area.

Cardinal McCormack stood, his black cassock a contrast to the red belt wrapped around his waist. All the other men took his que and stood as well. Cardinal McCormack waved the O'Maras into the room.

Gen spoke to Kelly telepathically. *"We found the camerlengo."*

The glow of Kelly's aura lit up the back of the conference room, she stepped out from within it. The gasps were audible, several cardinals held their hands over their hearts as if to calm themselves. A few of them even made the sign of the cross and kissed their crucifixes.

"Subtle," Gen snarked at Kelly.

"We don't have time for diplomacy," Kelly replied.

Gen entered the room followed by her brothers. The exterior wall of the room had panels of windows with views of Saint Peter's Square. The thick wine-colored carpet masked their footfalls. The twenty-foot square table and leather chairs was accompanied by a credenza. Tall glasses and a pitcher of ice water sat sweating on a silver tray.

The cardinal at the head of the table was short and stocky, with a ruddy face and a dimple in the center of his chin. He wore wire-rimmed glasses and a crucifix that hung from a long chain that reached his waist. His blues eyes seemed to sparkle with surprise.

"I'm the camerlengo of the Papacy." the cardinal outstretched his hand to Gen. "My name is Patrick McCormack. What brings you to Vatican City?"

"Do you know who we are?" Gen asked as she shook the cardinal's hand.

"Wrong question." Kelly walked along the wall of glass to join her siblings at the other end. "Do you know *what* we are?"

"As camerlengo I am privy to sensitive information that not everyone in the room is. Some here only know rumors and legends." The cardinal paused as if internally debating how to finish answering Kelly's question. "I know you are not of this world."

The cardinals' murmuring echoed off the glass, mixed with praying.

"That is correct." Gen addressed the other cardinals. "We're here to protect humanity, we're Guardians from Heaven."

The room erupted, a chorus of gasps, prayers, and pleas.

Maybe now they'll listen.

CHAPTER FIFTEEN

"I'm sorry for the bluntness," Gen said to Cardinal McCormack. "There is no time for diplomacy. We have come across a cure for the vampiric virus currently wreaking havoc across the world and we need your help."

"A cure?" One of the other cardinals at the table said in wonder.

"Of sorts," Gen answered.

"Please, come take a seat." The camerlengo said pointing to open seats at the table.

All of them sat except Kelly and Michael. Each choosing to stand on either side of the exit door.

The camerlengo sat and the other cardinals who were still standing followed.

"We have access to a unique type of holy water," Gen told them. "We can bring it to you in large quantities. We need you to put it in the fonts and distribute bottles of it to parishioners."

"A unique type of holy water?" One of the men

questioned. "I don't understand how there can be more than one type. Anyway, I'm afraid what you ask is impossible. As you said, there is a virus running rampant. We can't very well ask people to use a public font. With cross-contamination concerns, no one would currently trust using those."

"We're using the word virus, liberally," Tom stated.

"What does that mean?" Cardinal McCormack asked.

"It's not contagious," Greg answered. "It's contained within the person infected."

"Are you saying an infected person cannot spread it to another?" A balding, overweight cardinal asked. "We understood from the scientific community that the virus spreads through bodily fluid. A bite, a scratch, and other means."

"We understand your reservations, but we need you to trust us." Gen stated. "We have holy water that can cure people."

"If holy water cures people," Cardinal McCormack stated. "Then we have plenty here already."

"This isn't working." Kelly mumbled. "They aren't understanding."

"Cardinal McCormack," Gen said. "We can show you. As camerlengo do you know of anyone suffering from the virus, perhaps someone here in Vatican City?"

Several of the cardinals groaned, a few moved

about their seats uncomfortably. Clearly Gen had struck a nerve.

"Having an infected person within these walls is not allowed." Cardinal McCormack stated but couldn't meet Gen's eyes.

"We are not here to judge." Gen countered. "Please, bring us to the person afflicted, let us show you what our holy water can do."

More murmurs broke out in the room, most in Latin. Cardinal McCormack held up his hands and quieted the others.

"There is disagreement among them," Kelly announced. "There is someone in the papal apartments who was bitten two days ago."

Cardinal McCormack turned to Kelly. "I see you understand Latin."

"I speak many languages." Kelly answered. "Most of my family does."

"I assumed you could read Latin." Cardinal McCormack said. "Not everyone who can read it is able to follow it when spoken, or to speak it themselves."

"How do you know I can read Latin?" Kelly asked as her eyebrows came together in stern focus on the camerlengo.

"You've been using our library without authorization for a long time Ms. O'Mara." Cardinal McCormack responded. "Most of the books you borrowed are not in English."

"All books have been returned." Tom interrupted.

"Yes," Cardinal McCormack responded. "I am aware. I almost didn't recognize you Ms. O'Mara. You typically visit us in the middle of the night, in pajama's if I'm not mistaken."

"I do my best thinking at night." Kelly argued. "You have the most comprehensive library for research, and you keep it all to yourself. Though I know there must be more hidden elsewhere."

"We all have our secrets, Ms. O'Mara." Cardinal McCormack offered.

"Please Cardinal," Gen interrupted to refocus back to the matter at hand. "Bring us to the sick patient, now before their symptoms get worse."

Michael's phone rang and startled the room. Her brother turned away and hit the screen to answer it.

"We don't have a lot of time." Kelly said impatiently. "We need to get back to helping people."

Gen stood and walked over to Michael. "What is it?" she whispered.

Michael said the word *okay* several times and then hung up. "We need to go. Several guards are under attack in the square. Vincenzo needs backup."

Tom, Greg, and Frankie exited the room and teleported from the waiting area.

Several cardinals left their seats and raced to the windows to view the square.

Commander Grafton returned to the room. "Camerlengo." He said urgently. "We must go, it is not safe here."

"I'm done." Kelly responded. "This was a waste

of time. They aren't going to help us."

Kelly teleported from the room. The bright glow streaked across the black table and rippled along the glass.

Gen pulled a bottle of holy water from a satchel she brought along with her. "Please take this to the one who is sick. Have him drink it, all of it. The arch diocese in Boston will know how to get in touch with us."

"We will pray for you." Cardinal McCormack said to Gen as he picked up the bottle. "For all of you."

"Thank you." Gen said. "And pray for your fellow humans." She then exited the room followed by Dan and Michael.

When they reached the waiting room Gen asked Michael. "How bad is it out there?"

"There are several vampires." Michael said grabbing Gen's arm. "Garrick may be among them."

Gen's heart sped up. "Well, if Kelly gets ahold of him, it might be the last we see of him."

"That's what I'm afraid of." Michael said. "Kelly's anger is getting the best of her. Seeing him might send her over the edge."

"She's found a way to kill them, Michael." Dan answered.

"I'm not questioning her ability nor her strength," Michael answered.

"Then what?" Gen asked.

"Her impatience is growing." Michael said. "We just witnessed it in that room. If she doesn't get her emotions under control, it will hinder her in battle.

Being out of control leads to mistakes. Mistakes in war lead to death." Michael locked eyes with Gen. "I can't lose another family member."

Michael and Dan left the room in their aura before Gen could respond. Her eyes fell back to the room, most of the cardinals were pacing about or staring out the exterior windows. She prayed Michael was wrong, but deep down she feared he was right.

Gen's eyes watered as her aura carried her away from the cardinals in a sphere of lavender light.

***

Kelly arrived in Saint Peter's square first. Vincenzo, one of the tallest of the Orsini brothers, was engaged in hand-to-hand combat with one of hell's army. The female vampire was dressed in full garb. The red and black medieval jacket was buttoned up to the top of her neck. Her hair was braided and wound into a tight bun, leaving nothing loose to grab onto. Her dark gray fatigues and combat boots completed the uniform. The hilt of a falchion, the vampire's weapon of choice, stuck out from underneath her jacket.

Kelly locked eyes with her brother Tom. The female vampire appeared to be the only vampire on site.

"Where are the others?" Kelly yelled to Tom.

Tom shrugged his shoulders. "I don't know."

Kelly continued to span the square. Members of

the Swiss Guard flooded into the piazza. Kelly ran toward them.

"Get back." Kelly yelled to Commander Grafton who was wielding a sword. "You are no match for them."

Michael arrived on her left. "There are two vampires back in the garden area. Dan, Frankie, and Greg went there. Is there only one out here?"

"Yes," Kelly stated. "Vincenzo is keeping her busy, we should take her out before she calls for backup."

Everything okay, Dan? Kelly asked her brother telepathically.

Little busy, Dan replied. *Frankie and I brought the new weapons you made, no time like the present to test them out.*

A wave of relief washed over her.

"Why isn't the area cloaked?" Kelly asked Michael. "Dan can hear me."

"I'm not sure." Michael answered. "Maybe hell cannot cloak a holy site."

The female kicked Vincenzo in the stomach sending him tumbling backward. Michael engaged the vampire, in his typical stance, he waited for her to make the first move. She swung, Michael blocked and countered with a punch to the ear. The blow sent the vampire staggering back a few steps.

Kelly rushed over and helped Vincenzo back to his feet. The Guardian's cheek was split open, and he was sporting a fat lip. His broad chest heaved underneath the black T-shirt he wore. His black dress pants were ripped at the knee and the loafers on his feet were a clear sign he didn't expect a confrontation.

"Aim for the nose, ears, and knees." Kelly said intensely.

Vincenzo nodded but said nothing.

"Everything else is a waste of energy. Remember, you won't get through her skin, even with repeated strikes." Kelly told him.

Vincenzo stepped back toward the battle. Michael landed a punch to the vampire's nose, snapping her head back. Vincenzo punched the female's ear while Michael kicked her right knee. The vampire yelped and fell to one knee. Vincenzo took the opportunity to pummel the right side of her head. Michael struck the left. When the female fell backward, Kelly stepped behind the vampire. She reached down, wrapped her arm around the vampire's neck and pulled her up. Kelly grabbed the pipe from its sheath and swung down hard into the female's ear. When the arrow penetrated her ear, the vampire screamed. Kelly then grabbed a dagger from her jacket and used the hilt like a hammer smashing it against the end of the rod. The poker sank further inward, the female vampire convulsed spewing fluid all over the ground.

The vampire's body twitched and rolled to a stop a few feet from where they stood. Kelly walked over and yanked the rod free from the vampire's ear. The demonic fluid pooled underneath the vampire's corpse. The vampires near perfect skin turned gray, her hands decomposing into dust as they stood over her.

"How?" Vincenzo asked. "I thought they were near impossible to kill."

"They are." Kelly answered. "You need to hit them where they're vulnerable and apparently, they'll decompose on the spot.

Dan confirmed they killed the two in the garden and were on their way back.

"Tell your brothers." Kelly said to Vincenzo. She handed him the weapon so he could inspect it. "Make these and spread the word to every Guardian you know."

"Amazing." Vincenzo replied as he flipped the rod over in his hands wrapping his large hands around the end. "I will tell my brothers. They left just before you arrived in the square, called away by their marks to Charges in need."

Vincenzo handed the rod back to Kelly. "We will go to work on making these right away, thank you."

Kelly nodded. Her eyes were drawn to Gen and Tom alongside Dan and Greg. Frankie was making his way over to Kelly.

"That was crazy," Frankie told Kelly. "Once the arrow pierced the ear, the vampires were in too much pain to fight back. I shoved the pipe in, the vampire shook all over, and then collapsed. There was a lot of blood, same as her."

"Yeah." Kelly agreed. "It is strange, like the liquid is the first to go."

"Decomp is rapid." Michael stated.

"It doesn't matter how they die." Vincenzo said. "What matters is we have a way to defeat them. I must go, share this information with everyone."

Vincenzo grasped Michael's outstretched hand and drew him into an embrace with a strong pat on the back.

"Be safe my friend and blessings to your family." Michael told Vincenzo.

"You also, Michael." Vincenzo turned to the rest of the family. "My condolences for the loss of Xavier. He was a fine warrior. I will miss talking with him about futbol.

The O'Mara siblings stood in solemn silence as Vincenzo teleported from the square.

The Swiss Guard that had fled to the church rejoined them in the square. Commander Grafton was speaking with Tom and Greg. Gen and Dan moved to join Kelly.

"Are you okay?" Gen asked. "That was crazy, good thing the three of you brought those weapons."

"I just had a feeling." Kelly told her. "I was thinking it was only a matter of time before they attacked here. It's one of the largest religious symbols on Earth."

"True." Gen agreed. "We didn't exactly get what we came for, but I'm glad we were here to help."

"I was wondering why they attacked outside." Dan commented.

"What do you mean?" Michael asked.

"Just that they divided us, but didn't fully attack

or cloak the area." Dan answered. "Like they wanted us out here."

"Hey," Greg yelled to them interrupting their conversation. "The commander was just radioed that there are more in the building."

The O'Mara's teleported back to the conference room. There were broken bodies strewn on the floor. Two cardinals were slumped face down on the table. The balding, overweight cardinal sat back in the chair holding his stomach, blood seeping through his fingers as he tried to stem the blood loss. He was in shock and could not speak. His death was imminent.

The wall of glass to the right was smeared red, several of the panes separating the hallway from the conference room were smashed.

On the far side of the room the camerlengo was on the floor, two of hell's army looming above him, one female, one male.

The female turned back first. It was Keeva, the vampire who fought alongside Garrick at the house in Boston.

Keeva locked eyes with Gen, and immediately lunged at her. Gen used Keeva's own momentum against her, and in one smooth motion flung her over the partially collapsed wall.

Kelly ran toward the male vampire but stopped short when he turned toward her, it was Garrick.

Gen quickly pounced on Keeva, not giving her a moment to regroup. If she did, Keeva could focus and teleport away. Gen grabbed her by her uniform jacket and threw her back several feet toward Tom and Greg.

"Get away from him!" Kelly yelled at Garrick.

Greg, Tom, and Gen took turns pummeling Keeva. Gen punched her several times in the nose. Greg was behind Keeva and clubbed both fists at her ears simultaneously. Tom was to her right and delivered a side kick to her knee.

"He's no use to us now." Garrick smirked as he stepped away from the camerlengo. "You and I will meet again soon, Guardian."

Frankie tossed Greg the weapon Kelly made. Greg wasted no time stabbing the female vampire, but he missed a direct shot into the ear. The vampire lurched upright in pain screeching as she did so.

Keeva's scream drew Kelly and Garrick's attention. The vampire's blood disappeared into the thick red carpet below. Keeva vanished into her own gray aura as she teleported away from them.

Kelly swung for Garrick's head, but he teleported away in a mire of thick black smoke.

"It was a distraction," Michael said taking in the disastrous state of the room.

"They wanted us outside." Kelly's mind reeled.

Gen went to the camerlengo who was barely holding on and tried to heal him, Kelly joined her. Frankie grasped each of his sister's shoulders to amplify their powers. Cardinal McCormack hacked and spit until his breathing steadied.

"Where are you keeping the priest who was bitten?" Kelly urged.

"He is safe," Cardinal McCormack said in between panting breaths. "We sent the vial of holy water to him. We were waiting to hear the results when they attacked."

"Who is sick?" Gen asked. "What are you not telling us?"

The camerlengo's body shook, his still blue lips quivered.

"His Holiness," Cardinal McCormack whispered. "The Pope is the one that has been bitten."

CHAPTER SIXTEEN

Deb ran toward Marcus. He was nearly unrecognizable between the slumped posture, bruised body, and severe weight loss. He was a shell of the confident sentinel Deb had grown so found of.

"I was afraid I'd never find you," she said breathlessly as she knelt on the ground next to him.

Deb gently laid a hand on the side of Marcus' face. His left eye was swollen shut.

"I can't believe you're here." His voice was raspy. "I had given up hope. How did you get here?"

"I had help." She began examining his wounds more closely.

Marcus groaned when Deb peeled back a thin piece of cotton stuck to an open wound on his side. The mud below him was wet with his blood.

"What hurts?" Deb asked.

"Everything." He arched his back away from the wall.

"You need to be more specific. It helps to know where to concentrate my powers."

"No." Marcus grabbed Deb's hand as she was lightly pressing on his side trying to gage the level of damage. "Stop."

"It's okay. I can heal you and then we can get out of this cell."

"I would love nothing more," Marcus told her. "I'm afraid that's not in the cards for me."

"What are you talking about?" Deb asked, surveying the cell to be sure they were alone, something she should have done before entering.

"I've been marked," Marcus said simply.

"I don't care." Deb raised her hands above the deep gashes on his chest.

"Deb," he said breathlessly. "Listen to me." He grabbed her left hand and brought it to his lips kissing it gently. "I don't have much time left."

"No," Deb said emphatically. "I don't accept that. These injuries are bad, but–"

He brought his right hand up and touched her cheek. "Always the optimist."

"I came here for you, Marcus." Deb placed her head gently against his forehead, her tears dropping softly on his chest. "I'm not leaving without you."

The low hum of voices accompanied the creaking of metal on metal, a door was opening.

"It's the torture room," Marcus told her. "There's a small alcove behind the wall I'm leaning against. Go there now, they won't sense anything beyond me."

As the footfalls got closer, Deb stood and quickly maneuvered around Marcus. She squeezed herself into the narrow space behind the wall Marcus was leaning against. Her vision of the entryway was now blocked, but with the torture room door open the screams and cries of the damned rang out loudly.

Deb breathed in and out, slowing her racing heart.

Deb pictured herself small and invisible. Marcus' cough accompanied the rustling of a chain she hadn't identified when examining him.

He's in prison cuffs, Deb thought. *I didn't see anything around his waist or ankles. Nothing on his wrists when he reached out to me.*

The shuffling of movement in and around the hallway came and went. After what seemed like an eternity, Marcus called out for her.

"Deb, it's clear."

Deb came around the corner and crouched next to him. "No more fooling around. We need to go."

"Please, just listen." Marcus choked on his next intake of air. The spasm propelled him forward away from the wall. The sentinel's back became visible.

Fresh tears sprang from Deb's eyes. A large chunk of the chain of chaos was embedded in Marcus' spine. The sentries tethered the chain to a clasp on the floor behind him. Every movement caused the chain to slither underneath the surface of his skin. Torturously, the demonic weapon was ripping Marcus apart from the inside.

"We need to get that out of you," Deb told him. "The longer it's in, the more it will chew you up."

"It's too late for me, Deb."

"No." Deb shook her head, but somewhere inside she feared the truth of his situation.

"I'm dying." His lips quivered and his breathing labored further. "I'm so glad I got to see you one last time."

"Marcus," Deb pleaded. "Don't talk like that. I'm a healer and I'm strong."

"I know you are," he implored. "Some things can't be healed."

"You left me a ring and I wasn't putting it on without you." Hoping to spark hope and a reason to fight back into the sentinel, Deb dug into her jeans pocket. She pulled out the gold band and held it up. "Look, it made the journey and so will you."

Marcus smiled. His red stained teeth revealed internal bleeding. Marcus took his grandmother's wedding band and put it on Deb's finger. "It's yours. My heart is yours and always will be."

Tears streamed down Deb's face.

I may be in love.

Placing a hand on either side of Marcus' face Deb kissed him. "Don't you dare die on me, sentinel."

"Did Gardenia come to you?" Marcus asked.

"Yes," Deb answered. "Gardenia said you told her to find me if anything happened to you. Why didn't you come to me if you were in trouble, Marcus?"

"There was no time," he whispered. "I care for Gardenia, and I knew you would keep her safe."

"Of course," Deb answered, a twinge of guilt slapped her for having left Gardenia in Gen and Kelly's care while she searched for him.

"I need to tell you about the coin while I still can," he whispered. "It belongs to Miles, the last soul catcher."

Marcus yelled out in pain as the chain of chaos moved violently under his skin.

Enough, Deb screamed silently. *I didn't come here to just give up.*

Deb stood up and pulled off the jean shirt she wore. Rolling up the sleeve of the jersey she held it up to Marcus' mouth.

"Bite down," she ordered.

Marcus put the denim in his mouth and took a deep breath.

Deb pulled his shoulder forward off the wall. His back was raw flesh, the chain moved as if it knew she was coming for it. Deb placed her hand on the small of his back, the chain took the bait and grabbed for her. She knew the chain wouldn't pass up the opportunity to reach for an enemy from heaven. When the end of the chain wrapped itself around Deb's wrist, she yanked the remaining portion out. The shirt muffled Marcus' scream. Blood spurted from Marcus' back and the sentinel fell forward passing out.

Standing, Deb slammed the chain against the wall with force. The ragged edged chain broke in half, one piece falling to the ground. The black metal fragments skittered away from them. The remaining piece went slack in Deb's hand, she threw it into the far corner of the room.

According to Schlosser using heavenly powers in hell would be telegraphing your position, but she didn't care. Deb shielded her and Marcus and used her powers to heal the wounds on his back. Though Marcus' skin came together, underneath was entirely black as if his blood were poisoned.

She pulled him gently back to a sitting position healing the wounds on his face and chest. He came to and grabbed her hand.

"Thank you," he told her with a small smile. "That is a bit better, but it's not enough."

"What do you mean?" she asked. "What did they do? Have you been doused with something?"

"I wish there was more time." His legs jerked and his left ankle turned black. "Do you have the coin, Deb."

"Yes. But forget about that," Deb told him. "I can teleport us out of here and then I'll work to heal more of your wounds."

"The coin is the key to the soul room, Deb."

"I don't know what that is." She put the denim shirt back on and slipped her arm between Marcus and the wall preparing to lift him onto his feet.

"The soul room, Deb. It's where Miles brings the souls he steals."

"Okay." She moved close for more leverage. "We can deal with that later."

Marcus screamed before she could move him. His right leg shook violently left to right as if convulsing. "This is it, Deb."

"What?" Deb pulled her arm back and went to his feet. "What's wrong with your legs?"

Pulling back one of his pant legs revealed more pieces of the chain of chaos. On his left leg the demonic weapon was wrapped around the exterior of his leg in a snake-like vice grip. On his right leg it was fully embedded, when she lifted the jean material the chain swam away causing Marcus to yell out once more.

Oh my God. I can't get all this out without killing him.

The truth depleted all hope of rescuing the sentinel. Deb had broken all the rules to save him but for what?

Marcus pulled her into his chest. "Save them, Deb."

Deb sobbed, all she had been through to get him out of hell and none of it mattered. He wrapped his arms around her and stroked her back gently. The rhythm of Marcus' heart thumped unnaturally. Deb trembled with the fear of losing him just as she finally found him.

He's right, the end is here.

"Go to the soul room," Marcus said as his

breathing became thick with fluid. "Save those who are trapped here, including Christian."

"You know about Christian?" Deb lifted her head and Marcus wiped the tears from her cheeks.

"I know about all of it. The magistrate came to me, asked me to look into how Schlosser was able to find Vermillion and take his powers."

"And?" Deb asked her own heart thrumming heavily now.

"I always knew there was more to the story of Genevieve and Gabriel," Marcus told her. "When the magistrate came and asked me to help her, I told her she needed to tell me the truth before I would even start an investigation. That was the price for my help."

"She told you about what they did to Kelly?" Deb asked.

"Not just to Kelly." Marcus grasped her hand and held it firmly. "I know that Antonio buried your memories too."

"That information was private. It wasn't the magistrate's story to tell." Deb averted Marcus' gaze.

Did she tell him about Dmitri? Deb thought in horror.

"Hey." Marcus lifted Deb's chin. She was once again staring into bloodshot eyes. "I always knew you were too special to be unbound."

New tears sprang from Deb's eyes. "I'm sorry, Marcus. I truly don't remember a lot of things. Whatever Antonio did, it worked."

"What the magistrate ordered Antonio to do was

wrong," Marcus admitted. "But I think the magistrate really believed she was helping all of you."

"I don't see how any of that helped," Deb said. "I don't remember parts of my past, but the feelings you brought out in me were real, Marcus."

"I know," he agreed. "But you've always fought them. What if that's because you weren't sure those feelings were for me, or for someone else."

"I'm wearing the ring." Deb sat up and outstretched her hand. The piece of jewelry was glistening.

"Did it bind?" Marcus coughed and blood sprayed across his chest in reddish-brown splotches.

"Let me get the chains out!" Deb urged. "Let me at least try."

Marcus' legs bent toward his chest, and he let out a howling scream. His eyes filled with terror.

Deb reached inside the pant leg and grabbed a piece of the chain and pulled. Marcus hollered and grabbed her arm pulling Deb away from his ankle.

"No...stop...Just tell me one thing...before I die," Marcus said nearly panting between words and reflexively clamping his jaw to deal with the pain. "Did it bind?"

Deb grabbed Marcus' face. Blood seeped from his ears and trickled across her hands.

"Yes," Deb said firmly. "Stay with me Marcus, don't you give up on me."

Marcus leaned back against the rock wall and smiled. "Go give them hell, Deb. Don't stop...until you've saved every soul...every single one trapped down here."

The embedded chain of chaos swam up Marcus' right leg, across his stomach and pushed through his skin. The living weapon opened a wide gash in Marcus' chest.

"No!" Deb screamed in horror. "Please God, no!"

Marcus' chest heaved and then he collapsed back down to the ground in a pool of his own blood. The two pieces of the chain of chaos slithered away from his limp form.

Deb knelt next to Marcus' still frame. Her hands hovered inches above his body as she used her powers once more to try and heal him. The wounds sealed, but his heart would not beat.

Grabbing Marcus, Deb pulled him into her chest and wailed. Her entire body shook with the sea of pain his death unleashed.

"Wake up, Marcus," Deb whimpered into his soft hair. "I need you to come back to me."

Deb didn't know how much time had passed. She was lost in the perilous reality of her situation. The plan was to reach Marcus and they would escape together. Deb never allowed herself to think about the possibility of his death. She stayed hopeful until this very moment. Now she was alone, sitting with the decaying corpse of the sentinel she risked everything and everyone to save.

Something was coming down the hall. Just as on

Earth, Deb could sense evil approaching. Deb knew she should run and hide in the alcove behind Marcus, but she didn't.

I don't care who finds me. What difference does it make now? I'm never finding my way out of this literal hell hole.

Deb's eyes fell back to Marcus. It was as if he was simply sleeping. Deb had closed Marcus' eyes, his head rested peacefully in her lap, his body covered with her denim shirt.

The female sentry who had dragged her into the cell across the hall appeared in the doorway. Her long black hair fell beyond her shoulders. She peered down at Deb confused as to how Deb had managed to get out of the prison cuffs, over the rune, and into Marcus' cell, all without detection.

"That scumbag finally got eaten by the chain." Her smile revealed broken teeth and a decaying gumline. "You get around, girl. We got your other boyfriend on the table."

The female demon stepped into the room.

"Get out," Deb warned.

"The one on the table is still alive," the female taunted. "At least for now." The demon's laughed grated on Deb's last nerve.

"I said get out." Deb used her shield to push the demon out of the room with force. The sentry sailed backward slamming hard against the wall in the cell across the hall. Deb's shield retreated, yanking the door shut and locking the sentry inside.

The female demon scrambled back to her feet and ran to the door. She grabbed the handle and yanked on it violently, but the wooden door and frame held firm. Screaming in frustration the sentry began yelling at Deb in a foreign tongue.

Marcus' chest heaved and Deb nearly jumped at the sight. An aura of blue light left Marcus' body and hovered just above him. Within a few seconds the tiny glowing orbs swirled to form a small globe.

His soul. It will be trapped down here with the others if I don't get out of here.

Deb gently moved Marcus to the floor. Remembering their earlier conversation about Gardenia, Deb thrust her hand inside her pants pocket searching for the coin. Pulling her left hand out of the tight fitting jeans, Deb let the coin sit in the open palm of her hand. Marcus' soul gravitated to the old relic and was absorbed inside.

Miles himself doesn't have the power to catch souls. Deb's breath caught in her throat. *The coin absorbs the soul. It must belong to a reaper. Whoever has possession of the coin, has the power to take souls to Heaven or to Hell. Miles isn't a soul catcher, he's a thief of souls.*

Grasping her fingers around the coin she flipped her hand over. The ring had slipped off. Deb moved the coin to the other hand and patted down her pocket. The outline of the wedding band pushed against the fabric of her jeans, she hadn't lost it, but it hadn't bound.

"Forgive me," Deb whispered to Marcus. "I wanted you to be at peace."

"Soul catcher." The female demon hollered from her jail cell. "I will find you, and when I do–"

Deb's power left her body as her thoughts were forming. The female demon was lifted off the ground, her body thrust into the ceiling of the cell and then smashing down onto the floor with force. Deb walked to the doorway and peered inside. The sentry's neck was broken. The demon lay in an unnatural position dead on the floor. Black liquid oozed from every orifice of her crumbling corpse.

Deb pulled the door open, found the pair of scissors on the floor, and retrieved the satchel Schlosser dropped. Patting down the demon's sides Deb took several weapons from the sentry. There were four throwing stars, two daggers, and a pair of prison cuffs. Deb stuffed everything in the bag and made her way out of the cell.

Walking to the end of the hallway, Deb turned left toward the torture room. "You better still be alive, Schlosser."

CHAPTER SEVENTEEN

As Deb walked the path toward the torture room, the high pitched yelling from within reverberated through the thick stone structure. The screaming of the beaten and battered thrummed through the rock walls.

The massive steel door that creaked when it opened hung from a rail bolted into the surface of the rock. The squealing when it moved was caused by its massive weight riding along an old rusty track. As Deb approached, the smell of death hung heavy in the air.

How many souls have been exterminated in this room? The question would never be answered.

The thick black door was stained with splotches of red, Deb assumed most were blood. There were scratch marks, some deep enough to reveal the steel material below. The noise from within reached a fever pitch. A cacophony of hysteria, the sorrow of the afflicted mingled with the ecstasy of the torturers. There was crying and laughter, but there were prayers too.

Deb needed to find Schlosser in what she imagined was a sea of bodies. The slide of the door screeched an announcement as it moved.

Something's exiting, Deb readied her mind. *It's now or never.*

Projecting her shield Deb hoped to stay hidden from the entity when the door fully opened. She had used this power before on both Schlosser and her sisters and it had worked. She prayed it would work in hell.

The door opened and a slew of sentries walked out of the room, exiting all around her. The demonic guards took different paths away from her.

Deb stepped inside the room before the door slid shut. On her right was a row of dead corpses, each one in varying stages of decomposition. Their torsos were bolted to the wall behind them. On her left was a curved path that led toward the noise. Straight ahead was a weapons depot, the door lay wide open.

Just what I need.

There were no runes on the floor of the entrance and no guards in or near the room.

No need to guard what would be a suicide mission.

Entering the well-stocked room, Deb made quick work of stealing what she could hastily stash inside the satchel that was draped across her chest. More daggers, a double-bladed knife, and two metal batons.

As she turned to exit, Deb spotted a dark red leather case sitting on an end table by the door. The glossy exterior showed it had been polished to perfection. A replica of the attaché case Torin had with him when he extracted her blood.

It can't be the same case.

Deb's mind reached back to the day she asked Jade to call Torin and meet them at the Savoy Hotel. Deb's blood was the price for the information on Marcus' whereabouts. Torin was the Trader who told Deb about Marcus being trapped in hell. Information that turned out to be true. Torin also told Deb that Marcus had been taken by Wrath. One of the seven deadly sins, and Jade's older brother.

Voices grew louder from the hallway on her right. Deb moved away from the doorway and out of sight. Even though she was still shielded, Deb didn't want to take any chances. She wanted to get in and get out as quickly as possible.

Spotting her reflection in the mirror that hung precariously off the wall, Deb stopped short. She almost didn't recognize the image reflected in the cracked pieces of black glass.

Deb's cheeks were sunken, who knew how much weight she had lost. The jeans that were nearly impossible to put on when she first arrived, now fit snuggly as intended. Her beautiful long brown hair had been burned off during the violent journey. Though her hair had grown into a short crop, visible rubbery burn scars marred her scalp.

Deb's blue eyes were bloodshot from crying and lack of sleep. Her skin was a sickly pale color, and her body was covered in cuts and bruises that had yet to fully heal. The left side of Deb's face was still swollen, and she had a deep gash running through her eyebrow where the sentry had hit her.

Look what they've done to me, Deb thought in anger as she inspected the inside of her left arm. Her fingers lightly brushed over the bumpy scar Torin had left behind when he healed her.

They had no right to mark me, Deb flashed back to Torin.

The voices in the hall faded, no one came into the weapons room. Deb stepped right and opened the case. A stack of crinkled papers lay on top. Deb rifled through them searching for her own contract. As she neared the bottom of the pile, Deb recognized the handwriting on the second to last page. She peered down at the bloody smudge mark below the signature.

It's mine. This is the same briefcase. Why would it be here? Is this where they forge the weapons used against us?

Deb reached inside and lifted the tray. The vials of blood were still inside. There were ten niches in the case. Four vials were missing, the other six were nestled in their slots. There was no way to be sure any of it was her blood, but she wasn't leaving it behind.

Flipping through the pages Deb read the signatures but didn't recognize any of the names. There were seven pages of contracts, including hers. If each gave one vial of blood, plus Deb's four, that equaled the ten slots inside the case. None of the other five signatures were familiar, but the mark in black ink to the left of their printed names matched her own, a Chi Rho cross. The mark indicated that all the entities were from heaven. She brought the pages over to the torch and held them up to the flame. The paper ignited quickly.

Deb released the corner of the stack before her fingertips burned. The contracts had engulfed into a large flame that crackled like kindling and then broke apart. The remaining pieces of burning parchment floated to the floor and eventually created a small pile of ash.

Deb took the vials of blood from the case and stomped them on the ground. She found amulets of Hell Fire venom and larger black globes of liquid she assumed to be the same. Wrapping a nearby rag around her face she poured the Hell Fire over the spilled blood. The liquid sparked and then burned until it joined the pile of ash from the contracts. The larger globes she tucked inside her bag.

Satisfied, Deb left the weapon depot armed and ready to enter the main room. The hall emptied out into a cavernous space. Several surgical tables held the remnants of previously tortured souls, most of whom were bound with brown leather straps secured to the tables.

There were smaller cell-like rooms on the left and right side of the space, all were occupied with the souls of the damned. Deb's heart raced, the sheer volume of entities parading in and around the area added to the terror of the moment. Her shield was holding, but she could sense evil pressing in against her as if it were trying to break her defenses.

At the far end of the room the floor had a gaping hole in it. It was a Hell Fire pit. The scent of burning lava irritated her nose, the gaseous fumes from the pit dulled everything in a smokey hue. Screaming came from every direction. Some of the bodies were being thrown into the pit still thrashing about and very much aware of their fate.

Deb closed her eyes and tried to calm the sickening sensation rolling through her. It was too much evil crammed into a confined space. She turned away and her eyes fell to the body strapped to the table in the last room on her right. Bald head, dark green T-shirt, and big brown boots. The body fastened to the table was unconscious. The sentry facing Deb held a long spear in his right hand, it was drenched in blood, Schlosser's blood.

If this is what they do to their own, what did Marcus endure? What did they do to Kelly?

Imaging the pain and despair that had befallen those closest to her was too much. Deb's eyes filled with tears. Swirling images of Marcus and Kelly continuously tortured in this pit of hopelessness fueled her desire to cleanse it.

Deb took a deep breath and pictured a tornado in her mind. Fisting her hands on either side of her body she grappled with her power and envisioned all the sentries lost in the chaos of a twister. Directing the power in her mind to her hands, Deb visualized yanking the persecutors out of every dark corner they were hiding in.

The dry air churned and picked up speed. The wind encircled the space causing the metal tables in the middle of the room to smash against one another. Deb opened her eyes. The demons were sucked out of the smaller rooms and carried up toward the jagged ceiling. The dust and debris swirled into a funnel cloud of her own design.

Deb pushed the twister down the space, picking up more demonic entities along the way. She steered the giant wall of whipping wind toward the gaping hole in the floor. The clanging of chains and the screams of the tormentors melded into the wind. The storm moaned, much like the souls of the demented. Loose furniture and glass smashed against the walls.

Weapons were sucked up into the smoky cyclone, several of the demons were battered, stabbed, and decapitated. When the whirlwind neared the opening in the floor bands of lava were pulled up through the floor and consumed by the storm. The tornado was laced with streaks of orange from the fiery flame. The demons shrieked as the Hell Fire ripped open their skin and burned them alive.

Lava splattered across the stone walls, fire spurting across the landscape. The wind battered the rocky terrain. Bits of rock broke off and covered the room in a blanket of sandpaper. When the cyclone hovered above the chasm in the floor, Deb dropped her shield, and the demons were thrust into the Hell Fire pit below.

An eerie silence fell across the cavernous space. Deb was fatigued. The power it took to create and move the storm was both energizing and exhausting. The victims in the rooms lay still, not sure how to process what just happened. As she walked back toward Schlosser's cell, prayer rang out in her direction.

The hairs on the back of Deb's neck rose. Her scalp tingled, her injuries aching less than before. The souls of the damned were praying, and it was reaching Deb, working to heal and rejuvenate her body.

Praying internally for God to forgive the souls of the damned Deb stopped at the entryway to Schlosser's cell. The roamer demon stared over at her.

"Well you could have told me you were capable of that, Guardian," he snarked.

Deb unstrapped his bindings. The wounds on Schlosser's chest and stomach were raw and bleeding. Deb held her hands above his torso and used her power to heal him. As Deb removed the bag slung across her shoulder, she held it out to him.

"Try not to lose this again," Deb remarked. "I found better weapons than the scissors you left for me."

Schlosser sat up slowly, gauging his ability to move without pain. The demon slung his legs over the side of the table.

"I don't suppose there's a T-shirt in there?" he asked.

"Beggars can't be choosers," Deb derided repeating the phrase he jabbed her with when she first arrived. "I want out of here, now."

"Where's your boyfriend?" Schlosser asked as he hopped off the table and walked past her. The roamer demon took in the wreckage of the space with a whistle. "You unleashed holy hell in here!"

"Can you teleport us or not?" Deb asked not ready to engage in a conversation about Marcus.

Schlosser stared back, waiting for Deb's eyes to meet his. "Marcus didn't make it?"

Deb shook her head and turned away as a wave of sorrow pushed to the surface. She pressed down against it.

The door to the torture room shook as something was banging on it. Apparently, it only opened from the inside. Fortunately for them it was closed and there was no one left standing to open it.

"Why'd you come back?" Schlosser asked. "You could have left me here."

"I was keeping my end of the bargain." Deb paused. "Remember, or was that really just a dream I was having?"

"I don't know what it was," Schlosser acknowledged. "That never happened to me before, being pulled into someone else's head. Scary."

"That you found frightening?" Deb asked spreading her arms open wide. "Not this?"

"This is what I know." Schlosser peered up at the now molten ceiling. Cool globs of lava dotted the scene. "This is what I was born out of."

"It doesn't mean you don't have free will," Deb told him.

"Is that what this is?" Schlosser asked. "Nearly burning the entire thing down is exercising free will."

"No," Deb answered. "This is vengeance."

"This isn't vengeance," Schlosser paused. "You're vengeance. You, your siblings, your clans."

"And you're the physical manifestation of sin?" Deb asked.

"Not all sin," Schlosser corrected. "I'm just one of many mortal sins humanity has created."

"I want to tell you you're wrong." Deb paused.

"You know I'm not," he countered. "You know deep inside what I told you was true."

Humanity creates the saint and the sinner, Deb discerned. *Two sides of the same coin.*

"You can still choose your fate Schlosser."

"Fate." Schlosser spit the word. "Should I be like you?" The demon's crooked finger pointed over at her. "Breaking all the rules to pursue something no one else understands?"

Deb didn't answer. She simply allowed the seething roamer demon to vent.

"Well I did that already and look where it got me?" Schlosser yelled as he spread his arms wide. "I bet you'll go back home, run around helping the very thing that created me. Nothing will happen to you. You'll be just fine."

"You want me to admit humans are at fault?" Deb asked but didn't wait for an answer. "That they commit atrocities, war, famine."

"Yeah," Schlosser answered.

"They do," Deb said. "They also help people. They sacrifice. They love. And they get the chance to make the right decision after they've made a bad one. Just like you and I do."

The banging on the metal door intensified. Someone was using a battering ram of some kind to break the door.

"You know what I hate?" Schlosser griped.

"I imagine it's a long list," Deb quipped thinking he was ready to move on from the heavy conversation.

"Sun and beaches," he told her. "I don't care much for heights either. Next time you feel like pulling me into a dream, I'd like to be outdoors, laying in a sleeping bag, looking up at the stars."

"I'll keep that in mind." Deb rolled her eyes. "We better get moving before they break the door down."

"For once we agree, Guardian." Schlosser walked away from the entrance and back toward the Hell Fire pit. "You'll need new shoes. We'll be running from this mess for the rest of our time here."

When they reached the far end of the room Deb spotted what Schlosser was aiming for. Another pile of discarded clothing sat to the left of the hole in the floor. Schlosser reached down and put on a black T-shirt, grabbing a cleaner pair of gray cargo pants, he stuffed them into the bag. Deb picked up a navy blue T-shirt.

"No holes and no stains," Deb mumbled. "That's an improvement."

Deb dropped the blood-stained denim jersey in the pile and foraged for boots and dry socks.

When she stood back up, Schlosser held out his hand to her. "Let's go."

Slipping her hand into his, Deb's vision was obscured by the gray-black smoke of the roamer demon's aura. Deb's feet left the ground as Schlosser teleported them out, just as the torture room door exploded open.

CHAPTER EIGHTEEN

The Swiss Guard trampled through the room. They raced to treat the injured and took special care when removing the dead. Five of the cardinals did not make it out of the conference room. Kelly and Gen healed those whose hearts were still beating, including the camerlengo.

As Cardinal McCormack was being rolled out of the room on a stretcher, he grabbed Kelly's hand. "Find his Holiness."

"You have no idea where he is?" Kelly asked once more.

Cardinal McCormack shook his head. "I told her not to tell me. I didn't want that information in my head should I be captured."

"What woman?" Gen asked. "What did she look like?"

"Blonde hair, green eyes." Cardinal McCormack paused. "She almost seemed to glow. Her aura was strong, searing white light accompanied her into the room. The tips of her wings nearly reached the ceiling."

"I know this is going to sound strange," Dan asked. "What color were her wings?"

"White of course." Cardinal McCormack coughed at the strain of talking. "She wore a lone silver band around her ring finger. That is all I remember."

As the cardinal was wheeled off, the O'Mara siblings stepped away from the crowd to talk privately.

"I know I'm not alone in believing that's the magistrate," Tom said.

"How did the vampires get to the Pope?" Frankie asked.

"We'll have to ask the Arch Angels that later," Michael answered. "We need to find him. We can't have hell using the Pope as a propaganda tool in this war."

"Can you imagine?" Gen placed her hand across her heart. "People seeing the holiest of holy figures ravaging humans. It would be devastating and demoralizing on an unprecedented scale. People would lose hope. Lose faith. It would also affect all of heaven's warriors."

"That's exactly why they want him," Michael responded.

Dan interjected. "Let's agree it's the magistrate, even though she's not the only one with white wings. Where would she take him? It's not like she can hide him from the world, he's too well known."

"The commander said his security guards saw nothing definitive," Greg told them. "The security feed picked up glimpses of a person wearing a long cloak, with the hood up, heading into the basilica. The visual cut out for a few seconds and when it came back, the figure was gone. They could not track where the person went. How did she get him out of here?"

Kelly was pacing. "Maybe she didn't."

"What are you thinking?" Gen asked. "You know the layout here better than any of us."

"I'm thinking she took him to one of two places on the grounds without cameras," Kelly told them.

"Where?" Michael asked.

"The first is part of the private papal residence," Kelly answered.

"Unlikely," Dan commented. "That would be the first place a Guardian or vampire would check."

"Agreed," Michael answered. "However, we should still clear all the apartments."

"Michael," Kelly urged. "Call the Orsini brothers. Ask them to check the papal apartments. Have them split up and clear all the residence quarters."

Michael pulled out his phone and called Vincenzo. The conversation took less than a minute.

"They're heading there now and will call once they've gone through all of it," Michael told them.

"Where are we going?" Greg asked.

"The necropolis," Kelly told them. "Underneath the basilica. Phones won't work there, neither do cameras."

"How are we doing this?" Tom asked. "I'm assuming there's little light down there."

"There are small lamps that dot the way, that's partial lighting," Kelly answered. "We'll have to let our eyes adjust when we enter. The passageways are crampy, serpentine paths. Picture it like walking along a narrow alley with small rooms off to your right. We'll need to split up to cover more ground. Each group needs to have one of the three rods we brought with us."

"You think the magistrate brought the Pope to a vampire?" Greg asked.

"We shouldn't assume anything," Michael answered.

"Let's go," Kelly said. "Meet me beside the papal altar in the center of the basilica."

***

The stillness of the basilica would normally have been peaceful to Kelly. Absent the hordes of tourists, the presence of heaven was all around her. The anxiety over rescuing the Pope however, took away any sense of calm.

Her siblings arrived within seconds of each other, their auras glistening off the curved black pillars of the altar.

"The stairs are over there." Kelly pointed to the right of the altar. "Once we descend, we should split up."

"Someone should stay up here," Michael added. "In case we miss them, and they retreat back out."

"I'll keep watch," Tom said. "Michael hand me your phone, when Vincenzo clears the residences, I'll have him meet us here."

"The necropolis extends the farthest left, maybe a football field in length," Kelly told them. "The right side extends to the doorway over there." She pointed to the exit facing the courtyard. "The center will be near the bottom of the stairs and is the deepest."

"I've never been down there," Gen stated. "Has anyone other than Kelly been down there?"

Kelly's brothers shook their heads.

"We won't be able to teleport," Gen commented.

"True," Kelly agreed. "You'd need to know where you're going to teleport."

"We need to be efficient though," Michael urged. "Clear the areas and move on quickly."

"Gen and Greg are the fastest runners," Kelly said. "They'll head left. Run to the far end and clear back toward the center. That's where Dan and I will be. The two of us will clear everything upon entry until we reach the Tomb of the Valerii. That tomb is the largest of the mausoleums, you won't miss it. We should all meet there."

"Got it." Gen took one of the long black rods Kelly had forged into a weapon.

"Frankie and I will clear the right side," Michael confirmed. "We'll make our way back to the middle as well. Any way to signal each other?"

"Yes," Kelly answered. "There are whistles at the top of the stairwell. On tours they give them to people to use if they experience an emergency. Gen, whistle three times in quick succession if you see them, we'll all head to you. Michael, twice for the right side. Dan and I will be once for the center. Wait at least three seconds before repeating the signal."

"We should use the flashlights on our phones to descend the stairs near the altar," Gen said.

"Yes," Kelly agreed. "I'll flip on the emergency lighting when we reach the entrance to the necropolis."

"Assuming he's down there, let's go get him and get back here as soon as possible," Michael commented.

"Ready?" Kelly asked. Her siblings nodded.

Grabbing a whistle at the entryway, Kelly pointed to show the others where the whistles were stashed. Descending the stairs Kelly's cell phone lamp extended several steps ahead of her. When she reached the bottom of the stairwell she paused at the entrance. The door was tightly closed. Humid air swelled the wooden door, Kelly had to shimmy it open. Flipping on the lights she propped the wooden door ajar with a heavy metal door jamb left just inside the entryway. Balmy stale air rushed out to greet them.

Kelly used the clay wall on her right as a guide and walked forward several steps to leave room for her siblings to enter behind her. The air smelled musty like an old library. The sandy earth beneath her feet kicked up dust as she walked.

There were parts of the necropolis too small to

stand in, several of the claustrophobic rooms were roped off, but the inside was easily visible from the pathway.

When the last of her siblings descended the stairs, Kelly took a moment to adjust to the dim light. Gen and Greg took off running, their stampeding feet quickly faded the farther away they ran.

"Be careful," Michael warned. "Watch each other's backs."

Michael and Frankie ran off to her right, within a few moments their feet stomping on packed earth also dulled. The thick walls and mud floors seemed to absorb the sound.

Kelly walked straight ahead followed closely by Dan. The center section had two rows of rooms. They cleared the first row slowly stopping several times to crouch and evaluate the entirety of the tiny spaces. Every few rooms, Kelly paused, but there was only silence. As they went deeper into the space the air thickened, perspiration broke out across her forehead.

Kelly removed her raincoat and wrapped it around her waist. Dan carried the satchel Kelly had brought with her. The canvas strap crossed his chest, the bag of holy water fell at his hip. The iron rod weapon she made was fastened into a sheath behind her back. As they pushed further inward, the walls seemed to crumble. Tiny pebbles cascaded to the floor as they walked deeper into the space. Dirt stuck to her damp hands and dust tickled her nose.

They crossed over to the back wall and cleared

two more rooms, there were only two left before they reached the tomb of the Valerii.

Kelly turned back toward Dan. "We have one straight ahead to clear and then the Valerii is just two to our left."

Dan nodded and they continued their methodical pace.

When they entered the next space, the wall to their left shook. The string of small lights hanging overhead swayed as if wind were blowing, but the air inside the necropolis was stagnant.

"Cloaking?" Dan asked.

"Feels close. I think it's coming from the Valerii," Kelly said. "Let's go."

As they left the space and turned right, vibrations rippled underfoot. Kelly crouched and stayed tight to the wall as they peaked in the next room before passing it by to head straight to the tomb of the Valerii. Before approaching the entryway, muffled chatter echoed back to them.

Kelly got on her hands and knees, crawling the rest of the way. The wall connecting one room to the next was partially collapsed. Moisture added to the decaying conditions of the ruins. In some areas only half a wall separated one tomb from the next. As she reached the end of the wall, she lifted her head and peaked between the layers of stones. The Pope was slumped on the ground, his back against one of the mausoleums.

Kelly turned back to Dan who had stayed back several feet. She signaled with a thumbs up. He turned and ran between the rows back toward the walkway. Dan whistled one solitary note and then stopped. Three seconds later, her brother's whistle sang once more. Not wanting to risk the safety of the Pope and knowing back up was enroute, Kelly stood and quickly made her entrance.

A female was standing over the Pope. Kelly opened her mouth to yell but was punched on the right side of her face. Stumbling sideways Kelly slammed her left shoulder against a pillar of stone. The attacker came at her again. It was a female vampire in full regalia, the flash of red fabric a swirl of color against the muted backdrop. The vampire's hair was as black as night, it seemed to disappear into the fog of darkness in the tomb. The vampire's eyes were the color of coal, her second iris around the pupil was bright red.

The vampire pulled her right arm back and swung hard for Kelly's face. Kelly pulled back and grabbed the vampire's arm while punching with her left. The vampire absorbed the punch, her head snapped back only briefly. Kelly charged and thrust the vampire against the stucco wall, the ruins partially crumbling under the force of the collision. Using both hands the vampire pushed up and off the wall lunging toward Kelly.

Dan came from behind and hit the vampire in the head with a large rock, sending the vampire tumbling to the ground.

Kelly turned and nearly slammed into Gen.

"Where is he?" Gen said breathlessly.

"In here." A female voice called from deeper within the tomb. "We're in here."

Michael had grabbed the vampire from behind while Dan kicked and broke her kneecap. The vampire screamed in response, thrashing about attempting to break free. Frankie stood in front of the vampire with the pipe Kelly had made.

"Kelly come on." Gen pulled her into the space where the Pope sat on the ground.

The shriek that escaped the vampire's throat jarred the Pope awake. His eyes filled with terror as he swatted at the form standing above him. When the female turned toward Kelly the world crawled to a standstill.

The magistrate. Kelly held her breath.

"Get away from him," Gen yelled.

Dan grasped Kelly's shoulder. "Are you okay?"

"Yeah," Kelly mumbled. "I can't believe it's really her."

Gen knelt before the Pope trying to alleviate his fear. She held her hand over his injured wrist and healed it. The Pope whispered prayers in Latin. The vampire's body was engulfed in holy fire, the body decomposed quickly, but the acrid smell of burning flesh lingered.

"Where were you taking him?" Michael asked the magistrate.

"I was already watching over him," the magistrate answered. "I knew you were here. I saw you enter the square. When the guards brought me the vial of holy water, I almost didn't try it."

"Why?" Frankie asked. "Did you not want to help him?"

"What is this?" The magistrate snapped. "We're on the same side."

"No!" Kelly snapped. "We aren't."

"We don't have time for this, Kell," Dan warned.

"There's never going to be a good time." Kelly stepped toward the magistrate. "You ordered Antonio to remove memories from me, from my sisters. I want to know why. I want answers!"

"You know why," the magistrate replied. "It had to be done. You were broken."

Kelly's eyes watered. *She has no remorse.*

"That's cold," Gen replied. "Even for a magistrate. And you say we're on the same side?"

"I do what has to be done," the magistrate stated. "Genevieve, you nearly combed the Earth looking for your husband. You weren't going to stop."

"No," Gen answered. "I wasn't. How dare you send him away for rescuing my sister."

"I had a small window of time to keep things from escalating," the magistrate righteously replied. "And I took it."

"You mean you covered it up," Greg replied.

"You should have reported what Azza did," Gen added. "Why didn't you?"

"It's within my discretion what to report and when," the magistrate answered.

Kelly's mind tried to process the magistrate's explanation or lack thereof, but she was overwhelmed with anger.

Lurching forward Kelly slammed the petite blonde woman up against the tomb wall. Kelly's hands fisted the magistrate's jacket pinning her in place.

"You have some nerve talking to us this way!" Kelly yelled. "You owe us a better explanation. You owe me a better explanation. You're the magistrate! You're supposed to be the example for all of us!"

Rage coursed through Kelly's body. Blood pumped through her muscles like a thunderous river, her chest nearly heaving. Her siblings were calling for her to calm down, but the injustice of it all fogged her mind and muddied her thoughts. At that moment Kelly wanted nothing but vengeance.

"It wasn't your decision to make," Kelly seethed. "You had no right to take memories from me, to force Antonio to do the same. You are not God."

Gray black smoke billowed all around her. A rush of heat engulfed Kelly's body, flushing her cheeks and turning her hands candy apple red.

Dan was standing closest to Kelly. Reaching out he grabbed Kelly's shoulder to pull her off the magistrate and a thunderclap exploded in her ears. Kelly left the ground and sailed through the air landing several feet away from her siblings. Crashing down against the half wall on the far side of the tomb, pain seared through Kelly's back and shoulder. Rolling over she stared at the ceiling trying to make sense of what just happened.

"Are you alright?!" Gen leaned down to help

Kelly up. "What just happened?"

"I don't know." Kelly shook her head unable to think clearly.

Her hammering heart was thumping so loudly it drown out the voices in the room. Kelly's anger retreated as her mind raced to assess the situation.

Who did that? Confused, Kelly questioned. *Who hit me?*

Gen grabbed Kelly's hand and pulled her onto her feet while Greg helped Dan to his. He had been thrown in the opposite direction. His shirt was wet, and he was standing in a puddle of water.

"Are you alright, Dan?" Kelly asked from across the room.

Dan nodded. "Yeah. How about you?"

"I'll be okay," Kelly answered. "Certainly knocked me for a loop."

"We should get the Pope out of here," Gen commented.

Frankie helped the Pope to stand and escorted him out of the room.

Gen walked over to the magistrate. "Are you hurt?"

"No. Thank you." The magistrate's voice quivered. "What's going on with your siblings?"

"You don't get to ask questions, we do," Gen replied. "We want the information you have about Azza and Wrath."

The magistrate nodded. "I'll tell you everything I know."

"Good," Gen replied. "Let's get back up to the basilica."

They made their way out of the tomb. The magistrate avoided Kelly's stare as she walked past her.

"I don't know what that was," Michael said to Kelly. "We'll worry about it later, but we need your head in the game."

Kelly nodded. "Yeah, I know. I couldn't help it, the magistrate acted like what she did was justified."

"I understand," Michael answered. "But I need you to stay focused on the task at hand."

"Fine!" Kelly blurted.

"You need to work on controlling your anger, Kell," Michael warned. "Or one day you're going to wake up and it will be controlling you."

CHAPTER NINETEEN

A throbbing pain reverberated through Kelly's shoulder. The thump of a headache was knocking on her right temple. Dan reached inside the satchel he carried retrieving a bottle of water and handed it to her.

"Here," Dan said. "Drink some water."

Kelly reached for the water, hesitating a fraction of a second before taking the blue plastic bottle from his outstretched hand.

"Thanks." Kelly took a long sip, the cool liquid washing away the dry coating in her throat.

The Orsini brothers took the Pope out of the basilica and into the waiting arms of emergency personnel. Vincenzo spoke with Michael briefly and then left the church closing the heavy doors behind him. All eyes fell on the magistrate.

"We have a lot of questions," Michael told her. "Let's start with what happened down there?"

"I came to check on the Pope in his private residence," the magistrate answered. "The camerlengo had left the vial of water for me when I returned."

"I gave holy water to the camerlengo for whoever was sick," Gen said. "At the time, I didn't know it was the Pope that was bitten. In the necropolis you said you almost didn't give it to him, why?"

"The men here have already tried holy water," the magistrate answered. "It wasn't until the commander of the Swiss Guard explained the small bottle came from you that I understood it had to be actual holy water."

"You obviously gave it to him," Gen commented. "His injuries were minor when we got to you."

"Yes," the magistrate answered. "I gave it to him. He was sitting up when the vampire showed up."

"You fought off that female vampire?" Kelly asked, her voice lilting in disbelief.

"No," the magistrate answered. "It wasn't a female vampire that came to the residences. The vampire on the security feed was male."

"That's why you ran," Tom commented. "You realized with a vampire onsite you couldn't teleport. You also couldn't fight off a vampire and keep the Pope safe."

"I was originally going to try and get him out to the square, where either you or the other Guardians would be," the magistrate told them. "I took the Pope out through a secret exit in his bedroom. When we reached the ground floor and crossed the courtyard, I realized we'd be on camera. It wouldn't just be all of you who would know where we were."

"You thought the vampires would think you got away if they couldn't find you in the basilica?" Dan asked.

"I hoped," the magistrate answered. "Not the best plan I know. I'm not a warrior like all of you. I'm a diplomat. I had to hope you'd find me before they did."

"Let's say we believe all of this." Kelly rolled her eyes. "Why didn't the female vampire kill you?"

"I tried reasoning with her," the magistrate answered flatly.

"Are we talking about the same vampire that nearly took my head off upon arrival?" Kelly snorted.

"That's different. Once she knew she was outnumbered she reacted like a cornered animal. You would too."

"Are you defending her?" Tom questioned.

"Not defending. Simply stating facts."

"What made you think you could reason with a vampire?" Michael asked.

"Vampires are not zombies, Michael. They want to be relevant and empowered. I tried to appeal to that."

"I don't even know what to say to that." Kelly paused. "These monsters have been ravaging humanity. They are turning and killing at an unprecedented rate, and you're concerned about how they feel!"

"I didn't say that I agreed with their desires." The magistrate pushed a piece of loose blonde hair behind her ear.

"We can debate the flaws in your logic later," Michael interrupted. "We need answers now."

"Yes," Frankie agreed. "We don't have the luxury of time. We need to get back to helping people who have been victimized."

"We need to kill all the vampires we can find," Kelly added.

The magistrate bristled at Kelly's words, standing up a bit straighter she crossed her arms.

Curious defensive posture, Kelly observed.

"Why did you go to a Historian's safe house?" Michael asked.

"I go where I need to." The magistrate narrowed her eyes on Michael.

"Okay," Tom added. "But you must have known an angel of your stature crossing into a safe house would break the sanctity of the area."

I nearly forgot she was the one who showed up at Lacey's house, Kelly thought.

The magistrate didn't answer, it was as if she were trying to think of a reply to Tom's comment.

"Did you know you were followed by Miles?" Kelly waited for the magistrate to answer. "You know who I'm referring to, correct?"

"The last soul catcher." The words were soft as if speaking under her breath instead of projecting out for the group.

"The last one?" Kelly asked. "How do you know he's the last one?"

"None of this is relevant right now." The magistrate snapped, agitation streaking across her crumpled forehead for the first time in the conversation. "I need to find your sister, Deborah."

"Why?" Frankie asked sharply.

"I asked Marcus to investigate the Schlosser case," the magistrate answered. "Now, I can't find him."

"Explain," Gen demanded. "We heard nothing about an official inquiry. In fact, Harry told us there wasn't record of a case being opened for any of what happened."

"When you got overzealous and branded Schlosser," the magistrate huffed. "You squashed any hope of an inquiry by handing him over to the four demons of the apocalypse."

"What did you want us to do?" Kelly snapped, her voice echoing off the high ceilings.

"I wanted him to stand trial, to answer questions." The magistrate's arms fell back down by her sides. "A roamer demon happening to come across Vermillion. Did you ever ask yourself how Schlosser was able to overpower Vermillion?"

"You think he was working with someone?" Greg asked.

"That seems pretty evident," the magistrate said. "No Earthbound demon of his level could pull that off alone. I didn't realize how big a pawn Schlosser was until Azza showed up. And the arrival of a supercharged Wrath along with Azza doesn't feel like a coincidence."

"But wait. Back up. How does Miles fit in?" Kelly asked. "He showed up at Lacey's house looking for an old coin. He said it was his and that Marcus took it. Do you know anything about that?"

"I don't." The magistrate peered into Kelly's eyes for the first time since their encounter in the necropolis. "Marcus is a seasoned sentinel, one of the best. I asked him to investigate how Schlosser pulled off what he did, who else was involved, and I haven't seen him since."

"Deb believed Marcus was kidnapped and dragged to hell," Frankie told her.

"It's possible." The magistrate's shoulders fell. "I hope she's wrong, but I have been unable to find him anywhere."

"That's why you asked Marcus," Gen stated. "Any sentinel would know investigating something involving the horsemen and the seven deadly sin demons would put them in immense danger. You asked Marcus because you knew of his relationship with Deb."

"To be fair everyone knows about his relationship with Deb," the magistrate sniped.

Kelly took several steps in the magistrate's direction. The room tensed.

"You took advantage of Marcus." Kelly's jaw clenched as she tried to push down the anger. "Just like you did Antonio. You're a manipulator."

"That is uncalled for!" The magistrate snapped in irritation. "You have no idea what I have had to do to keep the Accord from being broken."

"The accord was broken already," Gen declared. "Many times over, but for sure when Wrath murdered an Arch Angel in cold blood."

Michael stepped forward and grabbed Kelly's arm. She peered into her older brother's big brown eyes. He was imploring her to stand down.

She has to pay for what she's done, Kelly pleaded silently. With a gentle squeeze Michael nodded back toward the altar. Willing herself to move, Kelly reluctantly stepped toward the altar and away from the magistrate's position.

"What can Wrath do with Jacob's ring?" Tom asked. "Antonio told us that he went to you after Jacob was killed. That he told you about Wrath cutting off Jacob's hand and taking it with him."

"I don't know Wrath's intentions," the magistrate answered.

"Antonio also told us he's been looking for you," Greg added. "Running from your own kind, never a good sign."

The magistrate held her hands up. "That doesn't mean what you think it does."

The tension in the room heightened. The shifting sun streaked through the darker colored stained glass windows casting a storm of shadows in every corner. The aroma of candles and incense swirled all around them. A virtual battle between good and evil, light and dark playing out all around them.

The magistrate took a couple of steps back away from them. "I have done nothing wrong. I don't know what Wrath is going to do with the ring."

"What can he do?" Dan asked. "Did the ring restore Azza's wings?"

"Not alone it didn't," the magistrate answered. "He would need to imbue the ring with power."

Wrath's siblings, Kelly's mind reached back to the night Antonio revealed what he had done. Deb told them Jade was in danger, that Wrath was coming for her power.

"I'm not on trial here." The magistrate took one more step away from Michael who stood closest to her. "I don't answer to you. I am the magistrate, and you will treat me accordingly!"

"You agreed to tell us everything you know," Gen implored.

"I have!" the magistrate argued.

"Have you?" Kelly asked. "You have no idea what Wrath and Azza are planning?"

"Why would I know that?" the magistrate answered.

"Let's calm down." Michael raised his hands as if it would quell the stress. "If you have nothing else to share, then I would recommend you check in with Heaven. They are concerned for your wellbeing. If anything else comes up, we'll make sure to inform

Harry so he can pass it along. I assume you will do the same."

The magistrate paused before finally nodding in agreement. The door at the back of the church creaked open. All eyes turned toward the thick wooden doors. The sun spilled through first obscuring the form looming at the entrance.

A breeze bristled up the aisle of the church. Several steps inside the doorway and Kelly identified the boots, and as her eyes worked upward and caught the bottom of the red jacket.

"Vampire!" Greg yelled already running toward the male.

Tom and Dan followed. Grabbing one of Kelly's metal pipe weapons, Frankie joined them.

Michael turned back toward Kelly and Gen. "Watch her, we'll take care of this."

Michael teleported to the other end of the church temporarily blocking Kelly's view of the vampire. The magistrate had retreated backward toward the side exit. The Arch Angel's frightened eyes told Kelly she wasn't sticking around to engage any vampires.

"I need to go," the magistrate mumbled. "I need to get back to Heaven."

"You're leaving?" Gen yelled. "I thought Arch Angels were able to smite vampires."

"Seems that's just lore," Kelly said as her brothers wrestled the vampire to the ground.

Why did he just walk in here like that? Kelly thought staring down at the melee playing out at the other end of the aisle.

The vampire was large, close to seven feet tall. His broad shoulders and meaty hands packed a wallop of a punch. So far, her brothers had avoided the direct hits and were getting plenty of their own in. The entire scene was curious, as big as this vampire was, he was sure to know the odds.

"Where is Vincenzo?" Kelly asked Gen. "Did none of the Orsini brothers stick around?"

"Look Out!" Gen screamed.

Kelly whipped her head around as a scabbard burst through the magistrate's chest. The petite blonde choked on her own gasp, blood spilling from her open mouth. The sharp blade penetrated through to the hilt. The magistrate's body was lifted off the ground, her feet dangling just above the decorative marble floor.

Standing in the magistrate's pooled blood were the black boots of a male vampire. He pulled the blade free from the magistrate, her limp body crumpled to the floor in a lifeless heap. The sky darkened, lightning streaked across the sky, and thunder boomed.

The male vampire smirked. "We meet again Ms. O'Mara."

Garrick.

"You're finished, vampire." Kelly unsheathed the metal pipe from its holster across her back.

"Not today." Garrick winked at her. "Don't worry, we'll dance again on the battlefield. I'll enjoy tasting you before you die."

"Taking out the weakest here," Kelly said with disdain. "You're a coward, Garrick."

Garrick laughed as he sheathed his weapon. "She was a traitor to us both."

The haze of smoke that enveloped him swam toward her. Kelly stepped back away from the fading strands of charcoal vapor as if they were poison.

Gen ran toward the magistrate and crouched beside her checking for a pulse. It was useless but she attempted to heal the Arch Angel anyway.

"It was a trap!" Kelly turned back to find that the first vampire had escaped from the church as well. "We fell for the distraction again!"

"She didn't deserve to die," Gen implored.

Vincenzo entered the church and ran down the aisle toward Michael. Their voices a mishmash of languages in an operatic song of confusion.

"The only ones who deserve to die are those in Hell," Kelly said enraged at what just happened. "I'm sick of this!"

"What do you mean?" Gen asked.

"We've been behind the ball this entire time," Kelly said as the Arch Angel's blood spilled out into the aisle and encircled the leg of the first pew.

"What did Garrick say?" Michael asked when her brothers re-joined them.

"Where were you, Vincenzo?" Kelly snapped. "I thought you guys were keeping watch."

"Hey!" Michael stepped toward Kelly, impeding her view of Vincenzo. "We're all in this together."

"What we are is losing." Kelly stepped back away from Michael. "Looking for help has gotten us nowhere."

"We can't just run off halfcocked, Kell," Dan warned.

"I'm not running anywhere," Kelly told him.

The flapping of wings came from outside. Kelly knew the Arch Angels were here to retrieve the magistrate's body. Antonio arrived first, his eyes finding Kelly's, he held them there. The weight of the loss bled through the Arch Angel's stern professional exterior.

The church filled with gasps, cries, and hushed voices as more of heaven's warriors filled the church to bear witness to the magistrate's death.

"I'm done," Kelly said under her breath to her siblings.

"Where are you going?" Dan asked.

"I'm going to hunt down Garrick and make him pay," Kelly said as she blocked out the pain that played out in front of her. "He's going to rue the day he ever met the O'Maras."

Kelly wrapped herself in her aura. Antonio yelled for her to stay. Kelly closed her watery eyes and let the heartache carry her far from the scene.

I'm coming for you, vampire.

Kelly's fury a siren's song of destruction.

CHAPTER TWENTY

Present Day

Kelly gripped the makeshift weapon in her right hand a little tighter. The fireplace poker was jagged on the end where she cut it in half. Her palms bore the scratches from continual use. Taking length off the household tool made it easy to wield. In her left hand was a large rock. Squeezing her hand, the sizeable chunk of jagged earth dug into her skin. The sharp edges pushed against the surface of her palm enough to send pain signals to the brain, but not enough to draw blood. The sensation broke through her scattered thoughts and helped her focus.

It was dusk and the darkening sky signaled rain with its thick heavy clouds looming above. The air was cool, the scent of alpine meadows masked by the wafting smoke of a nearby campfire. The vampire standing across from Kelly leered in disgust.

I feel the same about you.

He wore jeans and a heavy sweatshirt, no thick heavy coat of armor, no weapons. Kelly on the other hand was dressed for the engagement. She wore jeans with a thick black sweater under a mid-length raincoat. Her jacket hid a multitude of weapons, holy water, and pockets filled with holy oil.

"Are you just going to stand there, or run?" She bristled as a bead of sweat trickled down her neck before descending between her shoulder blades.

"I think you should be the one running." The vampire had brown eyes with a crew cut and a large tattoo of demonic writing on his left hand. "Poor little angel lost in the woods."

"Normally, I enjoy when things from Hell refer to me as an angel. It lets me know how out of their depth they are, but today–" Kelly paused using the back of her hand to wipe sweat from her brow. Her hand came away with a damp mix of dirt and blood, remnants from her earlier fight inside the necropolis. Her hair was swept up off her face and fastened into a tight ponytail.

"Today you're what?" Crew cut asked. "Are you tired? You look like you've seen better days angel. Maybe I'll show you some mercy and kill you quickly."

His boots were nearly covered in a hue of orange, red, and yellow leaves. During the day it would have been a beautiful kaleidoscope of the fall season.

"Mercy?" Kelly spat. "As if you know the meaning of the word."

The vampire laughed. Kelly smirked knowing his hubris would be his downfall. When he took a fraction of a second to snidely glance down at the weapons by his campsite Kelly launched. With a jump she kicked him square in the chest. He hurtled backward rolling over and landing face down in the dirt several yards away.

"Where is Garrick?" Kelly yelled. "I know you must have some way of communicating. Tell him I'm looking for him."

The vampire clawed his way back to his feet and pulled a doubled edged hunting knife out of an ankle holster. He swung it at Kelly. His weapon sliced through the air with a woosh. Kelly hoisted her right arm up and blocked his move. She was already swinging her left fist before he could attempt another blow. The rock in her palm smashed against the vampire's right ear. The crack to his skull reverberated down her wrist but she held on to her rudimentary weapon. He bellowed in pain and fell to one knee.

Kelly swung her right hand with force sending the tip of her weapon into the vampire's left ear. The vampire wailed in response, teetering on collapse. The vampire's weapon fell out of his hand and disappeared into the thickness of the underbrush below. Both hands reached for the object lodged in his ear. Before Kelly could push it in further the vampire threw his head back and collided with her chin. Stunned, Kelly stepped back several feet and shook her head trying to clear the fog. The vampire pulled the metal pipe out of his ear and dropped it to the ground.

They locked eyes. Not giving him any more time to think, Kelly charged forward tackling him to the ground. The two rolled away from the campsite with Kelly landing on top. Punching the vampire in the nose several times with her rock-heavy hand she drew blood. The vampire blocked her arm on the next swing and shoved Kelly up and off, then he scrambled to his feet.

Before Kelly could do the same the vampire kicked her in the jaw snapping her head back. The pain seared through her. Undaunted, she spun her body to the right, retrieved her weapon from the ground, and pushed off against the hardened dirt to get back onto her feet.

The vampire swung wildly for her head. She pulled back and he missed. Grabbing his arm Kelly pulled him toward the ground. With his momentum already projecting him forward he began to fall. She elbowed him in the spine forcing him to his knees. Kelly took the spear and stabbed his right ear.

"No!" The vampire screeched as he swatted wildly at his head.

Using the same motion she perfected from prior kills, Kelly slammed the rock against the handle. Since the vampire was thrashing the tip penetrated but not far enough to pierce the brain. The vampire panicked and bucked. He grabbed the pipe end of the weapon and yanked it out. He staggered to his feet and made it a yard or two before he fell once more to the hardened earth. Kelly pulled her weapon from his hands.

Digging his nails into the ground he crawled away from her. He reached a nearby tree and managed to painstakingly claw his way back up to a standing position. He left a muddy trail of blood-soaked leaves and broken branches behind him. Kelly retrieved the spear and sheathed it in a holster under her coat. Her black combat boots stomped through the underbrush snapping twigs as she came up behind him. The vampire's arms were stretched around the tree using it to steady himself. Slowly he turned to face her, coughing and gagging on his own demonic essence as it fled his body.

"I'm sending you back to Hell." Kelly pulled an amulet from inside her jacket pocket. "This time, don't come back."

Using her teeth she yanked out the cork-like stopper. She splattered Holy oil all over the front of the vampire's chest, then retrieved a lighter. Pulling down hard several times with her thumb against the metal starter did nothing. She shook the plastic device and tried again but could not produce so much as a flicker of light. The vampire started chuckling, an infuriating blend of laughter and choking.

"Be careful what you ask for." Demonic liquid leaked from his eyes and nose. His face was covered in varying shades of red, a hellish bloody rainbow. The crunching of leaves came from behind her. She turned and there stood Garrick. He wore black fatigues and a gray T-shirt. His long hair fell loose just above the shoulder. His thick neck and square jaw pulsed like the muscles on his arms.

"You came looking for me," Garrick teased. "I'm touched. That one's no match for you."

"Neither are you," Kelly said through gritted teeth.

Garrick smiled. "Let's get to it then."

Rage rolled through her like a freight train. The thunder of her heart thumped in her ears. She stared at the vampire who she had already gone several rounds with at Gen's house. The vicious creature who targeted the Pope and murdered the magistrate in cold blood.

"You are without mercy." Her voice dropped to a menacing whisper. "I will show you the same."

She was quick to reach him, throwing a right jab to his face. He tried to brace against the punch but could only raise one hand in front of him. Kelly used her weight to smash through his defenses and strike a blow to the face. As her hand collided with the bones in his nose, an image of Sonoran flashed in her mind. Thoughts of the gaunt figure with glowing green eyes who attacked her in the park between night and day enraged her further.

"You should have told your side to stay in Hell!" Kelly screamed.

Her hand swung through the air once more, but he blocked it and counter punched her in the chest. She slid back several feet pushing her weight forward and dropping her left hand to the ground to keep from falling.

He unsheathed his scabbard. Kelly unsheathed her pipe. He swung hard for her head and Kelly pushed her pipe forward to block the sword. Kelly's arms strained above her holding back the sword. She kicked the inside of his right knee with her foot. He yelled in pain and attempted to step back but limped. It was obvious he couldn't put full weight on his right leg. The kneecap wasn't broken but he was injured.

"You're wasting your talent fighting against us," he growled. "You're not like them, I can sense it. We're more alike than you think."

"You know nothing about me, Garrick," Kelly snapped.

"I know you survived hell." He snickered. "I bet that still burns in Azza's mind."

She went at him once more swinging hard with her right arm toward his ear. He blocked and grabbed her hand. He forced her into a circle, twisting her around, then pulled her toward him. He pushed her against his waist, wrapping his left arm across her neck. Kelly's back was snug against Garrick's chest. He leaned down close to her ear, sweat and alcohol bled together in a menacing stench.

"Any time you want me to stop," he whispered. "Just ask nicely."

With her left hand she reached in her jacket pocket for a bottle of holy water. She smashed the bottle open against his exposed forearm. The holy water burned his skin and he screamed yanking his arm away from her. She unwound turning back toward him and punched his left ear drawing blood.

Retrieving another bottle Kelly smashed it against the right side of his head. The water splattered across his neck and face tearing open his flesh and spilling into his right eye. He screeched and tried swiped the fluid off his face. His action only served to spread the water to more of his skin.

Kelly aimed for the wounded side of Garrick's face and punched him several times, upon impact she was doused with his blood.

The thought of being trapped in Hell and tortured by Azza came careening into her mind's eye.

How long was I beaten and healed? How much demonic blood runs through my veins?

"You don't know me!" Kelly's voice cracked against the strain. "I'm nothing like you."

She jabbed at the vampire's head no longer able to decipher the right side of his face. He blocked one punch and countered landing a jab to her ribcage. She yelped and backed off. He stumbled toward her with his hands defensively out in front of him. She grabbed another bottle and leapt on top of him smashing it down upon his head. The fluid splashed into his left eye. He moaned and flailed punching her in the side once more. He fell to one knee. She peered down at him blind to everything except the rage coursing through her.

A vision of Antonio's face flared in her mind. Her friend's betrayal gnawing at her like the open wound she knew it still to be.

"You think you can come here and do what you want?!" She yelled at Garrick as she smashed her fists down on both ears. His body listed, his breathing labored, but he was still very much alive.

Stepping back she searched for her weapon. Garrick pulled himself back to a standing position. Kelly quickly kicked him in the chest. Garrick staggered backward until he rested against a tree. She retrieved another bottle of holy water and threw it at his left shoulder. The water burned a hole through his T-shirt and opened a gaping wound on his shoulder. Blood poured from his mouth. His long hair was matted against his face. His neck was pulsing to the beat of his heavy breathing.

As he bent his head back to catch his breath, she unsheathed a dagger from her jacket and stabbed him in the wounded shoulder. With his skin severely weakened from the holy water the blade penetrated straight through to the tree. Garrick hollered and punched Kelly hard on the left side of the head. She staggered backward but stayed upright.

Garrick was effectively pinned and momentarily tethered in the upright position. As she approached, he weakly kicked at her. Kelly easily sidestepped his attack. Garrick grabbed for the dagger, but the movement tore open more of his skin. The blood-soaked handle was slippery, and the vampire struggled to grasp it. Kelly doused the vampire with holy oil. He cried out once more.

Finally, Garrick gave up trying to release himself from the tree and pulled a small knife from a holster by his hip. He threw the blade at Kelly. She moved her head but was too slow to avoid it entirely. The tip sliced open her skin and blood trickled down her cheek. Pain rippled through her strained muscles and Kelly grunted in response. The flashes of recent battles, laced with memories of Sonoran, Antonio, and Azza assaulted her. The idea that Garrick and Keeva came close to turning the Pope angered her further. Images of Joey, so weak from vampire venom that a demon invaded his body and almost succeeded in killing him, wreaked havoc on her soul.

"Don't do this O'Mara," a bloodied Garrick pleaded, his eyes filled with fear. "You don't understand who we are. We just want to go home. You're on the wrong side of this fight."

Kelly ignored him. She picked up the rock she had brought with her and made a fist around it.

Kelly brushed off Garrick's weak attempt to block her punch and she connected squarely to his nose. Garrick's body went limp but stayed upright still pinned to the tree.

Kelly continued to swing at Garrick's face. On her fourth punch, a sickening crunch of bone signaled a breaking of his nose and more. Kelly did not stop. She began thrusting harder, and with more might.

Kelly let out a long, guttural scream as the rock broke apart in her fist from the continued impacts. The skin in Kelly's palm tore open.

Kelly's face was sprayed with Garrick's blood mixed with bits of bone and brain matter. There was now just a raw, meaty hole where Garrick's face used to be.

Tears streaked down Kelly's blood-splattered cheeks as she screamed once more. Suddenly, fire broke out across Garrick's chest igniting the holy oil.

Kelly stumbled backward as Garrick's whole body became engulfed in flames.

"No!" Kelly yelled. "You're on the wrong side of this fight!"

Kelly's shirt was on fire. She swatted at her chest to extinguish the fire. As she pounded her chest the fire intensified. She gazed down at the cause and her hands were afire. Flames of red and orange light danced in the palm of both hands.

What's happening?

"Kelly O'Mara." A voice bellowed from behind. "Now, you are ready."

Panic coursed through her, spinning she faced the stranger.

"Who are you?" Kelly asked nearly breathless.

"I'm afraid I cannot answer that." He strode closer to her position. "For I cannot answer questions you already know the answer to. If you need a name, you can call me Sunny."

His brown eyes seemed to penetrate right through her. He wore dark colored fatigues with a red vest that zipped up the front. The uniform of sorts showcased his toned body and bulging muscles. His tan skin was covered at the wrist with dark leather straps bound to form a brace. His short jet black hair was as dark as the night that encroached.

"What do you want?" Kelly huffed as the flame in her palm dwindled. "I'm kind of busy."

"Your transition sent a signal. You effectively called me here. It's time for us to go."

"I'm in no mood, Sunny." Kelly stamped out the fire on the ground. Garrick's scorched body was crumpling to ash.

"If you want to know what you are than you need to come with me."

"I know what I am," she answered through gritted teeth. "Are you friend or foe?"

"You would already know if I was the latter." He paused. "I was referring to what you are becoming, not what you are leaving behind."

"I don't have time for riddles." Kelly sighed. "My head hurts and I still have to make my way home."

"If you want to learn how to use those powers." He pointed toward her hands. "You need to come with me."

"You." She pointed at him as the last strands of smoke billowed from her hands. "You're going to show me how to use powers. Thanks for the offer but I already have a trainer."

"Ah yes, Michael," Sunny stated simply. "He can't help you."

"You know my brother Michael?" Kelly asked. "That doesn't surprise me. He would take exception to your assessment of his training prowess."

"It's not an insult," Sunny answered. "It's just a fact. Let me demonstrate."

Sunny raised his arm and held his palm face up toward her. She was about to speak when a flame ignited in his hand.

"How?" she asked him.

"Training," he answered. "You want to learn how to harness your true power. You'll have to walk the path of totality."

The path of what? The adrenaline was wearing off and the pain in her ribs made every breath akin to a knife stabbing her.

"I know you have doubts, that's perfectly normal," Sunny stated. "But war is upon us so there isn't the luxury of time."

Thoughts of all she had been through continued to invade her mind. Jared was in the Pit for rescuing her from Hell. Time and place have been ripped from her memory by her friend and Arch Angel, Antonio. Sonoran, one of the demons of the apocalypse, nearly killed her. She had lost one sibling to hell and another by heaven.

He's wrong, Michael can help me, but is there time? Kelly's deliberations boiled. *If Michael works with me to control a new power, that's time we're not out there defending humanity.*

"Seems you've come to a decision." Sunny's lips curved into a small smile.

"Path of totality sounds precarious." Kelly kicked through the leaves until she found her weapon and sheathed it behind her back. Walking to the tree, Kelly pulled the dagger free. Garrick's ashen corpse had already scattered in the wind.

Turning, Kelly locked eyes with Sunny. "When do we start?"

"The question is not when," he answered. "It's where, and only you can answer that."

CHAPTER TWENTY-ONE

eb's feet sloshed through muddy puddles as she and Schlosser trudged their way along a narrow incline.

"When you said the desert saved us hours of walking," Deb panted. "I didn't know you meant that literally."

"When are you going to learn, Guardian." Schlosser chuckled. "I don't lie."

"We're walking uphill," Deb commented. "Where are we going?"

"Into the jungle," he said simply.

Jungle, Deb thought. *Seems hell has a little bit of everything.*

Fifteen minutes later Deb's shins strained as they pushed themselves up a steep ascent. Damp moss and rain permeated between long vines that hung across the exit to the cave they had been walking through.

Schlosser disappeared in the thick vegetation. Deb turned back, they had hiked several hundred feet above the cave floor.

When Deb exited, she joined Schlosser who was standing just beyond the rocky formation. Like the desert alcove, the cave entrance was small and led outdoors with little resistance. The sky was darker than a moonless night. The only light came from torches lit along a rough path to their left. The ground was covered in mushrooms. Along the path were Chinese evergreens and snake plants. There was the roar of rushing water in the distance like that of a waterfall. There were trees but most of them were thin and dwarfed with few to no leaves attached. The air was humid but chilly.

Schlosser walked off toward the path bending to pick a few mushrooms along the way.

"Make yourself useful, Guardian." Schlosser pointed to her right. "Pick the dark purple berries over there."

Deb moved to the thorny shrubs and started plucking the fruit off the vine. When her hands were full, she turned back toward Schlosser only to find he was gone.

"How many did you get?" Schlosser's voice came from behind her.

Spooked, Deb nearly lost the fruit. "Where the heck did you come from?"

"The path goes around in a circle," he told her. "There are some things hidden in a tent I left behind. Here, throw the berries in this."

Deb dropped the fruit in a plastic jug that had the top cut off.

"You spend a lot of time out here?" she asked.

"I used to," he answered, "I like the stars on Earth better. I haven't been here in quite a while. Someone else took it over when I left, but you can tell they've been gone awhile."

Deb filled her jug and Schlosser gathered mushrooms in his T-shirt. They walked off deeper into the thicket until they came upon a makeshift campsite. There was a black cast iron pot sitting on top of a broken grate. Sunk into the mud were bricks holding in varying lengths of wood and kindling.

"Is this going to light?" Deb wondered aloud.

"It should and we might as well use it," he told her.

Schlosser emptied the pot and threw in the mushrooms. Using one of the torches he lit the kindling. Beside the tent were several jugs of rainwater. He threw some in the pot and then told Deb to peel the berries and discard the skins in the underbrush behind her.

Deb sat on the ground and rubbed her fingers across the skin of the berry. With a little scratch of her fingernail the fruit split. With a gentle squeeze the softer inside popped out, nearly escaping her fingers and rolling on the dirt covered floor of the forest.

"Am I adding the berries to the pot?" she asked.

"Yup."

Deb tossed in the fruit and within a few minutes the fragrance of vegetable stew filled the air.

"Will we be attracting anything with this stew?" Deb asked.

"Not at night," Schlosser answered. "Everything sleeps at night."

"Dare I ask how many nights I've been here?"

"This is your first one." Schlosser ragged a couple cinderblocks over to sit on. "Night and day is not the same here as it is on Earth."

"How long do the days last?' Deb asked.

"Doesn't matter," Schlosser answered. "This is going to be your only chance to sleep. I would take it if I were you."

Sleep. I cannot imagine falling asleep right now. My body is exhausted, but my mind is probably not going to shut off.

As if reading her mind, Schlosser added. "If you don't sleep tonight, then I don't know that you're going to physically make it."

"I'll try," Deb answered.

Schlosser nodded and grabbed a metal stick from inside the tent and gave the contents a stir.

"It's gotta cook for a bit for those berries to no longer be poisonous." Schlosser opened the bag and removed the gray pants he took from inside the torture room. "I'll be back in a few. Soup should be ready by then."

Deb had to restrain herself from asking where he was going. Schlosser navigated around some evergreen bushes and disappeared.

"Don't go anywhere." His voice traveled back to her.

As her eyes adjusted to the dim lighting she paused to listen. There was only the crackling fire and the rushing water. No birds, no bugs, nothing.

Deb stood and walked a few feet away to check inside the tent. The side had a tear in it, but it was standing. Inside the tent was one sleeping bag and an uncovered pillow. Deb picked up the pillow, it was damp to the touch with the stench of mildew and wet dog. She brought the pillow outside and left it by the fire. It probably wouldn't dry anytime soon, but it made the tent a bit more palatable.

The sleeping bag fared better, it was dry and inside was a small black and white throw. Deb took the blanket outside and shook it out, no stains, no odor, that was a win. Following what Schlosser did, she went about searching for cinderblocks. No blocks, but she did find a worn out camp chair. Deb dragged the chair over to the fire and sat down wrapping herself in the small blanket. There was a sort of peace that settled over the landscape.

I can see why Schlosser spent time out here. Comparatively this must have been a breath of fresh air, literally and figuratively.

Leaves and branches swayed in the cool night air. She stared at the fire, occasionally stirring the liquid which she was not entirely sure how they were going to eat now.

The fire crackled and she added more kindling to it. Even though it wasn't a roaring fire there was a small bit of warmth from it. Deb nestled further into the chair and thought about her family. She hoped they'd forgive her and that they were okay.

Flashes of her brief time in hell invaded her mind. Every stolen moment of peace was ruined by frightening images of torment and death. She wondered if it would always be like that, or if it was a side effect of being in hell. A sort of cruel punishment where you never really rested. Where you were never free of the terror.

She thought of Marcus and her heart ached.

What if Schlosser was right? What if we don't have free will? What if it's all just a mirage? Like this jungle being safe. There's no such thing as being safe in hell.

The flickering of the fire soothed her, and her eyes grew heavy. Sleep was calling, her body beckoning to finally rest. The snapping of twigs didn't match the quiet surrounding and she straightened her posture. Deb recognized Schlosser's gate as he neared the camp site. When he reached her position, he held out a handful of berries.

"These you can eat without cooking."

Deb held her palm out and Schlosser filled it with round yellow berries shaped like a flower. Deb popped one into her mouth. Juice exploded when she bit the fruit, it was tangy and tart, like a cranberry.

"Not bad," Deb told him.

"When you're hungry, it all tastes good." He sat on the cinderblocks and eyed her blanket. "Find that in the sleeping bag?"

"Yeah." Deb nodded to the right of the fire. "Pillow is too wet to use, but the sleeping bag is dry."

Schlosser leaned forward his face lit by the dwindling fire. The wounds on his forehead and chin were healed. When he spoke the decaying gumline was imperceptible. His bald head glistened in the flickering light and the blood stains washed clean. He was wearing the gray cargo pants that he took from the torture room and the wretched odor he normally swam in was gone.

"You look refreshed," Deb commented.

"Do I?" he mocked. "I took a dip in the waterfall. I would have asked you to join me, but I didn't think you'd make the trek. I lost my footing once or twice and I'm used to this darkness."

"I can shower when I get out of here." She stirred the pot once more. "How are we eating this?"

"We aren't," he answered. "It'll be more like sipping."

He grabbed the hot handles and walked it over to a nearby puddle. The pot sizzled upon impact with the cool water. Then he went back into the tent and retrieved the empty plastic water jugs. He poured the soup in the jugs and placed one on the ground next to her.

"It will be a few before you can drink it," he told her. "I on the other hand can eat it hot."

"You're immune to the blazing heat of boiling soup?" Deb asked.

"Pretty much." He took a sip of the bubbling soup.

"Well?" Deb asked. "How is it?"

"It's not scrumptious, that's for sure."

Deb laughed, maybe for the first time since coming here.

"It's just sustenance," Schlosser added. "Nothing fancy. In hell, only a select few can expect more. It will do."

Deb picked up the jug and blew on it a little before taking a very small sip. The mushrooms overwhelmed the palate, but the berries mellowed it out on the backend. The fruit was firm like carrots and the taste was mild in comparison to the mushroom. The aroma of warm food caused her stomach to rumble. There was no doubt she was hungry.

"I'll take the sleeping bag out here." Schlosser dragged the bag out by the fire. He went about finding more kindling and adding it to the fire reigniting the flames.

Deb finished her soup and went inside the tent. She laid down on the ground and placed her elbow under her head. Wrapping the blanket around her upper body she tried to imagine herself back home, in the comfort of her own bed. The tent's front flaps billowed in the night air, the only repetitive noise to accompany the faint thunder of the waterfall.

Her belly was full, a testament to how much it had probably shrunk since arriving. Deb closed her eyes and thought about the first thing she was going to have when she got back home.

A cup of Scottish breakfast tea and a blueberry scone from the Tea Pot. The lilacs of spring would be long gone but there would be sunflowers, aster, and day lilies.

Finally falling asleep Deb tossed and turned in a fitful slumber. The nightmares seemed to crash over on themselves. Each harrowing image replaced by another more disturbing one. No matter where she was or what she was doing in her dream, Marcus' dead eyes were staring back at her. She was startled awake by the memory of the chain of chaos bursting through the sentinel's chest killing him.

The sky was less dark than when she fell asleep, she could make out streaks of white shining through the tear in the side of the tent. Sitting up Deb moved her neck around to stretch out the kinks from sleeping on the hard ground. Her shoulder ached but overall she was better having gotten some sleep.

She exited the tent. The fire was out and the sleeping bag empty. Deb walked toward the path. There was a vast landscape twenty feet below them. As she stepped across the rocky terrain, a large bird of some kind took flight in the distance. Deb stopped.

The creature spread its wide wings. It had a bird like head and talons at the end of its feet.

Gargoyle!

The monster landed on top of a large fountain and then dove down into the waters of the basin below. Continuing to examine the landscape Deb crossed over the cleared path and close to the edge of the cliff. Her heart rate picked up as she went, her mind reaching back to the story of Gen and Kelly's harrowing travel to purgatory.

As the night sky continued to lighten, warm rays of yellow seeped through the clouds in the distance. The valley to the right was full of lush trees and flowering bushes. Weeping willows basked in the warmth of sunlight, their long tresses dancing along the thick green grass below. Deb blinked at the sight of the stone staircase adorned with bright pink flowers, as if making sure it wasn't a mirage.

The park between night and day, it's here and it's as beautiful as Gen described it.

Footsteps shuffled through the underbrush behind her. Deb swung around with a wide smile on her face prepared to tell Schlosser she was going to teleport to the light side of the park. It wasn't Schlosser, it was Robino.

The god of darkness stood tall against the expansive rugged landscape. Hope evaporated like the brightness of the sun during a passing storm. Evil permeated from him, as if he exuded the very essence of what it meant to be demonic. His dark brown eyes narrowed in on Deb.

"You shouldn't be here, Guardian," Robino warned. "Someone is hunting you, and she wants your head on a spire."

CHAPTER TWENTY-TWO

The god of darkness loomed ahead like a tower in the dwarfed landscape. Robino's long hair fell to his shoulder blades, his axe glistened against the tree it leaned upon. He was alone, but his menacing presence exuded all the confidence needed to make an enemy stop in their tracks. Deb was betting not many beings went up against Robino and lived to brag about it.

"You hear me, Guardian?" Robino asked. "You're being hunted. You're as good as dead."

Deb didn't know where Schlosser was. She chose not to teleport away. Deb still needed the roamer demon's help navigating hell.

In false bravado Deb answered. "She's not just hunting me. I'm pretty sure she wants to be your boss."

"Keep mouthing off about her power-hungry ambitions," Robino taunted. "Eventually, Lucifer will come."

"I was looking for someone," Deb said.

"Schlosser? He's the only one unaccounted for in the torture room," Robino confirmed. "He your boyfriend or something? I mean I've heard of unholy alliances before, but that one repulses even me."

"No." Deb kept the answer brief.

Out of time and patience, the desire to get home weighed on Deb. Robino, this god of darkness, was now standing in her way.

"What do you want?" Deb asked.

"Torture rooms destroyed," Robino commented. "Any idea who did that?"

The outline of a figure shielded by a thick wall of dying bramble came into focus. Schlosser moved ever so slightly behind Robino.

"You short on rooms to torture people in?" Deb countered.

The seven-foot demon took a half step in Deb's direction as if to strike. She stood tall and didn't move assessing there was still several feet between them.

"You got a smart mouth, Guardian," Robino scolded. "You're either tough, or mad dog crazy, which is it?"

"Obviously, a little of both," Deb answered.

"Where's Schlosser?" Robino demanded. "That weasel's close by, I can feel him."

"You sense all the demons in hell?" Deb asked trying to keep Robino talking while she thought of a way out of this.

"Only the ones from my realm," Robino retorted. "Schlosser's one of mine."

"Which means?" Deb asked confused.

"Nothing to you, Guardian," Robino snapped.

"I overheard your conversation with Azza," Deb said.

"I should have known it was Schlosser when the hellcats went wild," Robino retorted. "You down here looking for that bitch, Azza?" Robino asked.

"No." Deb realized she may have an opening with the god of darkness. "I'm down here looking to stop her, you interested?"

"I don't get involved in heaven's bullshit," Robino tossed.

"Even if it affects your world?" Deb asked. "Like I said, it seems Azza is aiming for power. That day might come sooner rather than later when she's telling you what to do."

Robino belly laughed. "She can give it her best shot, but she's got no chance."

"She believes she's got more than that," Deb taunted.

"Azza's got a few alliances and a stolen hellcrux." Robino shrugged. "She ain't ascending through anymore ranks. She's topped out."

"You're dismissing Wrath?" Deb asked.

"That worm," Robino mocked. "He's always banging his chest making all the humans go crazy. He's a joke around here. I'd say it to his face if he ever dared show up in hell again after the bullshit he pulled on his sister."

"Jade?" Deb asked her interest piqued.

"Jade!" Robino derided with a stilted laugh. "Is that what she calls herself now? How fancy for a deadly sin spewing jealousy and resentment for all the world to consume."

"Wrath was hunting her before I left." Deb tried to draw more information from Robino.

"Again? Nothing surprises me about Wrath, he's an idiot." Robino scoffed. "Dragged Envy to hell, tortured and experimented on her, learned nothing if you ask me. Complete waste of time and then he got his ass handed to him by a horseman. Now that was some funny shit!"

That explains why Jade wouldn't take me to hell.

"What if Wrath and Azza get the gates open?" Deb asked.

"They have zero chance of doing that," Robino deadpanned.

Deb tilted her head. "You sure about that?"

"What do you know, Guardian?" Robino asked through gritted teeth.

"I want a deal," Deb told him.

"What kind of deal?" Robino asked. "Does it involve you leaving hell? Because that's not likely to happen."

"The kind of deal that keeps you in power," Deb brazenly added. "And yes, I'm leaving hell, with or without your help."

"You'd be wise to remember who you're talking to, Guardian." Robino reached for his axe.

Deb sent out her shield and pulled the weapon

across the path and into her own hand. The massive weapon was heavy, Deb used both hands to steady it.

"Torture room's not the only thing I can destroy." Dropping her voice to a menacing whisper. "You have no idea the lengths to which I will go to leave this place. You can't hold me, nothing can."

"You want to go one on one then?" Robino took several steps toward Deb. She pushed him back with her power. Robino used his considerable muscle to bend forward, digging his feet into the dirt, he stopped the slide backward.

"I get my hands on you and this game of yours is over!" Robino growled.

The tension between them escalated. Deb knew she had to bring it back down.

"Probably true." Deb paused while Robino's eyes narrowed in on her. "I'm not interested in fighting you and if you wanted to kill me, you would have done it before I turned around. What you want is information and I'm prepared to tell you what I know."

Robino contemplated her words. "Go on then, I'm listening."

Deb threw Robino's axe, it penetrated the tree closest to him.

"Not bad." Robino pulled the heavy blade out. "Now speak, before I change my mind."

"I don't believe Azza stole the hellcrux. I think she made a deal with Harac." Deb was making assumptions but at this point it was the only thing she had left. "Harac and his army get another crack at

Heaven while Azza uses the hellcrux to visit all the realms and recruit more allies."

Robino shrugged his shoulders. "Maybe. Even so, most of the other gods are not stupid enough to join her."

"What if she doesn't need all of them," Deb surmised. "Maybe with hell's first army she only needs–"

"Those snakes haven't led an army in over a thousand years!" Robino interrupted her. "Kelce isn't worthy of standing alongside demons, never mind leading them into battle."

Unworthy. I need to remind him that the vampires turned against Lucifer when they joined Harac's rebellion and escaped hell.

"How is Harac still a god?" Deb asked. "He led a rebellion and the vampires joined him."

"That's my point," Robino scoffed. "Kelce and his ilk will use anyone who comes out of hell. All they want is Heaven."

What do the vampires want with heaven?

Schlosser came out from behind the thicket.

"Your highness," Schlosser mumbled as he passed Robino on his way to stand next to Deb. "I think what the Guardian is trying to say–"

"Shut up, Schlosser!" Robino boomed. "You coward. Letting your girlfriend do all the negotiating while you're hiding in the bushes. I should slice you myself."

Schlosser thrust his hands in the air as he took a

tentative step backward.

"Apologies." Schlosser bowed his head several times.

"The vampires can't just walk into Heaven." Deb said it more like a question than a statement.

"Now who's unsure?" Robino laughed. "If they can handle a hellcrux, then they can sure as shit make it through the pearly gates."

Straining to put all these pieces of information together, Deb was no longer sure how to appeal to Robino.

"Whether Azza succeeds in opening the gates or not is irrelevant," Schlosser interjected.

"That's kind of the entire point, Schlosser," Deb argued.

"No," Schlosser said adamantly then turned to Robino. "What matters is what Lucifer does when he finds out and he will find out. Lucifer will hunt down those that sided with Azza against him."

"What do you want?" Robino asked Deb.

"I want a Hellcrux," Deb told him. "I need to stop Azza."

"As if you can." Robino spat.

"Not alone I can't," Deb retorted. "She's made a lot more enemies than just you, Robino."

Robino seemed to mull over the ask. "Schlosser stays here. He's owed punishment."

Deb shook her head. "I need help navigating hell. He comes with me."

"Fine," Robino snarked. "I'll give you a hellcrux.

But the others in my sphere will know it's been moved. They will feel it."

"What do you propose?" Deb asked.

"I'm going to send them after you." Robino paused for effect. "You want out of hell? You'll need to be faster than the hounds."

"Deal," Deb answered.

"Bring her to the dungeon." Robino pointed at Schlosser. "Don't think you and I are done, roamer. You're a demon, and you serve at my bidding, no one else's."

Robino disappeared into a haze of reddish smoke. Deb let go of the breath she didn't know she was holding.

"Well," Schlosser said. "You ready to get out of hell?"

"More than ready," Deb answered. Behind her the gargoyle took flight once more.

"Don't bother." Schlosser brought Deb's eyes back around. "Since your sisters traipsed all through purgatory looking for that precious husband, the place is crawling with ghosts."

"Ghosts?" Deb questioned.

"Not the apparitions humans are fascinated with on Earth," Schlosser retorted. "Here, ghosts are near transparent demons, like Sonoran. You never see them coming until it's too late. I'm assuming that's who told Robino we were up here."

"Robino said he could sense you," Deb stated. "Can you sense him? Is it that kind of connection?"

"Connection?" Schlosser shook his head as if he were trying to dislodge the thought from his mind. "More like a virus that's continually eating away at you."

Deb nodded, even though she would never really understand.

"I hope you're ready, Guardian." Schlosser took hold of Deb's upper arm. "We're going to be running from the moment we get that weapon."

"Wait." Deb pulled away. "Can't we open a portal once we have the hellcrux?"

"No," Schlosser answered. "We need to make it to a gate. Once we get through the gate, I can teleport out onto the Pit floor."

"How far away is the gate from the dungeon?" Deb asked.

"Far," Schlosser answered. "It's a good thing you had something to eat and a few hours rest. You're going to need it."

***

The dungeon was a large opulent room with hardwood floors, brass sconces, and lavish furniture. A stage the width of the room was hidden behind a red velvet curtain. Robino sat at the head of a banquet table. Servants were shuffling around pouring him drinks and laying out a feast of turkey, side dishes, and fruit.

Robino pointed at the seats to his right and left. "Sit."

Deb sat down, a glass of red wine already before her. Schlosser sat directly across from her avoiding Robino's gaze. Examining the space, Deb's eyes crawled up the twenty-foot high ceiling in awe. The numerous small seating areas and the massive stage were more akin to a club than the prison cell Deb had envisioned.

"Not what you were expecting." Robino took a sip of brown liquid.

"Not at all," Deb replied.

"Eat, Guardian," Robino ordered. "You're going to need your strength."

Deb glanced at Schlosser who was already gnawing his way through a turkey leg. Putting a small amount of pasta on her dish she was reluctant to eat, not sure it was safe.

"How do you plan on getting me back the hellcrux?" Robino asked as the servant took away his empty plate replacing it with a clean one.

"What are my options?" Deb asked.

"Schlosser," Robino paused. "If he makes it."

The god of darkness laughed at his own joke. Deb stiffened at the thought of Schlosser not making it out of hell.

"What's the matter?" Robino asked. "Having second thoughts or do you just not eat on Earth. You need meat on your bones if you ask me."

Picking up a fork Deb took a few mouthfuls and had to keep from verbalizing how genuinely delicious the food tasted. The mushroom soup paled in comparison to the buttery goodness of the al dente shells.

Schlosser never lifted from his plate, he mowed through several rounds of turkey and potatoes.

If we have to run later, Deb thought. *I don't want a stomach full of meat. That would just make me want to take a nap.*

"Feed the hounds!" Robino barked at the servant who was standing by the stage.

Deb jumped at Robino's sudden outburst. The servant ran up onto the stage and pulled back the curtain. Shackled to chains on the floor were several dog-like creatures. Each one muscular and furry like a dog, but larger in stature like an overgrown wolf. Their black coats were bald in several spots where they had been injured. Old scars and burn marks kept the hair from regrowing.

The hounds stretched and vigorously shook off the remnants of sleep. Sniffing the air, the two closest to Deb growled. Robino slammed his hand on the table and the hounds stopped.

Baring their giant teeth, the hounds bayed until the servant led several souls of the damned into the room and onto the stage. A male tried to retreat, but the servant pushed him onto the stage with the other two. The hounds attacked, ripping the souls apart. Blood sprayed across the stage. The dogs clamped onto the screaming men like they were pieces of the turkey laid out on the table before them.

The hounds shook the men violently, screams of terror continued to erupt, but were quickly drowned out by the caterwauls of the beasts. Within minutes the room descended into quiet once more, the souls consumed.

"Make sure you have a backup plan, Guardian," Robino warned. "If the hellcrux is not returned, I will come to Earth myself to collect it and you."

Goosebumps rode along Deb's arms. A wave of nausea threatened to make her vomit. She forced her mind to focus on something else in the room. Deb's eyes landed on an unlit candelabra. Staring at the object she managed to push the sickness down. Something she had to practice multiple times since arriving, for there was much to be sick over in hell.

Deb nodded at Robino not sure she could formulate polite words after the gruesome display.

"Excellent." Robino called a servant forward. "Bring me my hellcrux."

The servant left the room and returned with a square leather satchel. He placed it on the table next to Deb. She went to open it, but Robino grabbed Deb's hand and stopped her.

"You have what you came for, Guardian." Robino's eyes glistened in the light of the chandelier. "You have a fifteen-minute head start... clock's ticking... and my hounds are still hungry."

CHAPTER TWENTY-THREE

Deb pushed back from the table, the hounds jumped to their feet and lunged for her only to be yanked back by the chains that secured them. The unnaturally large beasts circled around and got back on all fours leaping once more. The clanging of the metal chain against the security of the bolt signaled it could break at any second.

Grabbing the strap of the black leather pouch, Deb pulled it over her head so the bag would drape across her body. Schlosser ran for the exit. Deb was on his heels. Schlosser's hands smashed onto the thick metal door slamming it open. Deb ran through the opening into the hallway. Row after row of cages came into view, most were occupied with the souls of the damned.

As they ran past, the imprisoned souls hammered their hands against the sides of their cages yelling for help. The high-pitched shrieks echoed off the rocky chamber walls.

Deb was within feet of Schlosser as he navigated twists and turns in the dimly lit serpentine pathways. They pushed themselves up steep inclines and crawled through damp dark tunnels. Finally, Schlosser slowed and then stopped to catch his breath.

"You okay?" Deb asked.

Schlosser nodded, his face reddened and covered in sweat, much as she imagined her own to be. She paced in the dark corridor, understanding there was no time to really rest.

"Let's keep moving," Schlosser told her as he began to run once more.

Before following, Deb paused to determine if anything was coming from behind them. There was the lilting of voices, but with it something else, snarling. The hounds, they were hunting.

Stampeding as hard as she could, Deb caught up to Schlosser. The roamer demon had stopped once more and was bent over trying to catch his breath. She was about to yell at him to keep moving when he stood back up, holding his side.

"I can teleport now," he said between panting breaths. "When we land, we need to run about another quarter mile. It's the closest gate, but they know that too. They're going to be right behind us, knowing where we're going."

Deb nodded unable to find her breath to answer. Schlosser grabbed her arm and took them from the darkened walkway.

***

Upon landing Deb's head spun. Between the running and Schlosser's aura, nausea overwhelmed her. Deb bent over her knees and vomited. The small pasta shells had not yet metabolized.

"You gonna make it, Guardian?" Schlosser was near breathless. "I had to land us here to avoid that giant hole in the ground you couldn't jump over last time.

Schlosser was about to keel over himself. Instead of answering, Deb spit out the last of the bile and took off running. Schlosser caught up to her and directed her north. They ran back through the level she had first encountered a Hell Fire pit.

Running down the long rows of doors they passed Lenny and Meena's hideaway with their honeysuckle wall. Speeding around the massive Hell Fire pit Deb averted tripping on the discarded clothing her and Schlosser had picked through.

Circling down two more levels, anyone in their path quickly moved out of their way. The thunderous galloping of the hounds hunting them drowned out everything else. Deb ran past Schlosser's prison cell where she encountered hellhounds tracking her for the first time. The beasts chasing them were gaining ground. The vibration of their giant paws striking the surface reverberated underfoot.

Turning the last corner, the gate loomed ahead

of them. No entity sat between them and the gate. There were two doors on the left, nothing on the right. Schlosser slowed as they passed the first door, peering inside before jogging past. The room was empty.

"Shit," he huffed. "It used to be a weapons depot."

Schlosser raced past the second door, but Deb was compelled to stop. The coin in her pocket began to flip and push around as if trying to escape.

"What's this room?" Deb asked heaving.

"No time, Guardian." Schlosser came back and pulled her arm forward.

The coin ripped free from Deb's pocket and flew to the door. Sliding along the exterior, the coin hovered in the crevice at the bottom of the door before being sucked inside.

"No!" Deb yelled as she pulled away from Schlosser. "That's Marcus' soul. I am not leaving him behind."

Pushing the door open with force Deb stepped inside and gasped. Above Deb's head were thousands of blue, white, and yellow orbs of light. They hovered toward the ceiling as if clamoring to escape.

The room was sparse, there were several bookshelves, two large chests, and a wooden table, but no chairs.

"It's the soul room." Deb exhaled, her eyes watering at the massive number of souls stolen and entrapped here.

The coin lay on the floor at her feet. Deb picked

it up and scampered to the center of the room. Unlike with Marcus, these souls didn't immediately gravitate to the coin.

How do I get them to enter the coin?

Schlosser hovered in the doorway. "There's no time for this!"

"I have to try!" Deb yelled back.

Pulling the table to the center of the room Deb climbed on top of it. She placed the coin in her palm and held it up toward the ceiling. Slowly, the circular balls of light approached. One entered the coin, followed by another and then ten more. It was working, but too slow to get them all before the hounds reached them.

Schlosser walked over to the chest and rummaged through its contents. He grabbed a bag and two glass bottles of brown liquid.

"What's that?" Deb asked after stealing a glance in his direction.

"A bomb," he answered.

"Guess it's good we stopped, then," Deb snarked.

"I don't know about good." Schlosser found a few daggers and some throwing stars adding them to the cloth bag. "The hounds are close. I can feel them, and they aren't alone. Robino sent sentries too. Those are the voices we hear."

Deb closed her eyes and pushed her shield toward the ceiling to encircle the orbs and pull them down. Within seconds her energy collided with the souls, and a small vortex hovered just above her hand.

The force of the light streaming down toward her nearly knocked her off the table. Schlosser steadied her legs and Deb remained on her feet.

When the last one was safely in the coin, Deb jumped off the table shoving the coin back inside her pocket.

Unzipping the leather pouch Robino gave her, Deb pulled out the heavy object from within.

"Is this a joke?" Deb asked involuntarily.

"Out of time!" Schlosser yelled as he yanked Deb from the room pushing her out and to the left. The first demon came into view. The hell hound attached to the sentry's chain was jerking to get free.

Reaching the gate, with no time to spare, Deb held up the hellcrux. It wasn't demonic, it was a Coptic Cross. The four-sided cross had three spikes on each end. In the center of the wrought iron gate was a cutout of the same size and shape. Deb shoved the hellcrux into it. Nothing happened.

The gate was over ten feet high and as wide and deep as a bank fault door. Through the slats of the black ironwork Deb could make out the tree covered landscape just beyond the exit. The gate was attached to a longer piece of fence that seemed to stretch as far as the eye could see.

With the growls of the hounds on their heels, Deb examined closely the center of the cross, there was a short metal pin protruding from the center of the embossed Christian symbol.

"If you're going to do something!" Schlosser

yelled. "Now's the time to do it!"

Pricking her finger on the pin, the cut drew blood that was absorbed into the cross. The gate swung open. The hellcrux moved through the width of the gate onto the backside. Running through the opening Deb launched past Schlosser. The roamer demon grabbed one of the bars and slammed the gate shut just at the hounds reached them.

The hellcrux was facing Deb. The silver cross once more ready for the operator to activate it and re-enter hell. Deb retrieved the cross from its carved space. The sentries and hounds faded, as did their obscenities, and promises of retribution. The gate was swallowed up in a haze of red smoke, just like Robino's aura.

Now standing before her was a rocky outcrop. Beneath Deb's feet was thick grass, trampled as if many a foot had passed over it.

"How would you find the gate again to use the hellcrux?" Deb wondered aloud.

"No time for that." Schlosser walked off along the rock wall. When the demon reached the end, he turned left.

Deb tentatively followed. "I thought we could teleport from here."

Schlosser mumbled something she couldn't make out. As she neared the end of the wall the raging of war thundered up to meet her. Deb stopped short trying to understand how there was only silence just ten feet behind her.

Schlosser came back around the corner holding

two wooden mugs. He handed her one. "Drink."

It was water and she threw it back. Some of the contents escaped down the sides of her mouth and dribbled onto her shirt. Wiping her mouth with the back of her hand she finally caught her breath.

"What now?" she asked Schlosser.

"Below us is the Pit floor." He drank the rest of his water. "I can teleport us down below, but once we get there–"

The wind picked up and Deb could sense something evil approaching. "It's what?" Deb glanced over her shoulder. "Spit it out, Schlosser. Something else is coming."

"It's going to be a free for all," Schlosser admitted. "The minute we land, they'll know what you are. You'll be behind enemy lines. No one can teleport on the pit floor. You'll have to run and fight your way to heaven's side."

Deb tried to wrap her mind around what she was about to walk into, but she knew there was no preparing for what the Pit was. Based on what she knew, it was nothing short of harrowing.

Schlosser opened the worn bag he found in the soul room. "Take these." Handing Deb a dagger and several throwing stars the roamer demon grabbed her elbow and turned them away from where he had just come. "Whatever you do, don't look back and don't stop until you find your people, Guardian. Understand?"

"What about you?" Deb asked. "What are you going to do?"

"What I've been doing my entire existence," he answered. "Survive."

"Schlosser," Deb began, but then faltered grasping for the right words.

"Don't thank me," he snapped. "You were my ticket out, that's all."

Deb inhaled sharply, the words affecting her more than they should.

If it was just that, Deb argued internally. *He would have left me the minute we got clear of the gate. He certainly wouldn't have gotten me water and warned me on what's about to happen.*

"And I thought you never lie…" Deb stated.

"Just give me the hellcrux." Schlosser smirked. "And don't take offense, but I hope I never see you again."

"None taken." Deb went to hand him the cross.

Schlosser balked. "In the satchel, unless you're trying to burn me."

"The cross would burn you?" Deb asked as she placed the silver cross back inside the leather pouch. "Simply by touching it?"

"Out of time," Schlosser said as a demon rounded the corner and yelled in their direction.

Schlosser's aura wrapped around them, and he teleported Deb for the last time. They landed to the tune of clanging swords. The grunts of male and female entities thundered in her ears.

Before she could get her bearings, a demon knocked her into the dirt wall on her left. From the ground she swiped upward at the figure coming down on top of her. The demon yelped and stepped back. Deb scrambled to her feet just as Schlosser stabbed the demon from behind.

"Thank you." Deb breathed out.

Schlosser stared in her direction. "I told you to run, damn it."

Grabbing her by the arm, Schlosser pulled her out of the pathway and onto the Pit floor. Fire engulfed part of the field to her right. The bodies smashing into one another were too numerous to count. The canyon floor was wide and long. The armies of hell stood on the cliffs above her. Heaven on the opposite precipice. In the valley below was the agony of full-on war. A sea of dead lay at her feet. Decomposition mixed with blood and sweat.

Focus your mind. Find your path out.

"You're going to have to go through!" Schlosser yelled. "I'll hold them off as long as I can."

"You can't help me!" Deb shouted over the rising cacophony. "They'll kill you for it."

"I've already helped you!" Schlosser hollered. "They'll kill me either way."

"Wait!" Deb yelled. "Come with me. I will use my shield to protect us."

"And then what?" Schlosser asked. "I'm a demon, remember? Your side will just kill me when we reach it."

Deb desperately searched for a solution. "I–"

Grabbing her hand Schlosser insisted, "It's okay,

Deborah."

The pain in Deb's chest when Schlosser used her name for the first time had no place on this field, but her heart cracked all the same.

The gutter demons reached Schlosser. Pushing out her shield Deb wrapped it around the roamer demon who had been her constant companion and partner on her harrowing journey through hell.

Schlosser gazed down across his body and then back toward Deb's position. The gutter demons bounced off Deb's protective shield and landed back where they had started.

Schlosser dropped her hand and removed the two bombs from his bag. "When you start running, count to ten and then drop your shield."

Deb nodded in acknowledgement as demons continued to bounce off the shield surrounding him. Schlosser had the full attention of the demons.

"So this is what it feels like?" Schlosser said in awe peering up into the dark and stormy clouds above.

"What?" Deb implored. "What are you talking about?"

"Free will." Schlosser's eyes met hers once more. "I understand why it's a big deal." Schlosser turned his head toward the melee. "Now go!" He yelled without turning back. "Run as fast and as far as you can!"

Deb turned away running deep into the midst of battle mentally counting to ten. Using her hands she pushed as many bodies as possible out of her way. The blade of her dagger slashed and sliced several demons already engaged in battle along her route.

When she reached ten, she dropped the shield surrounding Schlosser. A massive explosion rocked the canyon floor propelling numerous demons through the air. Large pieces of rock fell from the mountain wall. The shockwave sent several demons around Deb to the ground.

Numbness descended. Deb fell to her knees pleading with the sky above. Never have the battle lines been more blurred than they were at this moment.

As the demons recovered from the bomb and the fighting around her burst to life once more, Deb regained her footing. Standing she surveyed the area. Somehow, Deb had managed to reach a place in the center of the battlefield where heaven's encampment was visible. Heavenly warriors, Guardians, and Arch Angels were lined up several rows deep about a hundred yards from her position.

The wind picked up, Deb's shield burst outward smashing into demons and throwing them clear of her immediate area. Streaks of yellow light flared through the dark clouds. Her head was foggy, no longer engulfed by the noise of combat. Deb's body ached to lay down and sleep for days forgetting the realities of this world. Bloodshed was all around her, warfare up close and personal.

Pushing to her feet Deb stumbled across the valley falling yards from Heaven's position on the battlefield. Someone reached out and pulled Deb back up to a standing position. The male was asking her questions, but his voice could not penetrate her mind.

The six-foot Guardian had unruly brown hair and dark blue eyes the color of a stormy sea. Placing his arms around Deb's shoulders he ushered her across the remaining open field. Once they were standing alongside heaven's army, he teleported Deb up to the top of the cliffside.

When Deb's heart resumed a normal beat, tears exploded from her eyes. The Guardian's uneven gait walked closer to her position. Placing his hands on either side of Deb's arms he gently squeezed drawing her attention back to his face. Worry creased his forehead, alarm blazed from his concerned stare.

"It's alright, Deb." He met Deb's gaze and held it. "Are you hurt?"

"Gabriel." Her brother-in-law's name fell from her lips just before her body fell into his square chest. "Take me home."

CHAPTER TWENTY-FOUR

Staring into the forest that lay just beyond her brother Michael's house, Gen attempted to focus her energy and the ground below her feet trembled.

"Remember," Michael reminded her. "You want your power to follow where your mind is, to flow to the object you're either looking at or concentrating on."

Gen nodded trying to unwind the knot that was forming in her shoulders. They had been at it for hours. Gen had managed to crack open a few dead trees and a small corner of Michael's garage.

"Time for a break, Michael." Harry's voice rang out from his seat on the front porch.

Gardenia and some of her friends had been moved to a safe house being guarded by May, the Arch Angel that helped Kelly with the exorcism at the nearby ranch. Harry came to Michael's to check on them. He hoped Kelly had returned, which she hadn't.

There's a part of me that's empty. Gen surveyed the quiet landscape. *Xavier is gone. I can't feel Deb, and now Kelly is, what? Missing?*

Gen's somewhat normal life from six months ago was now exposed to be a house of cards. The stresses of that time proving to be trivial compared to the realities of war, famine, and death.

"I'm going to patrol the grounds," Michael told her. "Dan's on his way back, sounds like they were successful with testing his new power."

"That's great." Gen turned to head into the house.

Michael jogged through the yard and disappeared into the thick treelined edge of the property.

Harry was smiling, but the joy didn't reach his pale blue eyes.

"How about a cup of tea?" Harry asked.

"Yes," Gen answered. "I welcome the break."

Gen sat at the table stretching out the tension in her neck and shoulders. Tom came down the stairs, his hair wet from a recent shower.

"How's it going?" Tom asked.

"Well, I hit a few things I didn't mean to," Gen answered. "and I'm running about seventy percent on the rest."

"And Michael let you take a break with those numbers?" Tom asked sarcastically.

"Harry rescued me," Gen answered.

"Not all training is physical," Harry answered from the stove where he turned on the kettle.

"I'm going to go rummage up some food," Tom told them. "I'll be back in a few, if Dan tells his story make sure he includes me telepathically."

"Will do," Gen told him. "Be careful, call if you need us."

Tom nodded and teleported from the house in a hue of warm light.

"You want to talk about what's holding you back out there?" Harry asked getting right to the point as usual.

"I'm having a hard time concentrating," Gen admitted.

"I imagine anyone would under these circumstances." Harry pulled down mugs from the cabinet.

"Is Gardenia truly okay?" Gen asked.

Fit as a fiddle," Harry answered. "Honestly, she wasn't infected very long when you showed up. I think it would have been different if you hadn't arrived when you did. It was close, but she's strong."

"She would have to be," Gen commented. "The lost have had to fend for themselves for a long time. I'm glad that she has Gerry."

"And Lacey," Harry added.

"Yeah." Gen nodded. "A little family for all of them, it's nice. Wish it wasn't under these conditions."

"I don't know, maybe that's a silver lining," Harry said. "When things are tough it's sometime hard to recognize the good things that come about as a result of it."

"Very wise as usual, Harry."

"Well, when you get to be my age." Harry smiled. "You too will be wise. Are you getting any sleep?"

"Some," Gen answered. "Hard to sleep when you know people are hurting."

"There is some good news," Harry answered. "Governments have figured out how to kill the vampires. They're setting up safe zones, giving people food and shelter."

"I saw that," Gen told him. "We still don't know what Azza and Wrath are planning though."

The walls of the living room flashed with the brilliance of color and light. Dan and Frankie stepped out from their auras and joined Gen in the kitchen.

"I heard it went well," Gen said.

"Surprisingly well," Dan answered.

Coming up the trail to the house Greg jogged alongside Michael. Darkening storm clouds seemed to be chasing them.

"Tom is grabbing food," Gen told them. "He's on his way back."

Harry sat at the end of the table facing the front door. Michael and Greg walked in as Tom arrived in the kitchen with several bags of canned goods, boxes of pasta, and jars of sauce.

"Peanut butter and jelly?" Tom asked. "Or pasta again?"

"You found bread?" Frankie asked as he surveyed the contents.

"The farmstand two counties over," Tom answered. "Half the town is making bread and sharing it with anyone who needs it."

"The resiliency of people is inspirational." Harry winked at Gen.

"I'm good with peanut butter," Gen answered.

"Help yourself." Tom left the jars on the table along with a stack of plates, knives, and the package of bread.

"How did the test go?" Michael asked as he made his sandwich and ate it standing up.

"We went to several sources of water," Dan told them. "A beach, a lake, water from a hydrant, etc."

"Even tap water from a house we stopped in," Frankie added. "Once Dan was able to call forth his new power. He just had to touch the water to turn it."

"How are your hands feeling?" Harry asked.

Dan turned his palms outward. The outline of a cross was still visible on both hands. "I've hurt worse these last few weeks, that's for sure."

"Tap water to holy water." Harry shook his head. "With just one touch, miraculous."

"I still wonder what happened in the necropolis," Gen stated. "Why did you and Kelly fly apart from one another when you touched."

"Maybe visiting the Vatican escalated the arrival of Dan's powers," Tom surmised.

"Maybe Kelly has a power coming on too, then," Dan commented.

"Well, when Kelly returns," Harry said. "We'll be sure to ask about it."

The room fell silent. Kelly hadn't been seen or felt in days. No one wanted to say it, but Gen knew the real fear was that Kelly was gone. Another victim in this vicious assault.

Lighting struck and several minutes later thunder rang out in the distance indicating the storm was several miles out. Gen nearly missed the smashing light of Dmitri's aura as the heavenly warrior arrived on the front porch.

Opening the door, all eyes fell on Dmitri. "I found Jade."

Gen dropped the sandwich and stood up. "I'm coming with you."

"Me too," Frankie said.

If there was any chance this conversation would lead to Deb's return, there was no way Gen was going to sit it out.

"Don't go without weapons," Michael warned. "I refurbished the stockpile this morning. Take a bag and take Dan. We should test his new powers in the field."

"New powers?" Dmitri asked.

"Yes," Gen answered. "Dan can turn ordinary water into holy water."

"How?" Dmitri asked.

Dan finished his sandwich and washed his

hands before giving Dmitri a demonstration. Focusing on his breathing, Dan's hand began to shake. The surface of his palm stretched, and the imprint of a cross protruded upward turning his skin red.

When he calmed his heart rate it was as if someone had scarred his hands with a branding iron. Within a few seconds his coloring returned to normal, and you could trace your fingers across the raised surface. The embossed cross was smooth and cool to the touch.

"Wow," Dmitri said in wonder. "That looked like it hurt."

"I think the pain and heat are from resistance," Dan said. "I haven't completely figured it out yet."

"Mastering a power takes time." Michael's eyes fell on Gen. "You have to be patient."

"Patience during a war is nearly impossible," Gen answered.

"I take it she's a work in progress." Dmitri pointed at Gen.

"Very funny," Gen responded. "Let's go find Jade before she takes off again."

Frankie and Gen filled up two bags with daggers, knives, and several bottles of holy water and holy oil.

"Where is Jade?" Frankie asked.

"Hiding out in a sleepy little village town in England," Dmitri answered. "I don't know that we'll encounter any vampires. Vermillion cloaked the area, but the horseman is either losing his touch or the cloaking isn't working well."

"We've been noticing the cloaking the vampires use is covering a smaller area," Tom said. "It could be that the cloaking is starting to be glitchy, breaking down in spots, just like the veil is."

"That makes sense," Greg commented. "Of course that means you have to be more mindful of any humans that are around."

"True," Frankie said. "They don't necessarily know who's good and who's bad."

"Adds to the difficulty of the situation in an entirely new way," Michael said. "Be careful and check back in as soon as you speak with her."

"Assuming she will speak with you," Harry added.

"She'll speak with us," Gen said. "I'm confident she'll want to help Deb."

"With help like hers," Greg snarked.

"I think Jade believes she was helping," Gen said.

The heaviness in the room grew.

"We should go." Gen walked toward Dmitri. The Collector grasped Gen's shoulder as she held onto Frankie's hand. Dan was on the other side of Dmitri when he teleported them across the sea to find the goddess of Envy.

***

"Bollocks!" Jade bellowed. "You have any idea what you've just done showing up here."

"We just want to know where Vermillion sent our sister?" Gen pleaded.

"You bloody well know!" The demon spat. "She told you so in her own words, to which none of you listened."

Jade was wearing cream colored wide legged pants and a green silk blouse that was cinched at the waist. Her black high heel shoes were shiny patent leather. Even during war, the demon presented herself like she had just stepped off a runway. Her dark brown hair fell in waves down to her shoulder, her makeup perfectly in place.

"You are confirming you sent Deb to hell." Frankie said the sentence Gen could not muster.

"I did no such thing," Jade answered.

"No," Dan deadpanned. "You had Vermillion do your dirty work for you."

"Bloody hell, Guardian," Jade sneered. "At least Vermillion sent her to where Marcus was and didn't drop her in the middle of no man's land."

"How do we get her out?" Gen asked.

"I am in no more of a position to help you than I was to help Deborah," Jade answered.

"Meaning you won't help us," Dmitri said.

"Even though you are capable of going into hell and retrieving her yourself."

"I will do nothing of the sort," Jade answered unequivocally. Her heels clicked on the hardwood floor as she made her way over to the bar and poured herself a glass of whiskey.

"Why?" Gen implored. "Why won't you help my sister?"

Jade's eyes watered and she turned away from them and downed the contents of the glass.

"Please," Gen continued. "Help us get Deb back."

"I cannot." Jade shook her head. "I cannot go into hell, not ever."

"Why? What happened?" Dan asked.

"Hell is a place I can never return to. Not for Deb, not for anyone," Jade answered.

"How do you know Vermillion?" Gen asked. "Why did he show up that night?"

"How I met my husband is not a story for any of you lot," Jade insisted.

The revelation caused everyone to pause.

Oh my. Jade is not just a demon Deb befriended. She's a deadly sin married to one of the four horsemen of the apocalypse.

"Okay, fair enough." Frankie broke the silence. "If Vermillion sent her to hell, what about asking him to go get her?"

"Vermillion's debt has been repaid. If he were to help you now, then you would owe him a favor." Jade crossed her arms. "Are you prepared for that?"

"No," Dmitri said adamantly. "Do you at least

286

know which realm she was sent to?"

"Listen, mister tall dark and handsome," Jade snarked as she let her arms fall back down by her sides. "I tried to appeal to her not to go. Not sure why she'd choose to go into hell for Marcus, when she had you right in front of her."

"Do you know what realm or not?" Dmitri's anger bled through his words.

"Feeling insecure, are we?" Jade mocked. "It was curious how conflicted Deborah was. Then that snake of an Arch Angel admitted he'd buried memories about the two of you."

"What's your point, demon," Dmitri said through gritted teeth, his fists clenched.

Gen stepped between them. "This is not helping."

Dmitri turned and walked several steps away from Jade.

"Who else knows you're here?" Jade feverishly began pacing around the space.

"Just our siblings," Gen answered. "Why?"

The chill in the air put Jade immediately on edge. She retrieved a jacket from the sofa and put it on.

"Are you leaving?" Dmitri asked.

Before Jade could answer the lights in the house flickered. Gen and Frankie wasted no time retrieving weapons from the bag they brought with them.

"We need an exit strategy," Dan told them. "The room is cloaked now. We can't teleport."

"Bloody hell, he must have found me," Jade said

in barely a whisper.

"What's this address?" Dan asked as he reached into his pants pocket retrieving a cell phone.

"What?" Jade asked perplexed. A brief moment later Jade blurted out the address and Dan furiously typed it into his phone.

Wrath materialized in the room standing across from Gen. His blonde hair no longer slicked back. He wore camouflage pants and a tight fitting white T-shirt that gleamed as if it were brand new. His black shoes were as spotless and shiny as Jade's.

"Jade, darling." He reached his arms out as if she would run to him.

Gen peaked over at Jade who was visibly shaking as she stepped back behind Frankie.

"Peter," Gen said. "Or should we call you Wrath?"

Jade's brother resembled an actor, dressed for the part of a warrior. He appeared well rested, calm, like he hadn't missed a wink of sleep. Gen's anger swelled and the floor rumbled.

Wrath ignored Gen's question. "You're keeping odd company, sister."

"What do you want?" Gen stepped closer and Dan reached his hand out to halt her forward progress.

"World chaos," Wrath snarked. "I want a tidal wave of hate and anger to burn this world and all of you with it."

"You're having a bit of trouble on your side," Dan goaded. "Little disarray amongst the ranks. After we've killed so many of hell's first army, the vampires don't seem to be around as much."

"Yes, well," Wrath huffed. "The vampires were always more interested in heaven than they were with Earth, but hey, Azza and I can work around that."

Gen's mind grappled with the thought that the vampires wanted to take over heaven.

Michael appeared and hit Wrath from behind with a hammer. The demon stumbled forward. Blood streamed down the side of his face and dripped onto his pristine white shirt.

"Such need for violence." Wrath breathed in deep like he was relishing in the moment. "I'll be back, Jade. Once I have the rest of your powers all the gates will be open and none of you will matter anymore."

Before they could respond Wrath disappeared. Jade fell into the chair next to her.

"He's never going to stop," Jade said.

"We'll stop him," Gen assured her. "For now, you're coming with us."

CHAPTER TWENTY-FIVE

Kelly jabbed at Sunny who was wearing thick long boxing pads on each arm. He rocked back away from her as she continued forward. Coming at him again she threw right and left hooks before swinging her leg around to the right and landing a firm blow against his pads. Covered in sweat, Kelly's muscles stretched and responded to every maneuver.

"Are you tired yet, Guardian?" Sunny taunted.

"Funny." Kelly jabbed left and then swung up with an uppercut sending her partner back a foot. "I was about to ask you the same thing."

Sunny laughed, a deep genuine belly laugh. He was enjoying himself. Truth be told Kelly was also. Kelly's thoughts drifted to her family.

Sunny pushed against Kelly's chest, caught off guard she tumbled backward onto the ground.

"Distraction kills," Sunny lectured. "Get back to your feet, Guardian."

Kelly thought of Xavier. Understanding that if she were on the battlefield that day, it would not have made a difference, didn't assuage her guilt.

"Your head and your body are misaligned." Sunny groaned. "Focus!"

Kelly took a deep breath and went back to work on the combination of jab, elbow, kick. Repeat. They were outside, the ocean lay several hundred feet below the concrete platform they were working on. The sea crashed across the rocky shoreline with force. The crisp September air cooled her warm skin. They had been practicing combinations of Muay Thai.

"You know this artform," Sunny insisted. "You are not tight enough on the kicks. Your body needs to flow like one seamless movement."

"For the tenth time this is new to me," Kelly replied.

"You must focus," Sunny repeated. "Your mind buried the memories. They are not lost."

"What if I don't want to remember?" Kelly asked.

"Everything that has happened to you has happened for a reason," Sunny told her. "There are lessons in all things, even those that haunt us."

They practiced in the warm sun until the air turned chilly. Now the gray clouds swarming above threatened rain. Buckling down, Kelly ran through ten more combinations. When Sunny sidestepped her last jab, Kelly fell forward catching her entire body on one finger.

Thunder cracked in the distance. Sunny lowered his pads.

"You are ready for the next phase. Go inside, shower, and change."

"Finally," Kelly huffed.

When they first arrived on the island, Kelly was resistant to the process. She wanted it to be fast, arguing that she had to return to fighting vampires. Sunny convinced her to give him a few days.

"Nothing worth attaining ever came quickly." Sunny picked up all the equipment and made his way toward the shed. "We'll have tea in the temple."

The temple was a rundown building behind the cottage they were staying in. She hadn't been inside yet.

"Are you sure I'm ready for the temple?" Kelly asked.

Sunny focused on the racing clouds above. "The sky is ready."

"I'll take that as a yes." Kelly stepped inside the two-story gray shingled house.

The kitchen's blue and white floor tile was cold on her bare feet. Inside the bathroom, Kelly removed her damp clothing. Stepping into the steamy shower, Kelly washed away the sweat and salt air from the outdoor workout. The hot water pelted her skin massaging away the aches already setting in.

There was a serenity that enveloped the property. Kelly didn't know if it was the quiet of the island or the simplicity of their routine. When she laid down at night her body was exhausted in an entirely different manner than it had been. In the days leading up to her confrontation with Garrick, she barely rested let alone slept.

Turning off the water she grabbed a towel and fought to tamp down the anger flared by thoughts of Garrick. Kelly practiced breathing techniques for hours sitting crossed legged on the living room floor. Sunny insisted she do this before he would teach her how to manifest fire.

Every time Kelly thought of a vampire her heart rate increased, her stomach lurched, and her emotions threatened to sail off the deep end. Every night she dreamt of her brother Xavier's death at the hands of those in hell and she woke seething. When she thought of Deb trapped in hell, a place she barely survived forty years ago, the rage boiled. With Sunny's guidance, she learned how to recognize the signs and work to control the emotion.

Making her way into the cozy bedroom, Kelly changed into clean clothes, then sat on the floor crossing her legs. Straightening her back Kelly inhaled in and out until the spinning out of control that accompanied her anger subsided.

Getting up, Kelly made her way downstairs and exited through the back patio. The rain had started. Her feet splashed through the puddles as she briskly walked toward the building Sunny referred to as a sanctuary. Standing before the large ornate door she took a moment to gather her thoughts. Somewhere inside she knew things were about to change.

Path of totality.

Pulling open the heavy door Kelly stepped inside. Before her lay an open space, with terracotta tile floors and cream colored walls. At the front of the room was a small altar that held an abundance of flowering plants. The succulent flowers fell to the floor, their petals drifting in the breeze from an open window.

There were dozens of lit tea light candles on the floor to her right and left, the room's aroma was a mix of wax and potting soil. On the floor was a beautiful oriental rug with hues of orange, blue, and gray. The rectangular carpet was covered with several pillows. Sunny sat waiting for her holding two small cups of tea.

"Come," he told her.

Kelly stepped forward and took the cup he held out for her. The green tea smelled of citrus. She took a sip of the warm liquid and sat down on the rug across from him.

"If you want to calm the dragon inside," Sunny explained. "You must walk the path of totality. This is a commitment to seek the truth from within so that your body and soul will once again be aligned. You are fractured, you must be healed from the inside out."

"Finish the tea," Sunny told her as Kelly took several more sips. "There is no hiding from yourself. Your memories were not taken, merely buried. You need to face the source of your anger and conquer it."

"So." Kelly exhaled as she placed the empty cup on the floor next her. "Is this one of those movie moments where I fall asleep and relive my memories?"

"Not as dramatic."

Kelly cocked her head to the side. "What does that mean?"

"I am going to jog small images loose," Sunny explained. "I will ask questions. Your job is to answer them honestly."

The room darkened. A cold wind blew out all the candles. Goosebumps road her arms.

"That sounds a lot like reliving," Kelly answered.

"You will not relive anything. You will be forced to find and face your memories from that time, but not all of them," Sonny insisted. "Like it or not, there are key moments you need to remember."

"What if I'm okay with not remembering." Kelly sighed.

"That's your choice." Sunny paused. "But every choice has a consequence. Do you want to live a life where your memories are riddled with holes? Or do you want the truth to set you free?"

Kelly huffed and contemplated those choices. After a few minutes, she held Sunny's gaze.

"Let's do it."

Sunny reached out and placed his thumb on her forehead. Images of Christian's motionless body came first. Then Azza flailing to keep from being sucked into the vortex. Followed by a harrowing descent into hell accompanied by a sickening queasiness.

Kelly shook as if her body was being smashed along a rocky surface. The cracking of bone and the agonizing screams of pain bounced throughout the small space.

"I thought we weren't reliving anything!" Kelly yelled.

"These are remnants," Sunny explained as the noise faded. "Echoes from your memory core."

Sunny placed a hand on each of her arms. "Resistance is more painful, try to relax and let them come naturally."

Kelly steeled herself for the next memory. More fragments shot across her mind's eye. Tables were filled with souls being tortured. The sting of burns rippled across Kelly's lower body. Red welts appeared.

"It's just in your mind, Ms. O'Mara," Sunny explained. "Breathe through it, just like we practiced."

Breathing in and out could not stop the nightmare as it kept on playing in her mind. Azza stood over Kelly, a blood soaked dagger in her hand.

I'm sorry, Azza said in hushed whispers. *I'm not as strong as you. Antonio made me hate the world and everything in it. Now, I'm going to burn it down. Starting with you.*

Ominous laughter bellowed in Kelly's head. Her hands flew to cover both ears as if she could block it all out. The wind howled. The ocean breeze whipped around her dizzying head.

"It hurts." Tears streaked down Kelly's face.

"It's not real, Ms. O'Mara." Sunny's voice remained calm and direct. "You must see it for what it is, a piece of your history, a part of you."

The pain of the past seared through her. Though Kelly was aware these were mere memories playing out in rapid succession, her chest heaved. The mind was an easy thing to fool. Her body reacted as if she were living it all over again. Gasping, Kelly found it hard to catch her breath. Azza was sitting on top of her chest, battering Kelly with fists of fury.

"Stop resisting," Sunny urged. "You are in pain because you refuse to accept what you know to be true."

The last images were of Jared's face as he picked Kelly up off a table. Then he was running. The pounding of feet on pavement and the barking of monsters hunting them were almost too much. The images swirled again. A devastated Antonio wept over her battered and beaten body. The Arch Angel tried to soothe her, but Kelly wouldn't stop screaming.

The memories confirmed the story Dmitri and Antonio told her, but that brought little relief. Tears continued to stream down Kelly's face. The droplets doused the cushion that lay between her and Sunny.

"Where does fear come from?" Sunny asked.

"Many places, obviously," Kelly snapped.

"No," Sunny answered. "Look deeper, where does your fear come from?"

"You want me to say from within." Kelly whimpered as she wanted out of this waking nightmare.

"What are you afraid of?" Sunny asked.

"Hell winning," Kelly cried out.

"No!" Sunny scolded. "Dig deeper."

"I don't want to." Kelly shook her head.

"You will never be fully healed. Never become who you are meant to be," Sunny pushed. "Unless you face your fears."

"I don't want to lose anyone else," Kelly yelled. "Azza killed Xavier!"

"Yes." Sunny's voice mellowed. "What else?"

"I'm afraid of what's inside." Kelly pulled her knees up to her chest. "I'm scared that I'm something I don't want to be. That hell made me that way."

The scent of fire bolted Kelly to a standing position. She was alone in the temple.

"Sunny?" Kelly yelled.

The rain whipped against the exterior walls in hard pelting lashes, like that of a hurricane. Howling wind whistled as it rocked the small building.

The door to the temple flew open. Sunny now stood in the opening, behind him a raging fire burned through the trees.

"What happened?" Kelly shouted.

"You confronted your fear," Sunny told her. "And you set it ablaze."

The flames were batted down by the rain. Smoke drifted in from outside. Sunny walked toward her. His shadow twice as tall as he was. His looming presence heavier than she remembered it to be.

"Are you afraid because you started the fire?" Sunny asked. "Or because of something else?"

"I don't know." Kelly shook her head slightly. "I'm so confused."

"You called the fire forward," Sunny told her.

"Then you turned away from it. Turning away from your true self causes discord. That chaos is what you see outside."

"I didn't know that would happen," Kelly protested.

"If you don't accept who you are, the totality of who you are," Sunny warned. "You will drown in the spot you are standing in."

Kelly's mind was a swarm of muddled thoughts. Her temples began to throb. "How could I have possibly caused the fire outside while I was in here?"

"You are made of fire," Sunny told her. "Think it and it will burn."

Sunny turned back toward the door. "Come back to the house, you need water after such a journey."

I am made of fire. How can that be true?

Exiting the temple, she stood awestruck at the extent of the damage. The fire stretched a hundred feet across. Kelly jogged through the yard, the rain pouring down so hard it hurt. Inside the kitchen a single glass of water sat on the counter.

"Drink and get some rest," Sunny told her. "Tomorrow, we begin again."

"What if I can't do this?" Kelly was panting, the water from her drenched clothing creating a puddle under her feet. "What if I'm not strong enough to control that?" She pointed to the yard behind her.

"You'll be as strong as you believe yourself to be." He closed the doors to his study.

Hell broke me. Azza broke me. Antonio was telling

the truth. I was screaming when they brought me out of hell, and I couldn't stop.

CHAPTER TWENTY-SIX

Shivering, Deb sat on a worn out tree stump at the top of the mountain ridge overlooking the Pit. Despite being wrapped in a thin blanket and holding a steaming mug of tea she could not stop the tremors running through her body. The air was warm, with a peaceful lake just a few hundred yards behind her. The picture perfect view could not calm Deb's nervous tension. Deb had cleaned up as much as she could by taking a short swim in the lake. Her brother-in-law found her clean clothes along with bandages and salve for her more severe wounds.

What lay below her in the Pit was the tragedy and savagery of battle. The thunder and cacophony of war rose out of the valley in a continual rhythmic wave.

The smashing of heaven and hell was a devastating unceasing rampage. Blood, sweat, and burning bodies ravaged the landscape. Gabriel met up with her after her swim and settled her in by the warm fire before seeking out Jared.

They could not teleport out of the Pit. Any being sentenced to the Pit could only use teleportation powers to bring themselves up to the ridge and then back down to the valley floor below. Escape was near impossible. The hope she grasped onto was that Jared and Gabriel had managed to break free of this place and return to Earth. Dmitri had drawn them a map. A serpentine trail down the other side of the mountain until they reached a plateau they could teleport from.

We're making assumptions. Heaven could have added security after they learned of what Jared and Gabriel had done. Look what hell did after Schlosser managed to steal Vermillion's powers and return to Earth.

Deb's eyes watered once more. *Schlosser. I can't believe he's dead, that he sacrificed himself so that I could survive. What kind of demon does that?*

"Deb?"

Deb's eyes found Jared. His crew cut revealed fresh scars. His black fatigues were torn at the knees. He wore a red sweatshirt that masked the blood splatter stained across his chest. His penetrating green eyes met hers and held them. Jared holstered his sword before he approached. Crouching, Jared laid a gentle hand against Deb's arm.

"Jared, it's good to see you."

Jared nodded. "You too, I wish it wasn't here though, Deb."

"I know. Me too," Deb agreed.

"Gabe says you haven't really said much. You feel like talking now?"

Deb inhaled sharply and nodded. "Yes, but preferably on our journey. I really want to get going."

"Okay," Jared said. "Gabe is grabbing a few things. It's a hike. How far we get will depend on how often we stop."

"Understood," Deb stated. "I will try and keep up."

Gabriel walked toward them with three backpacks. Reaching their position he handed one to each of them. Deb stood, leaving her cup on the log she wrapped the thin blanket she had been using and stuffed it into the bag.

"There's water, a little food, and a small sleeping bag inside," Gabriel said. "We should get going, we have a few more hours before nightfall."

Walking along the lake the discord of war faded with each stride. The three didn't speak, each one waiting for the other to break the silence. The dirt path they were on was pristine, the grass to her right lush and full. Tree limbs swayed in the gentle breeze. Birds swooped up into the higher branches upon their approach. On the far side of the lake ducks swam in packs, bathing and diving underneath the surface of the water searching for food. When they reached the far side of the lake a wall of greenery encircled them.

"Where do we go from here?" Deb asked.

"It's just beyond the thick bushes over here," Gabe answered.

Stepping forward Gabe and Jared reached in and pulled the sandbar willow apart revealing a short path behind it. Stepping inside, Gabe followed, then Jared.

A few yards through and the trail reached a dead end with a rocky path spiraling downward on her left. Deb was grateful Gabe had found her thick soled shoes. The treads of her shoes were able to grab hold of the dirt and keep her from sliding too far forward. Once they were on the path, Gabe took the lead once more.

"There are several of these steep paths," Jared said from behind her. "The good news is they're short, then you hike over to the next one and descend again."

"We're slowly walking down the mountain," Deb said. "But now it no longer looks like we're on a mountain."

"Exactly," Gabe confirmed. "Once you leave the lake behind you have no sense of how far up you are."

"It's actually kind of nice," Jared commented. "At least it would be if you weren't so scared of getting caught."

They continued walking across wide open acres with bursts of yellow rattle wildflowers encircling them. The sky was cloudy, but visibility was not an issue. Once the sun went down Deb was guessing the trek would be near impossible. They would be forced to stop for the night, hence why Gabe packed sleeping bags.

"Nighttime must be beautiful out here," Deb commented. "Wide open space, bound to see your fair share of stars."

Just the type of place Schlosser would have enjoyed. Maybe it isn't just people that can change.

"We'll be fine as long as we can find shelter," Gabe said bringing Deb's attention back to the present. "It will be cold."

"I feel bad trampling through here," Deb told them.

"I know what you mean," Jared answered. "It's as if we don't belong. Like the flowers are saying, 'hey you're not supposed to be here'."

Gabe chuckled. "I think it's practical, used to help track escapees. Wide open spaces, pristine landscape."

"It would be easy to find where we've walked," Deb added.

"That's for sure," Jared agreed. "Assuming anyone is even going to notice with everything going on."

"What do you mean?" Deb asked. "You think they know I went to hell?"

Jared and Gabe stopped. Deb walked forward, then turned so she was facing them.

"Why don't you give us the sixty-second version," Gabe told her in a tone not unlike her brother Michael's.

"Ok, well where to start." Deb glanced between them.

The crease in Gabe's forehead screamed alarm. The gentleness in Jared's eyes conveyed concern.

"Wrath, one of the seven deadly sins," Deb began. "He kidnapped Marcus, a sentinel."

"We know Marcus," Jared answered.

"You do?" Deb asked confused. "How?"

"Later," Gabe interrupted. "Please, keep going."

"Wrath brought Marcus into hell," Deb told them.

"You went in after him?" Gabe asked plainly.

"Yes." Deb waited for their disagreement, but none came.

"Why would you risk your life for Marcus?" Jared asked, his deep furrowed eyebrows narrowing.

"What hell did was wrong!" Deb said emphatically, alarmed at how hollow her argument now rang.

"You broke the Accord, Deb?" Gabe asked. "For a sentinel? Was there something more between the two of you?"

"I don't know," Deb snapped. "I never will. He died in my arms."

Gabe stared down at the thick grass beneath his feet. Jared stepped forward and hugged her. Deb accepted the embrace. The first since escaping the hounds of hell and the ravages of the Pit.

"Thank you," Deb said as Jared stepped back. "I know what I did was wrong, but honestly, I was in a place where I just didn't care anymore. Wrath, or Peter as he refers to himself, murdered Jacob. He tortured and weakened his own siblings. And that's not even the worst of it."

"What's worse than all that?" Jared asked.

"Wrath is in league with Azza." Deb waited for that to sink in.

"She's out of hell?" Jared blurted. "I mean, we heard rumors about a fallen Arch Angel but not a name."

"I saw her in hell," Deb replied. "And she had a hellcrux."

Jared and Gabe exchanged a knowing glance.

"I know why you were sentenced to the Pit," Deb told them. "We all do. Dmitri and Antonio showed us all what happened. We used Greg's powers to pull their memories of that day forward."

"How did Kelly take it?" Jared asked.

"Not well. She screamed at Antonio and took off," Deb answered. "We were attacked at Harry's cottage, which I guess was Dmitri's at one time."

"On the Cape?" Gabe asked. "The one he built for you?"

"Oh boy." Deb sighed. "I keep forgetting we each only have pieces of this puzzle. The magistrate ordered Antonio to suppress memories of Dmitri. Worse, she had memories removed from Kelly about her time in Hell."

"She's not allowed to do that!" Jared yelled and walked off, clearly upset. "She's got some nerve. The magistrate has no idea what other things could have been affected by that. She doesn't know how many other memories were tampered with or have gone missing."

"I–" Gabriel paused. "I have too many questions."

"I'm sorry," Deb said. "It wasn't necessarily my place to tell you. I just think we need everything out in the open."

"Yeah," Gabe agreed. "How did you get through that all by yourself, Deb? Jared and I nearly didn't, and we had knowledge of the realm we were going to and a map."

"I had help navigating hell." Deb understood the next part might be the craziest of all the news she had to share.

"Something in hell actually helped you?" Gabe leveled a stare of disbelief.

"Helped me navigate and escape," Deb confirmed.

"And?" Jared asked. "What aren't you telling us?"

"He sacrificed himself." Deb's voice cracked. "So I could reach our side of the Pit floor."

"The explosion," Gabe said. "That was you?"

"No," Deb answered. "It was Schlosser, that's who helped me."

"The roamer demon that nearly killed Gen?' Gabe asked.

"In what universe would he help you?" Jared added.

"I know how it sounds." Deb held her hands up. "But it's the truth."

"Deb, we know the Accord's been broken," Gabe told her. "We've heard nothing but horror stories. Are you aware of what's going on?"

"No," Deb answered. "Tell me what you know, please."

"The vampires are unleashed," Jared answered. "We heard it's a blood bath on Earth."

Oh no, what have I done.

"I need to get back." Deb's mind raced through all the horrific images of humans in the path of a vengeful vampire army. "I should be down there helping them. I'm partly to blame for what's going on!"

"I can't fault you for what you did," Jared told her. "I went into hell for someone I loved too."

"I don't know that I was in love with Marcus." Deb sighed. "But now I'll never have the chance to find out because hell murdered him. What I do know is the Accord, as it stands today, is not worth the piece of parchment it's written on. Hell breaks the Accord all the time and heaven does nothing about it. I was not going to allow Marcus to become collateral damage. I am not sorry for my actions, but I'm sorry if my actions caused harm to anyone else."

Deb had no more words, the unfairness of it all jaded her thoughts.

"Deb, we understand, probably better than most," Gabe answered. "We're better off focusing our energy on what's happening now. Do you know what Azza and Wrath are planning?"

"Azza's had a long time to plot her revenge," Deb told them. "Wrath is somehow stealing the powers from his siblings. I saw that for myself before going to hell."

"I imagine he can do a lot with those powers," Gabe commented. "Do you know what she's planning?"

"Azza is lobbying all the gods of darkness to join her," Deb answered. "She claims with all the deadly sins powers, she can open the gates of hell."

"That would overwhelm the Pit," Gabe answered. "There's no way heaven could stop an army coming out of hell. Not with the forces we currently have back there."

"What are you thinking?" Jared asked. "We go back, warn them?"

"No." Gabe paced back and forth. "I don't know."

"Wrath murdered Jacob," Deb told them. "But I still went willingly into Hell. I'll take responsibility for my actions, but I need to help make this right. I need to get back to my siblings."

Gabriel nodded but kept pacing.

"Do we split up?" Jared asked.

"I think what we need to do is join forces," Gabe answered. "Let's get out of here, get home. Then we'll figure something out."

"Michael will know what to do," Deb added. "That's where you go when you need a plan."

Jared glanced over at Gabe. "She's right. We need a battle plan. There's no one better than Michael O'Mara for that."

"Let's go find him then," Gabe agreed.

"Are you sure we can't teleport?" Deb asked.

"Wait a minute." Jared perked up. "It's Gabe and I that don't have the power to teleport here. Maybe you do, Deb."

"I didn't even think of that," Gabe said. "Jared's right, you weren't sentenced to the Pit."

"Ahh." Deb's head swirled trying to remember all the rules. "The magistrate probably doesn't worry about those not sentenced to the Pit coming here."

"I think it's safe to assume they couldn't find it," Jared answered.

"That's it," Deb answered. "You can't teleport if you've never been here to see it. That's why they don't restrict it from those not sentenced."

"Let's try it." Gabe stepped forward.

Deb grabbed each of their hands. Streaks of yellow light encompassed the trio as Deb teleported them from the field.

***

They arrived on the beach where Deb kissed Marcus. The coastal landscape was empty. Waves rippled across the sandy shoreline leaving white foam in its wake.

"You did it, Deb," Gabe said. "But why didn't you just bring us to the house?"

"I'm sorry," Deb answered. "It's gone. Vampires attacked Gen and Kelly and the house was destroyed in the process."

"What?" Gabe was furious. "What happened? Gen and Kelly fought off vampires?"

"According to Robino," Deb answered. "Kelly's become quite adept at killing vampires. She's been sending demons back to hell with a message for Azza. I am paraphrasing here but something like 'tell Azza Kelly O'Mara is coming for her'."

"That does not surprise me," Jared answered. "If anyone could figure out how to kill vampires, it would be her."

"Why is no one showing up?" Gabe asked. "I can't feel Gen."

"If they're battling vampires there will be cloaking," Jared offered.

"I can't sense any of them," Deb answered.

Deb tried to remain calm, she was home after all. This moment should be joyous but not sensing any of her siblings was more than a little unnerving.

"This place is deserted," Deb said. "That's unusual, all year round people walk the paths in and around the beach, with no regard to the weather."

"If what we heard is true," Jared said. "People are in lockdown. The government is calling it a virus."

"You think it's just here in the northeast?" Deb asked.

"No," Gabe answered. "It's worldwide."

"I can't imagine the terror," Deb said. "The fear must be palpable."

"Is that your mark, Deb?" Gabe asked pointing at her left arm.

Deb moved her sweatshirt to cover the bright beam of white light.

"I hope no one saw that," Deb announced.

"They are seeing far scarier things than your mark," Jared declared. "If they can see vampires, it would make sense that they could see us."

"You're saying the supernatural veil might be broken?" Deb asked.

"I think we should be prepared for anything and everything," Gabe answered. "For now, what Charge is that?"

Deb closed her eyes but couldn't clearly identify the person who needed help.

"Normally, the name comes to you at the same time the signal does," Deb said.

"Do you know where?" Gabe asked. "We'll go with you."

"It's Saint Ann's church," Deb answered. "It might be Sofia. She is a relative of Marcus and the two angels Leo and Lucas."

"We know where Saint Ann's is," Jared told her. "Do you have a weapon, Deb? If not, stay close."

"I do not have a weapon," Deb said. "I haven't

needed one since my powers manifested."

"Looking forward to seeing that!" Jared chuckled.

Wrapping herself in her aura her feet left the cool rough sand below.

I'll be back, Marcus. This will be the perfect place to say goodbye.

CHAPTER TWENTY-SEVEN

Gen's back slammed against the concrete wall. The bottom of the decorative marble frame split her head open. Blood painted the wall red, and the female licked her lips. Keeva had her hands wrapped around Gen's throat.

"I underestimated you at the house. At the Vatican you needed your brothers." Keeva smirked.

"Looks like you haven't recovered fully. My brothers nearly killed you after you attacked the innocent at the Vatican," Gen snarked.

Keeva's chin lifted and Gen saw the bright red color of her second iris. The female vampire's nostrils flared in anger. "Today, I will taste your blood, Guardian."

"Looks like you're running around with these two idiots," Gen jabbed. "Garrick leave you again?"

On Gen's right Dan was locked in battle with Luca. To her left Frankie was exchanging punches with

Sky. Dmitri was battling an enormous male vampire on the far aisle.

Jade stayed hidden behind the enormous statue of Saint Francis on the altar with several humans. Sky and Luca has been tracking Jade right alongside Dmitri so encountering them was predictable. Keeva on the other hand was not. Her brothers had nearly killed her at the Vatican. She narrowly escaped being stabbed with Kelly's new weapon.

Pinned, Gen pushed her feet against the nearest pew and managed to lift herself above the vampire's head. Keeva stretched to keep hold of Gen, but the distance loosened Keeva's grip around her neck.

Gen eye's darted to the other side of the room. Dmitri must be on the ground because the vampire Gen didn't recognize was throwing punches at the floor.

"Where's your sister?" Keeva sneered. "When I'm done with you, I'll be gunning for her."

Gen punched Keeva several times in the nose. The vampire pulled one hand free from Gen's neck. Swinging down with force Gen landed a punch on both ears. Squealing, Keeva stumbled backward. Falling quickly to the ground, Gen retrieved her weapon. Bouncing back to her feet Gen stomped on the inside of Keeva's leg, but the vampire's kneecap held. Keeva screamed but it was more a rallying cry to herself to continue the battle.

The church was awash in afternoon sunlight. The aroma of incense filled the air. People's gasps and hushed whimpers bounced off the tall ceilings. Several of the stained glass windows were broken. The cool fall air relieved Gen's overheated body. Various lights flickered across the thick red carpet. Gen understood it to be people taking pictures or worse, filming video of the event.

Luca screamed and the air above Dan's head filled with smoke. Her brother's face was beat red as he ran toward Dmitri. The next yelp erupted as Dan's blade penetrated the unknown male vampire's ear killing him instantly. Dan helped Dmitri back to his feet. His focus then went toward Frankie and Gen.

"Two down," Gen goaded Keeva.

Tackling Keeva to the ground, Gen aimed for the vampire's nose and started punching. Blood gushed out, but to Keeva's credit she didn't panic. Rotating her feet she separated Gen's legs and rolled her over. Now Keeva was on top, her blood dripping onto Gen's face.

"You've already lost, Guardian." Keeva laughed as she unholstered a dagger and pulled her arm up in the air to strike.

Gen tried to buck the vampire off but couldn't. Keeva's legs straddled Gen's body pinning her to the floor. Dmitri and Dan were too far away to help her. Gen held her arms up to keep Keeva from stabbing her, but Keeva punched her several times on the side making Gen wince and weakening her defensive grip.

Jade pushed over the large statue of Saint Francis, and it crashed to the floor breaking apart. The distraction caused Keeva's head to turn toward the altar. Gen took advantage and grabbed the tight bun

Keeva wore yanking on it. The vampire's head thrust toward Gen's stomach. Punching at her ear several times Keeva screeched and grabbed for Gen's hands as her dagger slipped from her grasp. The light thump as the dagger hit the floor told Gen the weapon was close by.

Not letting up Gen continued to punch until Keeva yanked herself free and rolled away from her. Spotting the dagger Gen picked it up. Gen refused to take her eyes off the vampire as Keeva used a nearby pew to hoist herself back to her feet. Keeva shook her head as if she were trying to clear something lodged inside it.

Footsteps coming up fast behind her caused Gen to tilt her head. Sky had escaped Frankie's grasp and was heading straight for her. Frankie was chasing her down. The on and off glitch of the vampire's cloaking still prevented them from teleporting.

Caught between two vampire's Gen jumped onto the pew and took several steps back away from the aisle. Instead of attacking, Sky ran past the pew Gen was standing on and grabbed Keeva pulling her toward the altar.

Dan and Dmitri came from the other side. Keeva and Sky stopped short and took several tentative steps back toward Gen. Frankie stopped at the pew Gen was on.

"Why are they stopped?" Frankie whispered.

"No idea." Gen was confused. "Are they all that's left?"

"Yeah," Frankie answered. "Dan scalded Luca's face with his new powers and helped Dmitri kill the other one."

"Looks like your friends abandoned you." Dan made his way up the aisle toward Keeva and Sky.

"All we want is Jade!" Sky hollered. "Give us Jade and we'll go."

"Not going to happen!" Gen yelled stepping down to stand with Frankie. "She's with us."

Raised voices erupted as the doors to the church burst open. Inside the entrance to the church stood Gabriel and Jared. It took a moment for Gen to recognize the gaunt woman with the crew cut standing next to them.

Deb! The palpable relief nearly caused Gen to collapse onto the pew.

"Thank God." Gen's heart thumped. Tears sprang from her eyes.

Deb smiled as the three of them made their way down the aisle toward Gen and Frankie.

"You're home, Deb!" Frankie said in disbelief. "I can't believe it, you made it out."

"I did." Deb focused past Gen to the altar where Jade stood. "This is an interesting meeting."

"Not a meeting, Deborah!" Jade exclaimed as the demon strode down the middle aisle. When she reached the next opening Jade walked across to where Gen and Frankie stood.

"I'm guessing the vampire's sensed the three of you arriving," Frankie commented. "Explains Sky running away from the area where you arrived."

"Well," Deb answered. "Since they were not invited, how about I take care of them for you."

Deb pushed her shield out, wrapped it around the two female vampires and thrust them through the air toward the front doors. The two females cried out as they were sent violently through the doors and onto the street.

"I wish Kelly were here." Gen walked over and embraced her sister. Frankie joined. Slowly they let go and Deb made the rounds hugging Dan and Dmitri.

The people in the church began to applaud the heavenly warriors. No more doubts about whether the veil was down or not.

Jared and Dmitri began ushering people out the back door of the church while Dan confirmed Sky and Keeva had left the area.

Gen raced to her husband and melted into Gabriel's arms inhaling his scent. It was a comfort she felt blessed and guilty for being able to have in such times of strife.

As Deb approached Jade, the demon thrust her hand out in front of her. "That's close enough, Deborah."

Deb halted. Her face blushing, obviously confused at Jade's aloofness.

"No offense, darling," Jade said softly. "I can smell you from here. And this attire," Jade lifted her hand up and down as she tsked at Deb. "It does nothing for your excellent height and small waist. Don't get me started on your hair. What have they done to you, Guardian? No worries. I know someone who can fix all this. Once you shower and clean yourself up, we can be off to London."

Deb laughed. "I believe there are other more pressing matters to attend to."

"I'm texting the others," Dan announced. "I'll tell them to meet us at Michael's."

Gen squeezed her husband's arm and moved away to attend to people on the altar who were hurt during the battle. Sophia, Deb's Charge was among them.

Gen and Deb went around and healed the wounded, there were multiple hugs and many blessings. As they finished and ushered the last of the people out of the church, Gabriel approached once more.

"Ready?" he asked.

"So ready." Gen took his hand.

Strands of golden light bounced across the wooden pews as her family began to teleport away to Michael's house.

The pieces of broken stained glass crunched under her feet as she and Gabe took a quiet moment before leaving the church.

"I would ask if you're alright," Gabe said. "But after what I heard is going on down here and what I just witnessed, I'm guessing you're anything but alright."

"I didn't want to say anything to Deb yet." Fresh tears sprang from Gen's eyes.

"What is it?" Gabe asked, holding both of Gen's hands in his own.

"Xavier's gone," Gen told him as her heart burst open. "Azza murdered him."

Gabe pulled Gen into his arms. "I'm so sorry."

"It's been rough," Gen told him. "There's been no time to grieve. We're running around getting our butts kicked and now this thing with Kelly."

"What do you mean?" Gabe pulled back. "Where is she?

"Kelly's missing." Gen choked on the words. "We haven't seen her and none of us have felt her in days."

Gabe's eyes watered. "I can't believe she's gone."

"She's not," Gen interrupted. "I can't explain it, but I know she's alive."

"Then we'll find her." Gabe wrapped his arms around Gen once more. "Together, we'll find her."

"We have to," Gen admitted. "I can't lose another sibling, Gabe."

"You won't," Gabe answered. "We're staying until we get to the bottom of Azza's plan."

"It's not just Azza," Gen told him.

"I know," Gabe answered. "Deb filled us in. Including how you know about why we're in the Pit."

"I always knew it had to be something worth giving up your freedom for," Gen told him. "I would have done the same. I would have gone in after her myself. So thank you for doing that, for saving her."

"It wasn't a choice," Gabe admitted. "We're family."

Gen nodded. "Let's get going."

Gen hung onto her husband tightly as he teleported them to Michael's house.

***

Deb was given the news of Xavier's death and fell into the chair nearest her. She eventually went upstairs where the shower masked her heavy sobs. The cost of war pummels.

Pulling on a pair of her own jeans seemed an odd opulence. The waistline was a little roomier than it should be. Raising her arms over her head no longer hurt as she put on a blue sweater. The wounds, burns, and aching muscles were gone, healed by Gen's heavenly touch.

The scars across Deb's heart were pronounced and ever present.

No healing those. Deb's eyes watered once more. *I don't even know if time can blunt them.*

The aroma of garlic and oil drifted under the door. Her stomach rumbled.

Taking in her appearance in the mirror Deb was

fairly put back together. Her hair was short, but it covered most of her scalp. Her color was pale, but a good meal and maybe an hour or two of sleep could fix a lot of things.

Walking down the stairs she caught the rise and fall of a serious discussion taking place. The squeak of a marker told her Dan had dragged out a whiteboard.

As she rounded the doorway to the kitchen, Gen sat at the table alone. Her legs pulled up to her chest. She wore a yellow sweater, jeans, and fuzzy socks. Her thick curls damp from a recent shower.

"Hey," she said to Deb as she entered. "Kettle's still hot."

Deb walked to the counter and poured a cup of tea. "Where's Jade?"

"Jade insisted that Dmitri either take her home to get proper overnight attire or take her shopping."

Deb smiled. "Sounds like her."

"She's nutty," Gen commented. "Your life is in danger. Who cares about what clothes you're wearing?"

Deb walked back to the table and sat across from her sister. "I can't fathom that Xavier is gone and now Kelly's missing. I'm sorry I wasn't here for you, for any of you."

Gen squeezed the top of Deb's hand as it lay on the table. "I'll tell you the same thing I told Kelly. It's not your fault. Hell did this, not you. We have enough to worry about without adding unnecessary guilt to the mix."

"So," Deb said loudly. "Now that we're all

caught up, what are we doing?"

The guys in the living room turned toward her. "We're going to eat and then ask Harry to call Antonio."

Tom filled up plates with pasta and bread and passed them around. There wasn't enough room at the table so some of them ate in the living room. When Jade returned, she demanded Frankie give up the seat next to Deb; he did.

"Well," Jade said as her hand cupped Deb's chin and moved her face side to side. "Your sister is no plastic surgeon, but it's a marked improvement."

"I assume I no longer smell?" Deb quipped.

"Hmm, you may need another shower." Jade picked up her fork. "Hell does leave a unique odor."

"She does not smell!" Gen snapped.

"I beg to differ, Genevieve." Jade gently squeezed Deb's hand. "I know hell when I smell it. I am glad you're in one piece, Guardian."

They finished dinner and plates were loaded into the dishwasher. Cups of tea and glasses of whiskey were passed around.

Michael had stepped outside to try calling Harry one more time. As he re-entered the room all eyes fell on him.

"Harry can't leave yet," Michael said. "He's with Gardenia and he said she's pretty distraught over the news about Marcus."

"I should go there." Deb stood.

"No," Gen told her. "You should get some rest. We all should. This battle is far from over. There will be plenty of time to console Gardenia when this is over."

Deb wanted to argue but Gen was right.

Antonio appeared in the living room to the left of Dan. The angel hadn't shaved in days. The puffy dark skin under his eyes reminded Deb of her own fatigue. His shirt and tan pants were wrinkled like he'd been wearing them for days. Maybe he had.

"I need all of you to come with me," Antonio stated.

"Why?" Dan asked.

"I am the acting magistrate. As such, I am bound not to discuss these matters in front of hell."

"That's bollocks, and you know it!" Jade snapped. "Being the magistrate just means you have more power. How you choose to wield it, is up to you."

"It's the Pit." The Arch Angel paused.

"What about it?" Jared demanded.

"I can't tell you," Antonio told them. "But if you come with me, you can see it for yourselves."

"How can we go to the Pit," Gen asked.

"I can teleport you there," he told them.

"So can I," Deb added. "Only those who are sentenced to the Pit are unable to use that power. The rest of us can."

"It is so nice to see you alive and well, Deborah," Antonio said.

"Fine," Michael interrupted. "We'll go with you to the Pit, on one condition."

"What is it?" Antonio asked.

"Tell us what you know," Michael demanded.

"All of it and fast. We don't have time for long drawn out stories."

"Oh pity, I love a good story," Jade cooed from across the room. "Why don't you start with who hell's first army is?"

Antonio's nostrils flared and Deb got the sense if he could have put his hands on Jade at that moment, the war torn angel might have choked the demon. The quiet that fell across the room was disturbing. Chills ran up Deb's arm, she crossed them instinctively.

"Well," Michael demanded. "Spit it out, what is Jade referring to?"

Antonio glanced up at the ceiling and then back toward Deb. "Hell's first army are the Arch Angels that fell to Earth with Lucifer."

Deb grabbed the kitchen chair for support.

Vampires are fallen Arch Angels! Deb's mind screamed.

Antonio continued. "When they fell to Earth, God banished them to the underworld. Lucifer embraced the punishment. He swore to prove he was right about humans being undeserving of God's love and this world. He then created the seven realms of darkness."

"Oh don't stop now, angel," Jade taunted. "You're getting to the best part."

"Stop," Michael demanded of Jade. "If you're not going to be helpful, then sit there and keep quiet."

"Fine." Jade pouted. "Vampire's drink blood to sustain life, isn't that right Antonio?"

"Yes." Antonio sneered at Jade. "When they fell, their wings blackened. The blood coursing through them turned rancid and dried up. They were outraged that God had banished them. They came and went from hell, ravaging Earth and drinking human blood. It kept them alive but also restored them, made their skin resilient and youthful."

"They want Earth?" Gen asked.

"They want heaven too," Deb added. "They feel they deserve it."

"I think I feel sick," Gen admitted. "Something from heaven turned that ugly and that cruel."

"Not only that," Deb said. "Schlosser told me he was born of the sins of humanity. That each deadly sin humanity commits, causes a demon to be created."

"That can't be true!" Frankie said.

"Oh it is, darling," Jade confirmed.

"Humanity is plagued by the very thing they created," Deb stated.

"This is horrific," Gen blurted. "How could we not have known this?"

"We'll deal with that later," Dan said. "What happened a thousand years ago?"

"Lucifer created seven gods of darkness," Antonio admitted. "To rule the seven realms of the underworld. They can never leave hell. Harac was goaded into war by General Kelce.

"Harac is ambitious," Jade added.

"He was led to believe he could win," Antonio said. "Kelce just wanted to slaughter those in heaven who had caused him harm."

"Heaven successfully ended the conflict," Greg said.

"That was the origin of the Accord?" Frankie asked.

"Yes," Antonio continued. "The demons were pushed back into hell. The fallen were made Earth bound, but without the taste for human blood. They had to drink demonic blood to stay alive, but it doesn't sustain them, or keep them young and virulent. That is where they were given the name vampire."

"All this time we've worked alongside you." Michael's voice was laced with anger and disappointment. "We're down here fighting hell and you're telling me this is a civil war."

"I've told you everything and you can hate me forever," Antonio said. "Please, just come with me now."

Deb reached into her pocket and grasped the coin containing the souls she liberated from hell. "Antonio, I have something I need to show you."

"There's no time, Deborah," Antonio responded. "Please. All of you, come with me to the Pit, now."

Michael nodded to Antonio and the family. Deb dropped the coin back inside her pocket.

The splashing auras of light enveloped them, and they were teleported to the place Deb had only just escaped.

Deb blinked several times not wanting to believe her eyes.

"What happened?" Gabe asked.

"We don't know," Antonio admitted. "But it's not a good sign."

"Explain what we're looking at," Michael snapped.

"The field," Jared said. "It's normally crawling with demons. Heaven battles here to keep them from crossing."

Deb spotted angels and Guardians roaming aimlessly on the clifftop.

Deb's mind spun. *The pit, it's empty.*

CHAPTER TWENTY-EIGHT

The Pit was a plethora of activity. Gen spanned the wide valley. She could barely identify the end point of the warring line Michael was pointing at.

"We have an opportunity here," Michael said. "We have the element of surprise and time to deploy defensive tactics ahead of when Kelce arrives."

"Kelce definitely won't be expecting us," Gen confirmed.

"How are we doing on numbers?" Michael asked Dan.

"We're getting about two out of three Guardians to say yes and come here," Dan answered.

"Is that enough?" Gen asked. "Why aren't they all coming?"

"Some don't believe war is coming," Frankie answered.

"Others think it's not our war," Greg said. "They implored us to return. Lectured us about how a

Guardian's job is to fight back against the vampires on Earth."

"The vampires invaded Earth to distract us," Michael interjected. "It was a rouse, one that wore us down and strengthened their side."

"There are those that don't know what to think," Frankie added.

"Fair," Gen said. "I'm not sure what to make of them pulling back myself."

"You pull back when you need to resupply and reposition," Michael answered. "Now that we're here, what they did on Earth makes sense. If Antonio had never brought us to the Pit today. Kelce would have arrived and marched right over this field and up this mountain range."

"I guess the disconcerting part is that they could show up at any minute," Gen said.

"Or three days from now," Michael stated. "In which case we would have all the time we need to hide bombs and setup our weapons."

Angels and Guardians were spread over the field below hiding holy water bombs. The valley floor was still covered with demonic corpses. Those sentenced to the Pit gave Michael a crash course in what the rules were and how hell typically engages and from what openings.

"The entire point of this battlefield," Michael said firmly. "Is to keep hell from breaching to this cliffside. If they make it past us, they make it to Earth."

Gen shivered at the thought of hell fighters roaming Earth annihilating humanity.

"We make a stand here," Michael warned. "Or Earth falls."

How did it come to this?

Deb arrived with Harry, Gardenia, and a slew of young members of the lost.

"Are you sure it's safe for them?" Gen asked.

"They said they were coming whether I brought them here or not," Deb answered.

"We can use them up here on the ridge," Michael answered. "Direct them over to Tom. He's setting up the catapults. He can teach them how to use them. We can use all the help we can get."

Deb brought Gardenia and her friends over to Tom's position. Harry walked over to stand beside Gen.

"How are you holding up?" Harry asked.

"As good as can be expected," Gen answered. "This is crazy. I can't believe we're about to engage in a major battle with rebels from hell."

"You've been preparing for this for a long time," Harry reassured. "All those hours of training with Michael. The various entities you've driven off Earth and sent back to hell. You're ready."

"I appreciate that," Gen told him. "I guess I just didn't think it would come down to this. I mean it's not the end of days. You always think that's the big one you're going to face. You never stop to think there may be several in between that are just as perilous."

"I think Guardians." Harry paused. "The O'Mara family in particular, are good at expecting the unexpected."

"Thanks Harry." Gen turned and hugged her angel. What a blessing he had been in their lives. "For everything."

"Oh come now, Genevieve," Harry told her. "This isn't the end. Have faith, there will be better days ahead."

Gen nodded as Harry walked off to speak with Frankie and Dan. Michael was on the phone directing the Guardians below to move a few of the bombs out of view of the oncoming army.

Gen thought of Kelly. *I don't know where you are or what you're doing. If you can hear me, please come. We need you!*

Deb's aura glowed across the mossy ground. Stepping out from within was Jade with five other beings.

"Michael," Gen called over her shoulder. "What do you want the demons to do?"

"What?" Michael snapped as he came to stand next to Gen. "Are those Jade's siblings.

"I've only met one other," Gen answered. "The brunette is Dee, short for Desire. She's the one I told you set her own house on fire running from Kelce."

Jade and Deb walked over to their position.

"Hey," Gen greeted. "I'm assuming those are all your siblings?"

"All but one. Unfortunately, Languor is..." Jade

paused as her eyes scanned the enormity of the battlefield. "Well, let's just say he's unavailable. But the rest are here to help, obviously."

"Obviously." Gen leveled a stare at Deb.

"They truly want to help," Deb said. "And we need all the bodies we can get."

"Fine," Michael said. "Any one of them steps out of line or gives away any part of what we're doing, and I'll personally pitch them off this cliff."

"I see diplomacy is not your strong suit, Michael," Jade snarked. "If you must know, my siblings and I did not stand up to our brother when we had the chance. We aren't letting another occasion slip by."

"Why don't you go join Tom," Gen told Jade. "He needs all hands on deck to set up the catapults."

Jade turned and sauntered back toward her siblings. She wore fashionable fatigues and a pressed olive green T-shirt. The ankle boots were better than heels, but Gen couldn't imagine her breaking a nail, never mind entering the fray of battle. A few of the siblings were forlorn and nervous to be surrounded by so many heavenly beings.

"This will be a first," Gen stated. "Demons fighting alongside heaven to squash a revolt from hell."

"Harry always said there's a first time for everything." Deb smiled.

"That he did," Gen agreed. "Who's the one in the three-piece suit with matching cuff links?"

"Decadence," Deb answered.

"Of course," Gen said. "That wasn't hard, guess

I'm just distracted."

"I saw Harry," Deb said. "I see he's brought Gardenia and other members of the lost. I thought they didn't pick sides."

"I don't think there is such a thing as neutral anymore," Gen stated. "Not after what the vampires or shall I say fallen angels have done."

"It seems that revelation is still bothering you, why?" Deb asked. "In the end does it really matter who the vampires were."

"I guess I just feel betrayed," Gen admitted. "History matters. That part of the Arch Angel's story was something I think we should have been privy to."

"Maybe," Deb said. "In the end what matters most is what someone does, not where they came from. Those aren't just human lessons."

"I know," Gen said. "It's just all a bit much. To think something that was born from heaven could have killed Xavier."

"I get it," Deb confirmed. "The world was clearer when there were dividing lines. But maybe that was never reality, maybe we were in a bubble of our own making."

Gen nodded. "I'm coming to that realization. I guess I was naïve."

"I don't know about that," Deb commented. "Death teaches different lessons. There is no manual for how to deal with that."

"Thanks, Deb." Gen bumped against her sister's shoulder. "I miss our chats. It seems like the three of us sitting around the kitchen table was years ago, not months."

"We'll have that again," Deb told her. "I feel it deep in my bones."

Flapping wings drew their attention to the sky. Antonio landed a few feet from them, his wine colored wings folded in on themselves.

"No sign of Kelly?" he asked. "I can go and look for her before heading back to rally the Arch Angels."

"Kelly will come when she's ready," Gen stated.

"Yes," Deb agreed. "And you have more important things to do first."

"I do?" Antonio tilted his head in confusion. "I think this is pretty important."

"I tried telling you at the house." Deb's voice lowered. "I have something I need you to bring to heaven. Something you need to do personally."

"What is it?" Antonio eyes narrowed in concern.

Deb reached in her pocket and retrieved the old coin that Gardenia had given her. Antonio gasped.

"How do you have this?" Antonio held out his palm and Deb gave him the coin. The Arch Angel's hand seemed weighed down by the brass object.

"What is it?" Gen asked.

"Miles isn't a soul catcher." Deb turned her head toward Gen. "The coin absorbs the soul. Whoever has the coin can bring the souls to heaven or to hell. Miles was more a thief of souls."

"How in the world did you figure that out?" Gen asked in wonder.

"Before Marcus died." Deb's voice cracked. "He told me to take the coin to the soul room and rescue all the souls trapped within it, including Christian's."

Antonio wrapped his hand around the coin and brought it to his chest as tears fell across his cheeks. "Christian will be at peace."

"When Marcus died." Deb paused. "His soul went into the coin. That's how I figured out what it was."

"Deb, I'm so sorry." Gen grabbed her sister's hand. "What you did wasn't just brave, it was heroic. To bring those souls out of hell and deliver them to heaven, it's incredible."

"Thank you," Antonio said. "It's not enough but please, I hope you know how truly grateful I am that you brought my love back to me. Now Christian can finally go home."

Antonio embraced Deb and the two of them wept. Stepping back Deb wiped the tears from her face.

"Take them to heaven before you go to the Arch Angels," Deb stated. "They deserve it for what they've been through."

"Yes." Antonio took several steps back and unfurled his wings. Keeping the coin tight to his chest his feet left the ground and flew skyward toward the heavens above.

For a moment Deb and Gen stood together as the Arch Angel ascended.

Voices rose from the valley below and brought their heads back around to the battlefield. Down past the catapults several Guardians were waving red flags.

Oh no. That's the signal.

"They're coming," Deb implored. "I'm going to get in position."

Gen jogged to the edge of the cliff and peered down. Gabriel was below on the front lines with Jared, Dmitri, and several other heavenly warriors assigned to the Pit. From here they were like tiny fragments of a broken mosaic. She couldn't pick out Gabriel, but she felt him all the same.

"The first battalion of demons just exited the gates," Michael announced. "Are you ready?"

Gen nodded even though she was nowhere near ready.

"Hey." Michael turned her toward him. "You can do this. We have everything we need."

"Each other." Gen breathed through the panic.

"That's right," Michael told her. "I'm going to be right there with you. The first wave are gutter demons. We're going to fight back to back and move counterclockwise. Push outward, the swarm is most lethal up close. Stab and pull up, the more fluid the demons lose the better."

"I remember," Gen answered. "No wasted movement. Aim for the thighs and kick to the knees, stab in the chest."

"That's right, focus on your targets. Nothing else matters." Michael grabbed Gen's arm and teleported the two of them down onto the Pit floor.

The valley was so wide that even on the ground

she couldn't point out Gabriel. Her husband wanted to stay with her, but Gen convinced him to go to the front where he was most needed.

The ground vibrated by the running of tens of thousands of feet. The gutter demons were running straight at them. Their battle cries thundered ahead of their massive numbers. Gen's heart hammered and she took several deep breaths to calm it.

"Four hundred yards!" Michael yelled to the line of warriors who pushed ahead bracing for impact.

Gen counted the seconds in her head. Before she reached ten Michael's voice rang out again.

"Three hundred yards!" Michael hollered. He was receiving the information from Tom who was signaling from above.

The sun was setting, Michael assumed Hell would deploy at night since demons had natural night vision. He knew Kelce would think it was to his advantage, but Michael had a plan to counter it.

The demons were clawing at one another to get ahead. She remembered that fervor when they fought them last time. Gutter demons don't work in unison, they fight each other to get ahead. It was a competition for who could kill more heavenly entities.

Frankie arrived just behind her, "You got this," he told her.

The gutters demons were so loud she almost missed Michael's order.

"Now Genevieve!" Michael yelled.

Gen pictured the ground under the gutter

demons' feet. She closed her eyes and her power swirled through her body. Frankie grasped her shoulder and when their powers intwined Gen released it through the ground and across the field.

Explosions rocked the battlefield. Gen used her power to detonate the holy water bombs upward as the gutter demons ran. Dozens of demons fell to the ground no longer able to run or move. The water tore open their skin and weakened the bone underneath. Their battle cries turned to screeching panic as they weren't sure where to step. Several stopped moving forward, but hundreds of others ran haphazardly onward. Their cold blood caked the ground in a slippery blue mess.

Despite the damage and chaos the bombs caused, more gutter demons kept coming. Their numbers were unlike anything Gen had ever witnessed. Panic ripped through her. Gen knew if they didn't do something soon the gutter demons would be able to encircle them.

"We have to do something." Gen turned back toward Frankie. "I'm going to open a crack in the ground, maybe we'll bury several hundred."

"Let's do it." Frankie grabbed her shoulder once more.

Gen pictured the ground as she did from above. Visualizing the thick mass of dead demons in the center of the field she pushed her powers through her feet. The ground rocked and those in heavens ranks struggled to remain standing.

Gen's powers ripped open the ground, like a

giant maw ready to swallow whole the stampeding gutter demon clan. Hundreds of sprinting gutter demons fell to their death in the deep trench. Before the swarm understood what was in front of them, more stepped off the precipice and died. Still the horde kept coming. Never retreating, thousands hurtled into darkness. Continuing forward the chasm filled and the boots of their comrades pounded them into the earth.

Heaven's warriors regained their footing and held firm to their positions. As the first several rows of demons reached them, the warriors moved in the manner Michael described. Genevieve got back-to-back with Michael. Frankie teleported back up top to Deb.

Gen held her double curved knife in her right hand. Her and Michael moved in tight circles, stabbing, and punching outward. Just as before the demons were unable to counter their superior fighting stance.

Michael and Gen stabbed and slashed. Their faces and clothes were stained blue. Gen lost her footing several times for she and her brother were now spinning in puddles of demonic liquid.

Pushing and punching outward the fight was a tornado of movement. Michael and Gen killed dozens of demons. The pair were ankle deep in demonic corpses when the field directly in front of them cleared.

Relief flooded through her when heaven's warriors started hooting and hollering victoriously.

"What now?" Gen asked panting from the intense fight.

"They're going to keep coming," Michael said.

"We just have to see how quickly. There are more bombs. See if you can detonate them. It looks like we've got about three rows left to battle."

Gen breathed in and out and sent her powers out once more. Fatigue encroached as she pushed her body to respond. Explosives shook the valley. The demons screamed from within the chaos, some choosing to retreat. The final two rows of battle-hardened demons pressed forward.

Once more Gen got back-to-back with Michael. The gutter demons reached them swiping with shivs and broken bottles. Gen's arm split open, and her blood gushed from the wound. Pushing the female gutter demon back Gen stabbed her in the thigh pulling up to open the demon's veins. The female wailed. Gen kicked repeatedly, caving in the female demon's kneecap causing her to fall.

Gen and Michael never stopped moving. Each turn of Gen's body brought her face to face with a new demon. The mass of bodies pressed closer. One gutter demon swiped at Gen's head. Ducking Gen stabbed at the demon's leg, but he moved out of the way. Gen fell to the ground, and the gutter demons encircled her.

The right side of Gen's body took several kicks before Michael was able to reach down and pull Gen back up to her feet. Now they were out of position, facing the gutter demons one-on-one. Punching and pushing back was making little progress.

A stabbing pain rang through Gen's head. Blood ran down the side of her face as demons were floating all around her.

Michael pulled Gen away from the gutter demons who were now suspended in midair.

Deb was holding her hands above her head. Hundreds of gutter demons were launched higher into the air and then slammed to the ground. Before the demonic scavengers could attempt a recovery, they were hauled up into the air again and smashed down even harder. Deb used her power to perform this task several times until the last of the gutter demons lay dead at their feet.

"I didn't know she could do that." Michael steadied Gen.

"She told us her powers intensified in hell," Gen told him.

"She just killed hundreds of demons," Michael said. "The rest of the swarm are retreating."

"Good," Gen said. "I need a little help with this head wound."

Michael examined Gen's wound. There was blood above her ear. "I'll bring you up."

Her brother's blue aura teleported them to the top of the cliff. Deb ran over to them.

"Are you okay?" she asked viewing the blood from Gen's head wound. "That was terrifying to watch."

"I'm okay," Gen answered. "Nothing a little healing can't fix."

Deb used her powers to seal the wounds. It wasn't fully healed, but it would get Gen through to the next battle.

"I had no idea your powers were that strong, Deb," Michael told her. "Good job, they were taking it to us."

"No time to celebrate," Deb replied. "There's another wave coming."

"Are the catapults ready?" Michael asked.

"They are," Deb answered. "The Orsini brothers showed up with a ton of weapons and holy oil."

"Just in time," Michael commented. "I'm going to go catch up with them."

Michael ran off toward the catapults. Deb handed Gen some water.

"Thanks, Deb."

"Of course. Feeling better?" Deb asked.

"Much," Gen answered. "Though I'm afraid to ask what's next."

"It's another wave of demons," Deb answered. "Not sure what kind."

Gen and Deb jogged to the side of the cliff and scanned the ground below. Hundreds of demons were running toward heaven's warriors once more.

"I bet those are the demons the vampires turned," Gen told her.

"I didn't know they turned demons into vampires," Deb said.

"They're immune to holy water," Gen said loudly. "I hope I told Michael that."

"You must have," Deb told her. "He's deploying the catapults of holy fire."

The catapults were separated into two sections. One was down at the opposite end of the cliff where the lookouts were positioned. The other was about hundred yards from Gen's current position.

Michael had a flag in his hand, he stood in front of the group of catapult operators imploring them to remain calm.

Spanning the group Gen spotted Gerry, Lacey, and dozens of other historians. "Wow, everyone is here."

"Yeah," Deb agreed. "It's amazing how many came when we asked. Even Leo and Lucas. Though, I'm not sure how helpful Leo will be."

"Yeah," Gen agreed. "For an angel he's a little high strung."

Michael directed everyone to clear away from the cliffside in front of the catapults. As the demons marched closer to the frontlines Michael's voice rang out.

"Hold!" Michael warned.

Another hundred yards the demons pushed.

"Hold!" Michael shouted again.

The demons charged closer, as hell reached about two hundred yards out from the warriors' frontline, Gen held her breath.

"Now!" Michael ordered as he waved the flag sending the signal for the group further down the cliffside to deploy their weapons as well.

Balls of holy fire sailed through the air. The Orsini brothers had created thick rolls of cotton soaked in holy oil. When ignited the catapults sent them careening into the air, gravity reigned them down onto the demons below. The screams of terror rang out as the demons were enveloped in holy fire.

The catapults reloaded and launched another round. Soon the air filled with the stench of kerosine and death.

Michael had separated the catapults to land at the five-hundred-yard mark and the two-hundred-yard mark. The demons were trapped between two walls of fire. There was no escape and the demons who had fallen behind the marching brigade retreated.

The heavenly warriors erupted in celebration. Smoke billowed up obscuring parts of the land mass below. Gen and Deb teleported to Michael and Tom to get a better vantage point. Gen could tell something was wrong, they weren't celebrating.

"What's wrong?" Gen asked as she stopped next to Michael.

"That was just the first wave," Michael answered.

A large portal opened. General Kelce stepped through it assessing the damage that lay before him. hell fighters crossed the portal as did Azza and Wrath. Gargoyles flew through the opening and sailed up the cliffside.

How are we supposed to counter that? Gen's pulse quickened. *Where is Antonio? We need the Arch Angels before it's too late.*

CHAPTER TWENTY-NINE

Kelly woke with the book she had been reading resting comfortably on her chest. After her and Sunny's training rounds, she jogged around the property several times. Kelly even scaled down the rocky cliffside to stick her feet in the frigid ocean waters below. It was no wonder she fell asleep while reading.

The aroma of fresh vegetables, garlic, and sauteed chicken drew her from her slumber. Kelly's stomach growled. Getting up she placed the book on the small wooden box next to the twin bed. The cozy bedroom had thick white linen curtains, with a comfy chair and hassock that sat by the window. Her bed was covered in fresh white sheets and several thick blankets that smelled like lavender.

Coming down the stairs, Kelly's eyes fell to the grounds beyond the front door. Several square feet were burned to the ground. This was in stark contrast to the rest of the vegetation surrounding the property.

Passing through the tidy living space she eyed the handmade furniture. Sunny had a woodshop in the garage. He spent hours in there before the crack of dawn. The bedroom Kelly was sleeping in was on the opposite side of the house. Yet Kelly was still amazed there was never any hammering, or the buzzing of a saw, or even a yelp or two. Sunny had plenty of scars and burns on his hands. Kelly assumed some of them had to have come from his woodworking hobby.

"How was your nap?" Sunny asked as she entered the kitchen.

"How do you always know what I'm doing?" Kelly asked as she poured a glass of water and sat at the large counter in the kitchen. Sunny was bustling about cooking dinner and chopping up lettuce for a fresh salad.

"You were too quiet," Sunny answered. "Normally, I hear you walking about or coming in and out. Living here for so many years alone, your ears are tuned for things out of the ordinary."

"I feel restless," Kelly admitted. "Like something's going on?"

"It is," Sunny admitted. "Now, let's eat and then we'll have our final training lesson."

"Final?" Kelly asked. "Are you kicking me out?"

Sunny laughed, "I know you're itching to go."

"Well, I have made progress," Kelly told him.

"That you have." Sunny scooped food onto oval wooden plates. "Now fill the salad bowls and let's eat."

Kelly moved around the counter once Sunny had taken the plates to the table. She doled out generous portions of salad into the dark brown bowls Sunny had left on the counter. Grabbing them, she joined Sunny at the table which was already set. Sunny took his usual seat at the end of the table with a view of the property. Kelly sat on his left.

"How many have come and stayed with you?" Kelly asked.

"Truthfully, not many," Sunny answered. "I have trained dozens of fighters over the years. Bringing them here wasn't always called for."

"I was a unique case then," Kelly answered before digging into the hot food.

"Indeed you were, Ms. O'Mara."

"You know you can call me, Kelly."

"And you know you can call me by my real name." Sunny smiled. "All in due time."

"Yes," Kelly answered. "Well, I hope I remember it. As you've said *you can't tell me anything I already know.* That means we've met before, and the memory is still buried."

"How are you sleeping?" Sunny asked. "I don't hear as much disturbance as when you first arrived."

"Every night I guess I process more," Kelly answered in between bites. "The nightmares have lessened in intensity. Last night they didn't even wake me."

"That is excellent." Sunny held up his glass of water. "Let's toast to conquering our fears."

Kelly smiled and clinked his glass. *I don't know about conquer, but I definitely feel better.*

"I'm calmer here," Kelly said. "I don't know what it is, the tranquility of the island, the quiet of the space, or the company."

Sunny winked at her. "One at peace with who they are will live a life of serenity."

"What happens when I return?" Kelly asked. "When I come across a vampire, will I still be serene as I raise my blade and spill blood?"

"I cannot answer that," Sunny told her. "Only you can. Being here is not a cureall. It can't fix everything all at once."

"A work in progress, then," Kelly admitted.

Sunny nodded. "As are all."

"Thank you for brining me here," Kelly told him. "No matter what happens now, I have hope. The training, the techniques, the eating regimen. Which I'll be honest, is not my favorite thing here."

Smiling Sunny shrugged. "You needed to get in tune with your entire self. To bring harmony to your mind, your soul, and your physical body. Glazed donuts were not helping you."

"But they taste so amazing," Kelly insisted.

"I guess there's some things even I can't fix." Sunny laughed.

"In all seriousness," Kelly said moving on to her salad. "I do feel incredible. It's almost as if my body is waking up. I feel it responding while we're training in a way I never have before."

"Are you still afraid of your power?" Sunny asked.

"I was afraid it came from hell," Kelly admitted. "Now, I don't believe it does."

"Well, well," Sunny declared. "We have things to celebrate indeed."

"The fear was real," Kelly said adamantly.

"No doubt about that," Sunny said. "Fear is powerful. Like a great hurricane fueling off the ocean, fear can do much damage. Its real power is how tenacious and malleable it is."

"Yeah." Kelly sighed. "I see that now. How I pushed it down, but it just turned to rage and then boiled over."

"When you ignore fear, it lies in wait," Sunny warned. "It beckons in the dark and burrows deep within. When you're weakest, it will come for you. Like a demon in the night it has no mercy. Fear will devour anything that threatens its survival. Morphing until you can no longer distinguish between what is real and what is not."

"That is a terrifying story." Kelly sat enraptured by Sunny's words.

"Hopefully, you'll remember it then."

"I won't soon forget it."

"Then you'll always be centered." Sunny smiled. "An anchor for those who need it."

Kelly reflexively rubbed the mark on her left arm, an anchor. It was barely visible now, not having gone off for several days.

"I don't suppose you'd be up for telling me where we are," Kelly said.

"That's impossible." Sunny paused. "You are welcome home here, anytime. When and if you ever need me, you will find your way to the island."

"That's very Yoda." Kelly smiled broadly. "I love it."

They ate the rest of their dinner in comfortable silence. The sun waned in the sky. Streaks of golden yellow and pink that turned orange spanned the horizon.

"It will be dark soon," Sunny told her. "I'll go light the torches."

Sunny left out the back as Kelly piled the dishes in the sink.

Something is beckoning me home.

Following Sunny outside, Kelly walked toward the shed to grab the training gear.

"No gear tonight," Sunny announced. "Tonight you make fire."

Kelly met Sunny in the center of the slab they worked on.

"Breath in and out," Sunny told her. "Reach down and find your power."

It didn't take long to connect with the energy within. Kelly's powers were like a runaway train, careening over an endless track.

"In your mind, create a circle of fire," Sunny told her. "See the ball of light, small at first. Tiny sparks of flame, just dancing in and around themselves."

They had done this visualization exercise before, but she never manifested anything.

"Focus now." Sunny broke through her thoughts. "Don't think about whether it should or shouldn't be possible. Don't think about anything other than the fire."

Sunny moved to stand next to her. Kelly found a rocky formation in the ocean and let it ground her thoughts.

"Raise your palm," Sunny ordered. "Submit to the power, accept it as part of you and draw it forward."

The power moved through Kelly as her thoughts were forming. She didn't force it, she found her power and released it.

The ball of fire burst to life in her hand and stayed there.

It worked and it's beautiful.

"Good." Sunny sang the word as his voice lowered. "Now direct it out and into the ocean."

Kelly thought about the salt rocks straight ahead. She imagined the fireball taking flight and landing on them. As if on command the fire left her palm. The ball of light sailed through the air and exploded onto the salt rocks. The flickering light blazed brightly before being consumed by dark ocean water.

Kelly's heart raced. Adrenaline was pumping through her veins. Raising her hands victoriously in the air, she reacted like a champion.

"I did it!" Kelly hollered. "It worked, it really worked."

"Well of course it did." Sunny laughed. "You had an excellent teacher."

"I can't believe it." Kelly's words stumbled out. "I mean I can believe it, I just watched it happen. It's just so crazy. In the best possible way I guess."

Elation was not the correct word, but it was close. "I gotta do it again."

"By all means," Sunny responded. "Throw all the fireballs you want into the ocean. Practice is good for the body and the mind."

For the better part of the next hour Kelly manifested and moved fire. Sunny helped her morph it from balls of fire to long arrows of flame. Some of those went astray, but considering this was brand new, she'd take it.

Beads of sweat broke out against her forehead. "You will tire less often the more you practice calling the power forward."

Taking a break, Kelly went inside and gulped down several glasses of water. "It's amazing and it doesn't feel demonic at all."

"Well that's because it's not," Sunny confirmed. "You're calling forth holy fire. Nothing demonic about it."

Relief wrapped around her like a warm blanket on a cool night.

"What's next?" Kelly asked.

"I have one more memory to pull forth," Sunny told her. "After that, you'll need to go to your siblings."

"Why? Are they okay?" Kelly asked. The mood dampened from the growing concern in his eyes.

"Come into the living room." Sunny walked off.

"Please." Kelly's voice cracked. "If they're in trouble, I need to know."

"Sit here." He pointed at the largest cushioned chair in the space, the one Kelly used for mediation or occasional reading. The air was filled with the fragrance of juniper from the basket of berries that sat on top of the mantle above the fireplace.

Kelly sat down. Sunny sat on the wooden coffee table in front of her.

"You remember your fight with Sonoran?" Sunny asked.

"Yes," Kelly answered. "I told you I did, that I know I nearly died."

"Well, it's time to correct that last little bit." Sunny reached up and placed a finger in the middle of her forehead.

The images came in rapid succession. The Vatican library. The black and white marble floor she woke up on. The rows of books she walked along trying to decide what to pick. An image of Sunny standing beside the table that she and Gerry were sitting at. Kelly tried to pull back, but Sunny steadied her.

"It's just a memory," Sunny's voice cooed. "You are safe."

"I remember." Kelly's eyes watered. "I didn't nearly escape death. I died in Gen's arms."

Kelly opened her eyes. She stared at Sunny for what seemed like hours. Then she finally spoke.

"Your name, it's not Sunny," Kelly admitted.

"That is correct," he told her. "You know who I am. You've known it since that night."

Tears streaked down her face. "I remember running through the library, looking for an escape. Every door led me back to that room. I haven't been able to return to the Vatican library since. I didn't understand why until now."

"Go on, Ms. O'Mara," he encouraged. "You've already faced so many fears. Who am I?"

"Abaddon." Kelly's voice was but a whisper. "You are the angel of death."

"Kelly, I can show you no more than this." Grasping both of her hands in his, Abaddon continued. "War has begun. The Arch Angels are in crisis. I send you forth to May and Samantha. Be the anchor they need."

"Wait," Kelly pleaded. "What do you mean, be their anchor? What war and why have you been helping me?"

"There are so many more chapters of your life yet to be written," Abaddon answered. "I cannot wait to read them."

The smile on his face faded as the room descended into darkness. A wave of nausea assaulted Kelly's body. Her feet hit the ground, but it took her several seconds to adjust to the dim light. Sprawling oak trees lined either side of a large white farmhouse in the distance. The air was cool and dry, she was wearing the same clothes from the night she met Sunny.

Except it wasn't Sunny. Kelly shook her head trying to make sense of her troubled thoughts. *It was Death.*

Kelly couldn't hear or sense any of her siblings. Not sure she was even on Earth, she walked toward the front door of the property.

Halfway across the lawn rustling came from behind and Kelly turned in time to face an attacker coming up behind her. Running fast he nearly fell over when he forced himself to pull up short.

"Kelly O'Mara?" he said breathlessly.

"Um, yes," Kelly retorted. "Who are you?"

"I'm Billy." He pushed his hand out and Kelly shook it. "If you're looking for the meeting, it's in the barn."

Through the bushes came Billy's backup. This group wielded swords and crossbows.

"Billy!" A looming figure in front bellowed. "Back away."

"Stop," Billy ordered. "It's Kelly O'Mara."

The men approached tentatively. A flashlight came across her face, she put her arm up to shield her eyes.

"Ow." Kelly shielded her face. "A flashlight in the eye, hurts fellas."

"Take her to the barn." They lowered their weapons. "May will want to speak with her."

May. Kelly relaxed. *These are Arch Angels.*

Kelly followed the angels through the treelined yard that lay to the left of the house. They walked for several yards before there was a fervor of yelling voices.

"They're fighting?" Kelly asked out loud not really expecting a reply.

"Antonio came and asked us to fight," Billy answered.

"It's not our place to tell this story, Billy," snapped an angel to her right.

"Why isn't it your place?" Kelly asked. "You're all equal here, are you not?"

A bend in the path brought them to a two-story weathered barn. The doors were propped open, Arch Angels were everywhere. The heavenly warriors were three rows deep in the yard. Several of them sat on the roof. Still more sat on tree limbs or hovered in the air close to the building.

"Clear a path!" One of the angels behind her bellowed.

The sea of bodies, moved to their right and left. Out of the barn came May and Samantha.

"How in the world did you find us?" May asked.

Sam sprang forward and wrapped Kelly in an enormous hug. "I'm so glad to see you."

"I'm always happy to see you as well," Kelly responded. "What's happening here? What are you fighting about?"

"Antonio came to see us." May walked toward their position. "He ordered us to come and fight alongside your siblings in the Pit. But after what he did to you and your family the army won't follow him."

The Pit. Kelly's heart threatened to break the calm she was holding onto for dear life.

"Your brother Michael sent him," Sam told her. "He's convinced that General Kelce is going to lay siege to it."

"If Michael thinks that," Kelly stated. "Then why are you all still hanging around here?"

"Perhaps the three of you should speak alone," an angel to her left suggested.

"No!" Kelly barked. "Whatever is said should be said in front of all of you."

Gasps and hushed whispers ran through the crowd. May raised her hands in the air to quiet the group.

"If my brother sent for you, then you can be sure he needs you," Kelly told them. "You are being called to take up arms against hell."

The angels inside the barn had been flowing outside. They spread through the yard to better participate in the conversation.

"Why should we fight your war?" a female on her right yelled.

"Your sister broke the Accord," a male barked from behind. "This is your fight, not ours."

"Is that what you think?" Kelly asked. "Is it?"

The crowd fell silent, no one retorted. Kelly walked past May and Samantha and hopped up onto the roof of the barn so that she would be visible to all.

"It's true," Kelly said. "My sister went into hell to rescue a sentinel. A friend of our family who risked everything to save me from certain death."

Kelly paused waiting for a response, none came.

"But that was after Wrath murdered Jacob." Flashes of anger crossed May and Samantha's faces. "I saw it with my own eyes, I was there. I witnessed Wrath's cowardly maneuver to come from behind and stab Jacob through the back with a sword. I watched in horror as he cut Jacob's hand off and teleported away before I could reach him. Jacob died in my arms!"

"You can't kill a deadly sin," one angel urged from her right. "What are we to do?"

"You can't kill a deadly sin." Kelly nodded. "You're right. But you can smite demons. You can slay vampires. And you can, as sure as the sun rises, send the rest back down to hell."

Voices in huddled conversation broke the silence. They were arguing the merits of her case amongst themselves.

"This war is not between vampires and angels." Kelly paused to allow the crowd to settle. "And it's not between Guardians and demons. My family doesn't need you because your fallen brethren have been restored. They haven't asked for your help because they did something wrong."

Kelly peered through the crowd. All eyes were on her. There wasn't an angel among them not fully focused in the moment.

"This war is between heaven and hell," Kelly shouted. "God sent all of us to protect humanity. Face your fears and fight through them as I have."

"Yeah!" Billy held his sword above his head. More woops came from her left.

"We are the greatest threat against the demonic world," Kelly yelled to more clanging swords and fisted cheers. "We win because we're united in our cause. No demon will rule this world while I'm still standing. I'll die in the Pit before I let that happen!"

The cheers grew thunderous. May and Samantha were clapping from below.

"Now!" Kelly shouted. "Are you with me?!"

Holding her breath Kelly waited for the response and prayed it was the *yes* she needed it to be.

CHAPTER THIRTY

Running, Deb waved Gardenia and Lacey away from the catapults. The gargoyles swooped through the open portal so quickly there was barely any time for people to react.

The winged creatures attacked the catapults, their talons swiping at anyone that interfered. Flapping wildly to stay hovered above the tall wooden weapons the gargoyles unleashed Hell Fire from their enormous mouths igniting the catapults on fire.

"Lacey!" Deb yelled. "Take as many out of here as you can."

The historian nodded, huddled Gardenia and her friends together and teleported them from the cliffside. Jade and her siblings ran back toward the lake. They hid under the large oak trees.

"Watch out," Vincenzo Orsini hollered.

A gargoyle was aiming right for Deb. Pushing her shield, the bird-like beast smashed against the invisible barrier and rolled ten yards away from her.

Vincenzo Orsini lit a small ball of cloth laced with holy oil and threw it at the gargoyle. Upon impact the gargoyle's wings ignited. The creature squawked loudly flailing to put out the fire. The movement had the opposite effect, and the fire spread. Vincenzo brought his crossbow up to shoot. Dipping an arrow in holy water, he loaded the weapon and shot the animal square in the chest. The gargoyle stumbled backward falling to its death on the Pit floor.

"Both holy water and holy fire work on the gargoyles!" Vincenzo yelled to the others.

Within minutes several Guardians were spread out defending the cliffside from the flying demonic creatures.

Chaos reigned down below. The Pit floor was a sea of clashing forces. The heavenly warriors sentenced to the Pit floor were immune to hell fighter venom. The rest of the Guardians had to wait above hoping the gaseous fumes of demonic venom lost their potency the further into the atmosphere it rose.

"Did you get everyone pushed back?!" Gen yelled as she ran to Deb bringing her a crossbow along with a few freshly wet arrows.

"I think so." Deb's eyes spanned the open space once more for anyone she may have missed. "There are just Guardians up here now. Everyone else is either hiding or teleported away."

"What about Harry?" Gen asked.

"He wouldn't leave." Deb raised the weapon in front of her and loaded it with an arrow. "Harry is staying out of sight behind Tom."

"He's so stubborn." Gen pulled the trigger of her crossbow and landed a kill shot at the gargoyle closest to them.

Shrieking rang through the air as the beast fell to its death.

"How many are there?" Deb yelled. "They're moving around so quickly I can't tell."

"At least a dozen." Gen pivoted, dropped to one knee, and shot another.

"Your aim is amazing." Deb missed her first attempt.

"I don't know where Vincenzo got these." Gen took two steps to her left and shot again. "They're so lightweight."

Deb lifted the weapon in the air once more and shot again, another miss.

"Ok, I am not helping." Deb brought her spare arrows to Gen. "It's probably best to be smart with the limited ammo."

Deb snuck up to the edge and peered over. The first hell fighter was within a hundred yards of heaven's front lines. The beast was over nine feet tall and fully engulfed. It stomped across the field like a hungry lion hunting small prey. When it was fifty yards from the front lines the beast exploded. It was shot from behind by someone on hell's side of the field. The demons body broke into a thousand fireballs of poisonous gas. The remnants of the demon rained down on heaven's warriors. Though it couldn't kill them, enough of it could hurt them.

"What was that?" Gen yelled as she ran to Deb's side after killing a fifth gargoyle.

"Hell killed their own hell fighter," Deb explained. "Shot it from behind."

Before Gen could retort another hell fighter exploded and then another. The field became hazy, dozens of venomous balls of fires ricocheted in every direction. The line between heaven and hell blurred.

"They're killing their own fighters!" Gen yelled at Dan who ran toward them.

"It's Kelce," Dan yelled. "He's sacrificing them, using them like bombs."

"What do we do?" Deb's chest heaved. "It's only a matter of minutes before the poison drifts up the cliffside and envelopes all the Guardians up here with us."

"We're making progress on the gargoyles," Dan told her. "Can you direct your shield to blow the wind away from us?"

"I can try." Deb searched for a safe spot to stand, but there wasn't one.

Frankie teleported from the far end of the cliffs. "Gen's the best shot up here. I brought her more arrows." Dropping a bucket by her feet Gen wasted no time loading and shooting as she moved along the edge.

"The gas is drifting up fast," Gen told them. "I can see it through the scope."

"You got this Deb," Dan told her. "We'll guard while you and Frankie work to push the fumes away.

More explosions rocked the canyon. Deb swayed but stayed on her feet. Several yards away, Vincenzo Orsini and a few Guardians standing too close to the edge pitched forward and fell over the side.

"No!" Deb yelled pushing her shield out and reaching for the falling Guardians in her mind.

"It's too late, Deb." Frankie pulled her back from the side. "Vincenzo's gone. You can't save them, but you can save all the others still up here."

Deb's powers reacted. She envisioned a wall of giant fans blowing the noxious gas away from heaven's side of the ridge. Wind swirled past her picking up speed and blew out across the open expanse. Deb's hair blew outward around her face, but it didn't matter, her eyes were closed. She fixated on pushing the toxic fumes away.

"It's working," Gen yelled. "The gargoyles are momentarily retreating. We should restock while we can. They'll be back."

Gen and Dan ran toward the stockpile of arrows. Several Guardians were already doing the same and reloading their quivers.

Greg and Tom teleported over. They consolidated the holy oil. When Gen returned, Greg handed her a different crossbow.

"This holds three arrows inside," Greg explained. "One in the chamber, two below. The arrows have been soaked in holy oil. Just before shooting, ignite the arrow by clicking the red button. When you shoot, the arrow should come out enflamed. The only caveat is that you only have seconds to shoot once you click the red button. Otherwise, the arrow will melt the device and probably explode in your hands."

"Got it." Gen repositioned herself behind a nearby boulder and set the crossbow up on a stand. Once attached Gen could swivel freely to take out gargoyles from any direction.

Greg hauled the arrows in a large duffel bag leaving them on the ground to the left of Gen's position.

"The air is clear," Frankie said. "You can take a break Deb. Everyone is back in position."

Deb dropped her arms. "How many more hell fighters?"

"The few that remained ran back toward the portal." Tom pointed. "They were shot and killed by the vampires before they could escape."

"I don't understand the rationale there." Deb took a cup of water Frankie held out for her.

"Kelce has no loyalty to anything in hell," Dan said.

"Look." Greg pointed. "Azza and Wrath are yelling at Kelce."

"I bet Azza and Wrath were not let in on Kelce's strategic planning," Tom commented.

"No." Deb walked to the edge. "If the hell fighters belong in Harac's realm, this is a problem for Azza."

"What do you mean?" Frankie asked.

"Azza *borrowed*." Deb's hands formed an air quote to accentuate the word, "a hellcrux from Harac. If he gave her the hell fighters too, and Kelce just murdered them. Harac is going to be more than a little upset about losing his greatest weapon against heaven."

"Wait." Gen stepped away from the scope. "We just found out what the vampires were."

"Yes," Dan confirmed. "What are you thinking?"

"We didn't know what the vampires were before today," Gen repeated. "What if Azza didn't either?"

"Meaning she didn't realize the vampires were fallen angels?" Deb asked.

"Correct," Gen confirmed. "If Kelce ordered the hell fighters to be killed, perhaps that venom is poisonous to the vampires too."

"That would make sense," Frankie stated. "If Kelce's ultimate agenda is to help himself and not Azza, then he would want to leave hell as few weapons against vampires as possible."

"He's looking past us," Gen said. "He doesn't think we're a threat. He probably doesn't even realize the Guardians he's facing off against aren't all from the Pit."

"No reason for him to think that," Tom said. "Michael has us up here partly to hide that fact."

"There are no Arch Angels here either," Dan added. "Kelce is doing this for the element of surprise, and he probably believes it's working."

"The gargoyles are airborne again," Greg warned. "The sun is nearly down. I think it's time for the lights."

Gen went back to peering through the scope. Tom and Greg teleported back to the other end of the cliff. They planted hundreds of lamps along the wall and on the field, all facing toward Kelce. When the vampires march, Tom and Greg were to turn them on. This would obscure Kelce's view of what's in front of him.

Deb walked to the edge. Heaven's repositioned army was barely visible in the dim light below. They were wounded and fatigued but they would fight to the end.

We're out of tricks, Deb thought. Catapults are down. Our ammo is running low. We've lost Vincenzo and countless other heavenly fighters. And all the while hell's first army hasn't even taken the battlefield yet.

Antonio teleported onto the cliff next to Genevieve just at the field was illuminated by the bright lights her brothers had switched on.

"Where are the rest of the Arch Angels?" Deb's palms fell open in exasperation.

"Most are not coming," Antonio announced. "I'm sorry. I was able to convince a dozen or so to help me, but that's it."

"What?!" Gen shrieked. "What do you mean?"

Arch Angels flew through the air, temporarily distracting the gargoyles that were aiming for the cliffside. Tom and Greg teleported back.

"Kelce just got a glimpse of the Arch Angels overhead," Greg relayed.

"Where is the rest of the army?" Tom asked.

"They're not coming." Deb's eyes watered. "It doesn't matter why. We don't have the numbers."

The O'Mara family walked to the cliffside as Kelce emerged onto the battlefield leading his army.

"This is it. Our final stand." Deb paused. "If we fall, so does Earth and maybe even heaven itself."

Harry gathered the Guardians who remained on the cliffside and brought them to Antonio.

Harry held his hands up to Deb and Gen. "I know it looks bad."

"It doesn't just look bad, Harry," Gen said. "This is bad."

"When all hope seems lost, what do we lean on?" Harry asked.

"We have faith." Deb ran over to the black bag Vincenzo brought with him.

"Everyone, take one of these rods," Deb explained. "Kelly had Vincenzo forge them. They are the perfect weight and length to kill vampires. Aim for the ear and don't stop until the sharp end pierces the brain."

Deb carried the bag around until everyone had a weapon, including Harry.

"We teleport down and join forces." Deb stood next to her siblings.

God help us, Deb pleaded silently. *We're going to need it.*

Thunder rolled through the clouds and lightning crackled. The whooping noise ringing through the air was akin to a hundred helicopters descending.

"What is that?!" Gen yelled.

Please God, Deb prayed. *Don't let it be another creature pulled from the depths of hell.*

CHAPTER THIRTY-ONE

Kelly was swarmed by hordes of Arch Angels pledging to fight. She thanked them and made her way down onto the ground and over to May and Sam.

"That was some rallying speech," May said. "When are we leaving?"

"Now," Kelly urged. "Have them gather their weapons, we need to teleport to the Pit, assuming we can.

"We can," Sam answered. "Do you know where it is?"

"No," Kelly answered. "I'll definitely need a ride and a few weapons wouldn't hurt either."

"Can you at least tell us what we're up against?" May stared at Kelly concerned.

"Hell's first army," Kelly retorted. "I don't know how many there are, probably too many to count."

"Okay, okay." May raised her hands in the air. "We need holy fire, and lots of it."

"I've got that covered." Kelly smiled.

May ordered the Arch Angels to gather their gear. The field descended into an orderly fervor of activity as heaven's army readied for battle.

"Are you okay?" Sam asked. "You look a little like the cat that ate the canary."

"Someday soon," Kelly pledged. "I'll explain everything, my friend. For now, what happened when Antonio came here?"

"Walk with me." Sam snaked her way through the sea of Arch Angels hauling weapons out of the old barn. "When May and I returned from the exorcism, we told the others about what Antonio did to you. What the magistrate ordered him to do to you and your family."

"Ahh." Kelly inhaled sharply. "I'm guessing that did not go over well."

Sam leaned down and opened a crate just inside the barn entryway. Pulling out small handheld spears, she handed one to Kelly.

Kelly flipped the rod over in her hands. "This is perfect for killing vampires."

"Yeah, we know." Sam smiled. "Vincenzo told us how you made them. We figured these were sharper at the end for faster penetration."

Kelly chuckled. "Word travels fast."

"Anyway." Sam returned to the story. "We took a vote. We've never done that before, but it seemed only fair that the Arch Angels have a say in who they follow."

"The result?" Kelly waited.

"Before we had the chance to tell Antonio," Sam answered. "The magistrate was murdered. As next in line Antonio was automatically made acting magistrate."

"I assume that didn't help matters." Kelly took the bag Sam held out for her.

The beautiful blonde pulled her hair back into a tight bun. "Not well at all. Everyone felt their vote was rendered meaningless by his promotion."

"I can understand that." Kelly zipped the bag closed and hoisted it over her shoulder. The weapons inside clanged against one another.

"Then," Samantha continued. "Antonio showed up tonight unexpectedly. Pulls dozens of nearby Arch Angels to this barn. Claims the Pit is empty. Can you believe that? Hell pulled their armies off the field."

May had rejoined them for the end of Samantha's statement. "You know what that means, don't you?"

"I know how my brother Michael would have taken it." Kelly let out a deep breath. "He would have assumed Kelce was resupplying and repositioning his armies for war."

War. The word sat heavy in Kelly's chest. *My family's at war with General Kelce in the Pit. I need to get moving.*

"He'd be right," May confirmed. "After we rejected Antonio's plea, he was furious and tried to command us to help him. We stood firm, told him we stripped him of his command. We would not follow him in battle."

"Wow," Kelly blurted. "That is intense and a little rebellious."

"We felt we weren't being heard," Sam insisted.

"We sent someone to the Pit after Antonio left," May added. "He was telling the truth. Heaven and humanity really are in danger. So we voted on whether to go or stay out of it."

"That's what you were about to do when I showed up?" Kelly pointed at the barn. "You were about to vote on whether to join the fight?"

"No." May smirked. "We already voted. We were arguing about who would lead us when you showed up. I suggested an O'Mara, but some among us disagreed. After what Deb's done you can't fault them for having reservations. Hence the heckling when you arrived."

Kelly nodded. "I told them what they needed to hear."

"More importantly," May said. "They needed to hear it from *you*."

"I loved the speech." Sam wrapped an arm around Kelly's shoulders.

"I don't know as I'd give up your day job or anything," May mocked playfully.

"I won't," Kelly answered. "I promise."

"Good," May answered. "Because right now your family needs your badass self to show up and kick butt with us."

"And we found our leader," Sam said.

"Wait." Kelly felt the gravity of the last statement. "You mean me?"

"Yes," Sam and May said in unison.

"When you said *an O'Mara* I assumed you meant Michael."

"No." Sam shook her head. "Michael isn't one of us."

"Michael hasn't fought alongside us," May added. "He hasn't bled with us. You have."

"I'm humbled." Kelly stood tall. "And I'm ready."

"Not dressed like that you aren't," May told her. "Put on your fatigues. You're leading this army onto the battlefield."

Kelly ran back into the barn and changed into the Arch Angel uniform of blue fatigues and a navy blue long sleeved cotton shirt. Sam found her a pair of black combat boots and made quick work of lacing them up.

"May has everyone briefed and ready to go," Sam said.

Kelly walked out of the barn to a battalion of Arch Angels. There were hundreds of angels poised and ready to take flight.

"Wow!" Kelly shook her head at their sheer numbers. "That was fast."

"Ready!" May yelled from her position in front of the barn.

The Arch Angels smashed their swords against their shields in response. The clanging of metal on metal reverberated through Kelly's chest.

May and Samantha turned toward Kelly.

"We're awaiting your command." May nodded at Kelly.

Kelly took a deep breath and replied, "Let's go kick some demon ass!"

The Arch Angels roared in response as they took flight, their wine-colored wings flapping in harmony. Sam grasped Kelly's shoulder and teleported the two of them from the yard.

Kelly left the ground in a swirl of heavenly white light.

Hold on, Kelly pleaded silently to her family. *If you can hear me, we're coming.*

***

Kelly's feet landed on a grassy surface next to a lake. It was peaceful, nothing like what she believed she would encounter.

"The Arch Angels will make entry over the ridge line there." Sam pointed north.

Kelly squinted. Two figures were running back and forth several hundred yards away.

"I think those are my sisters," Kelly announced.

Closing her eyes Kelly attempted to reach them telepathically.

"Don't bother," Sam told her. "Telepathy will be intermittent at best now that Kelce has taken the field."

Sam unsheathed her sword and unfurled her wings. Kelly was about to teleport to the cliffside when a thunderous roar came from above. A moment later, Kelly's sisters teleported away.

"Wait." Kelly's mind raced. "Where did they go?"

"Down to the Pit itself I imagine," Sam said. "Ready? We're going straight onto the floor and into battle."

"Yeah," Kelly grasped the strap of the bag she brought with her. "Bring me to the fight."

Within seconds of teleporting, the roar of battle flooded her ears. Sam dropped Kelly ahead of heaven's front line and two hundred yards from the vampires charging toward them.

The field was stained purple from a mix of blood and the blue essence ripped from the gutter demons. The ground was singed, and fire still burned on both sides of the long rectangular battlefield. The dead lay scattered and Hell Fire venom drifted in the air even though no hell fighters could be seen.

The sky above crackled with sparks of light and smears of pastel color. The Arch Angels arriving created a beautiful kaleidoscope above the blackened hellish landscape below. The angels engaged the gargoyles, quickly overwhelming the winged creatures and obliterating hell's air superiority.

The sheer number of Arch Angel warriors all in battle formation had not been seen since the first war more than a thousand years ago. The shock and awe of the sight caused the thousands of gutter demons still on the field to retreat. They chose to flee back to their desolate wasteland rather than meet certain death.

Sam and May landed on either side of Kelly.

Kelce slowed his pace and stopped a few hundred feet from their position ignoring the fleeing gutter demons. He swore at the hundreds of angels hovering in the sky. Turning he yelled at this troops and they unsheathed their falchions preparing for battle.

"You wanted a war!" Kelly screamed at Kelce who leered at her in disgust. "Now you've got one!"

Kelly sprinted forward, May and Sam kept stride. The warriors behind her hollered out their battle cries, their swords clanging against one another. The ground thundered as they too followed Kelly into battle.

Vampires flooded in front of General Kelce. He stayed protected behind his front lines. Kelly clashed with a male vampire. He raised his falchion above his head with both hands preparing to thrust it down upon her head. Kelly kicked him in the chest knocking him on his back. Jumping on top of him she said nothing. Stabbing the spear into his ear the vampire was killed instantly.

The clash of bodies meant you couldn't see more than a few feet in front of you. Grunts and labored breathing rode through the air like a wave. Every few seconds a vampire screeched as they were slaughtered with the pipe weapon. Dirt, decay, and burning embers floated through the air.

Back on her feet, Kelly swung the pipe end of her weapon against the head of a female vampire. The female swayed. Kelly kicked her left knee bringing her to the ground. Twirling the weapon Kelly thrust it into the vampire's ear before she had time to react. The screams of death escaped her mouth as blood seeped from her nose and eyes.

Pushing up an incline of the dead created in the middle of the field, Kelly took a moment to search for her family. The mash of colliding bodies was too thick to locate them. Turning left, she spotted a familiar warrior with a crew cut and three-day old beard.

Jared, Kelly's heart leapt.

Pushing toward him, Kelly bashed a vampire from behind. Brought to his knees Sam stabbed him in the ear before Kelly could. Jared killed the female vampire he was locked in combat with. Their eyes met.

"Woman!" he yelled in Kelly's direction. "I knew you were trouble!"

Kelly leapt over a wounded vampire on the ground and flew into Jared's arms nearly knocking him to the ground.

"Stay alive." She placed both hands on either side of Jared's face. "You die and I'm coming to haul your ass out of heaven."

"No doubt." They broke apart to fight the next onslaught.

A male vampire punched Kelly in the face with the handle of a falchion. Her head snapped back, and blood trickled from her mouth.

As he pulled back to slice with his sword, she kicked his left knee. Wailing at the unnatural crack Kelly swung the pipe like a club. When he fell to one knee an arrow entered his head and killed him.

Sweat made the shirt Kelly was wearing stick to her body. Her mouth was dry, the coppery taste of blood lined her mouth, but she kept going.

In time, the line thinned. Between the mass of violent struggle, Antonio wrestled a gargoyle to the ground. Fire escaped the beast's mouth and ignited more of the dead. Kelly battled her way toward Antonio, Deb faced off against Sky.

Her sister's hair barely covered her scalp. She had lost weight but fought valiantly. Sky sliced Deb's shoulder. Kelly nearly yelped at the site. Deb kicked Sky back, raised the female vampire high off the ground with her shield, and thrust her to the ground.

Grabbing the pipe Deb stabbed Sky several times in the ear. The female vampire who had terrorized Jade and hunted Deb screamed. Deb smashed the weapon further into Sky's skull, killing her.

Bodies were piling atop bodies, the scene devolving into violent chaos. Arch Angels scooped the vampires off the ground and tossed them into a pool of hell fire. The vampire's cries of terror made some of their ranks retreat. Kelly made it through the lines, Antonio spotted her and took a single step in her direction. A blade burst through the Arch Angel's chest bringing him to his knees.

"No!" Kelly screamed as she raced to get to the Arch Angel. Azza ripped the blade from his back and teleported away from him before Kelly could reach her. Antonio slumped forward, Kelly caught him and cradled him in her arms.

"Antonio." Tears burst from Kelly's eyes.

"It's okay..." Antonio coughed on his words, blood splattering her clothes.

"No." Kelly leaned her head down on top of his and rocked his limp body back and forth.

"I'm glad it's you," Antonio whispered.

"Antonio, I'm sorry," Kelly cried. "I understand now, and you didn't take my memories, merely buried them. I remember now. I remember."

"I'm ready." Antonio grabbed her arm and squeezed. "I'm ready to go home... and be with Christian."

"Antonio, no," Kelly wailed. "This can't be how it ends. Forgive my behavior at the house. I wasn't ready to hear you out. But I am now, please stay. I accept your apology."

"Thank you..." Antonio struggled to speak. "...my friend."

Those were the last words the Arch Angel spoke. Kelly screamed at the heavens and buried her face against his warm cheek.

Deb reached her first. "Where's the wound, Kelly?"

Kelly lifted her head just as Gen ran up alongside Deb. The three of them used their powers, but it was too late, the Arch Angel had died in Kelly's arms.

Michael reached down and pulled Kelly up and into his arms. She sobbed into her big brother's chest. The Arch Angels formed a circle around the small group. They kept the vampires at bay while Kelly pulled herself together.

Fear isn't the only thing that hides in dark places. Kelly agonized. *Vengeance does too, and when you're low, it beckons. A sirens song to slaughter.*

"We need to end this." Kelly wiped the tears from her face.

"How?" Michael asked.

"Azza," Kelly said. "It will take all three of our powers. We need to do this, together."

"I can bring her back here," Deb said.

"I can break her," Gen added.

"I will end her and her reign of terror," Kelly said.

Sam pointed to the far end of the valley. "There she is."

Deb sent her shield out. Wrapping it around Azza's body she yanked her across the field. Azza screamed. Wrath grabbed her from behind trying to keep her grounded, but it was no use. Deb's power dragged the two of them forward. Wrath let go and fell to the ground. Azza flailed as she spiraled through the bloodied dirt and over the dead bodies of the fallen. Deb brought her right to Kelly's feet.

Panting and crying, Azza got back on her feet and unsheathed a dagger. Her eyes flew between the O'Mara sisters.

"He deserved what he got!" Azza screamed. "You all do. I will have my vengeance!"

"No," Kelly defiantly stated. "You won't."

"This is for Marcus," Deb said as her shield lifted Azza off the ground.

"This is for Xavier," Gen added as her power thrust the fallen angel's arms apart and broke her wrists.

Azza screeched. Her eyes filled with terror as she could no longer hold her weapon and it fell to the ground below.

Kelly held out her palm, fire exploded into a shining ball of light in her hand. The crowd halted and audible gasps erupted all around them.

"This is for me." Kelly forced the fireball forward hitting Azza in the chest with it.

The fallen angel's body ignited and became engulfed. Her shrieks of agony bellowed over the hundreds of entities on the field.

Deb let the fire-ravaged corpse fall to the ground.

"It's over," Kelly yelled toward Kelce. "You cannot win. Lay down your weapons and leave this field."

"No!" General Kelce yelled.

A cold wind whipped through the valley. The bodies of the dead were pulled away disappearing into a dense fog behind the vampires.

Wrath crawled away seemingly trying to hide from whatever was coming. The Arch Angels flew into the air and positioned themselves in attack formation. Gen and Deb pulled Kelly away from the mounds of the dead as they disintegrated. Their ashes rolled like tumble weeds into the massive storm cloud brewing on the opposite end of the field.

The bodies buried in the trench were engulfed in flame and pulled toward the swirling blackness. The ground rumbled as the crack Gen had opened re-sealed.

The vampires dropped their falchions. Some tried to run back toward the portal, but it was too late. The portal closed and out from the blackened storm cloud stepped Abaddon, the angel of death.

The gasps fell to silence as the form Kelly came to know as Sunny marched forward.

Abaddon stopped in front of General Kelce. "You know who I am and the power I hold. You have three choices."

"One." Abaddon pointed to a large portal he summoned to their right. "You can leave this field and return to the life you've led for the last thousand years on Earth."

Abaddon paused to let the first option sink in. "Two. You can step through the gates of hell, but I'll be sealing them, and no Hellcrux will open them again until the end of days."

General Kelce brazenly took a step in Abaddon's direction. "And number three?"

"I can bring you home." The words hung heavy

in the air.

"That isn't how I want to return home!" Kelce yelled. "We were right, all this time and we were right. Humans do not deserve this world. Look at what they have wrought onto themselves."

"Choose now, General," Abaddon warned. "Or I will choose for you."

As the swirling fog in the distance faded, a thousand reapers stood at the base of the valley ahead. Male and female entities standing more than six feet tall, wearing all black and carrying Coptic crosses. Heaven's warriors involuntarily took several steps back. Gen pulled at Kelly's arm.

"It's okay," Kelly told her. "You have nothing to be afraid of. They aren't here for us."

Dozens of vampires walked through the portal leading back to Earth. Scores of vampires dropped their weapons and willingly approached the stoic figures in black. As the vampires reached the reapers' position, they simply vaporized and disappeared.

"I refuse to return to a God who won't admit when he's wrong." Kelce stood firm and others stepped forward to join him.

"General Kelce, you and the remaining army have made your choice." Abaddon raised his hand. Kelce and his followers were sucked into a portal below their feet. The vampires screamed as they were swallowed by the abyss.

Jade and her siblings teleported down onto the cleared field next to Abaddon. Wrath was all that was left on hell's side of the millennia's old battleground.

"Kelly," Abaddon called. "Please bring me Azza's ring."

Using a sword, Kelly shuffled through the charred ground until the shiny silver band glistened against the dusty background.

Kelly held the ring out to Abaddon, but he shook his head.

"The ring needs to be cleansed in holy fire," he said simply. "As hot as you can bear."

Kelly placed the ring in the palm of her hand, focused, and set it ablaze. The flame shot six inches into the air encompassing her entire hand. She soon let the fire dwindle until it became small enough for her to snuff it out with a closed fist. When Kelly opened her hand, the ring had turned to ash. Tilting her hand, Kelly let the particles fall to the ground.

"The power of the deadly sins is now properly restored," Abaddon announced. "My time here is done, but you and your family have many years ahead. Hundreds of chapters yet to be written."

Facing Wrath, the angel of death shot him a warning. "You may be immortal, but what has been granted can always be revoked." Wrath cowered, like a snake he slithered a few steps backward.

Jade's siblings grabbed hold of Wrath and teleported away with their brother.

Deb approached Jade. "Fully restored powers, congratulations."

Jade's eyes sparkled in the bright lights still

humming along the far wall.

"Thank you, darling." Jade enveloped Deb in a tight embrace. "Let's go shopping soon. And you." Jade winked at Kelly. "Come and see me before the wedding. I throw a smashing bachelorette party."

Kelly hugged her family and told them she would meet them at Michael's. She needed to say goodbye to the Arch Angels.

The O'Mara family teleported from the field. Kelly walked to May and Sam.

"Well that was unexpected," Sam said.

"Death showing up," Kelly acknowledged. "Yeah, it was."

"We mean you manifesting holy fire." May crossed her arms in mock anger. "You didn't tell us you could do that."

Kelly laughed. "There's a lot I haven't told you, but I will. I promise."

Sam hugged Kelly. "We'll see you soon I hope."

"You will." Kelly smiled as the angel flew into the air.

May grabbed Kelly's hand and pulled her into a quick embrace. "I expect to see you at the next training session. But you can take a break during your honeymoon."

"Of course," Kelly answered. "I'll be there, you can count on me. We're family."

"We are," May agreed before flying up into the air and leaving with the rest of the Arch Angels.

"You still here, Abaddon?" Kelly asked the now

empty field.

"I am." Abaddon appeared to her left.

"I just wanted to say thank you." Kelly paused before continuing. "But I've got to ask. You have the power, why didn't you stop Azza from the beginning, before she and Wrath killed Jacob, Xavier, and Antonio?"

Abaddon took Kelly's hand in his. "Trials and tribulations forge the characters we all become. Take you for instance. If you hadn't been tortured in hell, and forced to face your fears, you wouldn't have been the leader the Arch Angels needed at this moment."

"So, what you're saying is that everything happens for a reason."

"Something like that, yes."

"So what now for the pit?"

"It can go back to its original purpose." Abaddon began to fade away. "Don't be a stranger to the Vatican library, they miss you over there."

Kelly teleported to the cliffside. The dirt floor below transitioned into a thick carpet of lush green grass.

"Show off." Kelly wrapped herself in her aura and left the field formerly referred to as the Pit.

Remember you are dust, Kelly prayed, *and to dust you shall return.*

CHAPTER THIRTY-TWO

Grasping the wreath Gen made, Deb walked alongside Gardenia heading for the breaker wall. The beach was near empty, cool winds pushed around gray clouds. The earlier rain and dropping temperatures made the late September afternoon raw. The ocean churned. The dark green waters of the bay sloshed against the cement passageway they were walking on. The wreath was made of ivy and covered in white roses, baby's breath, and lilies. It was a beautiful tribute to honor Marcus' life and legacy. Leo and Lucas stood off to her right. Harry, Gerry, and Lacey off to the left. Further down the beach, Dmitri stood alone wearing a three-piece suit.

The mood was somber, Gardenia's tears fell freely. After some brief prayers by Harry and a moving rendition of "Ava Maria" by Lacey, the service concluded. Deb and Gardenia locked arms and moved down the plank toward the end of the dock to drop the homemade wreath.

Gardenia huddled against Deb when they neared the edge. Bending down, Deb leaned over and tossed the wreath onto the water. Using her shield, Deb ensured no one would see any of it and guided the wreath out to the open sea.

"I don't know what to say," Gardenia mumbled.

"You don't have to say anything." Deb put her hand over Gardenia's. "You can speak to him anytime you want. He's always with you."

"I just miss him so much." Gardenia sniffled. "He was the first one to ever pay attention to me, to really care about me in this crazy place."

"He was an exceptional listener," Deb added. "He always made whoever he was interacting with feel like they had his complete attention."

"I feel guilty sometimes," Gardenia admitted.

"Why?" Deb asked as she handed her a clean tissue.

"Because of him." Gardenia wiped her eyes. "I have Gerry and Lacey. Not to mention Harry, you, and all your family. Even Leo and Lucas check in on me."

"I'm not usually one to tell people how they should feel." Deb paused as some of the lilies came loose and trailed the large wreath. "But in this case, I know Marcus would not want you to feel guilty. He would be incredibly happy you found all these folks who love and care about you."

The two of them said their final goodbyes and made their way back down toward the small crowd waiting for them. After several hugs and promises to meet up again, Leo and Lucas left. Gerry and Lacey walked with Gardenia along the waterfront before heading back home. The three of them now living together, a chosen family.

Harry grabbed Deb's hand. "Come see me anytime."

"You know I will, Harry."

"Now go talk to that fella down on the beach waiting for you." Harry winked.

Harry left the waterfront and Deb teleported down to Dmitri.

"How are you?" he asked, "I didn't want to intrude, I figured you might want some company after."

"Thank you for coming." Deb grasped his arm. "It means a lot."

"I don't see Gen and Kelly?"

"They came here with me last night. It was nice just the three of us."

"Thick as thieves the three of you have become." Dmitri smiled. "It's nice to see,"

"Yeah." Deb smiled. "I know we haven't had much time to talk."

"You don't owe me anything, Deb."

"I know." Deb paused fighting back the tears. "The ring Marcus gave me didn't bind. I know he wasn't the one. Harry says I may have transferred some of the emotions for you over onto Marcus. Side effect of suppressing memories I guess."

"Are you remembering things now?"

"Some." Deb's eyes spanned the beach. "I may never get all my memories back, but if you're willing, I wonder if we might start over."

"Well." Dmitri sighed. "As it turns out, I'll be sticking around a while. Seems heaven doesn't know where to place a former collector with forty years of service in the Pit."

"Perfect." Deb beamed up at him. "Let's start with tea."

"And a blueberry scone."

"And a blueberry scone for sure."

CHAPTER THIRTY-THREE

Kelly sat on the front porch of Michael's house basking in the late May sunshine. Gen had kicked all the males out of the house on Friday and ordered them not to return until the wedding this afternoon.

"Are you recovered yet?" Deb asked as she brought Kelly a fresh cup of coffee.

"All I can say is that Jade did not disappoint." Kelly sighed. "Good decision to go to London last weekend, Deb. If we went out with her last night. There might have been a real possibility of me being drunk for my own wedding."

"I don't think I ever danced as much as I did Saturday night," Gen added.

"Me neither." Kelly laughed. "I'm exhausted just thinking about it."

"There's a delivery truck coming down the driveway." Deb shielded her eyes from the sun as she stood at the railing.

"Must be a mistake," Gen commented. "I can't imagine Michael having anything delivered out here."

Changing into human form, Kelly went inside and waited for the driver to ring the bell before opening the door. The house was filled with the perfume of fresh roses and lilacs. Deb teleported to Boston that morning for fresh flowers for the wedding. Once the truck was clear of the property Kelly changed out of human view and re-joined her sisters on the porch, bringing the package with her.

"It's for me!" Kelly announced.

Sitting on the cushioned bench Kelly tore through the package pulling out a white box. She opened it and peeled back the tissue paper to reveal a white cotton dress.

Standing Kelly held the dress up in front of her. Spanning down the decorative cutouts along the top and bottom of the dress she spotted the purple nail polish on her toes.

"Oh my." Kelly sighed softly.

"What is it?" Gen asked. "Who sent it?"

There was a card at the bottom of the box, Kelly opened it. Inside was a short note wishing her and Jared many years of happiness.

"Well?" Gen's voice a tick higher than normal. "Don't keep us in suspense."

"I know this is going to sound crazy." Kelly sat back down.

"Oh boy," Gen whispered.

"A few years ago." Kelly paused trying to pull the date forward. "I went shopping and I found this pretty, white cotton dress. I thought it would be perfect for an outdoor wedding. I brought it home and tried it on. I decided right then and there it would be my wedding dress. I wrapped it up and stored it in the closet."

"The closet in Gen's house?" Deb asked.

"Yes," Kelly said emphatically.

"Are you saying that's the same dress?" Gen asked.

"It is." Kelly stood once more examining the dress. She turned it front to back. "That's what I'm saying."

"And the card?" Gen asked.

"It's signed with the letter *A*."

Gen picked up the card and read it as Deb peeked over her shoulder.

"*A* as in?" Gen hung the sentence out there.

"Abaddon." Kelly turned toward the front door. "Let's head inside. We have a new wedding dress to press!"

Thanks for bringing the dress back to me, Kelly thought. *Someway, somehow, I know you can hear me.*

***

Standing on the porch smiling at the crowd filling up the yard, Gen thought of how full her life was and smiled.

It's amazing we're able to stand here today and celebrate. Gen thought. So much heartache, but so much joy too. I *wish you were here Xav, you would have had so much fun hanging with this many Arch Angels.*

The yard was set up with hundreds of chairs and a flower-covered aisle down the middle. At the end, sat a wrought iron arch draped in purple and white roses. The hustle and bustle of the crowd drowned out the soft music playing in the background. It was a perfect spring day. The sun was shining, and yellow and blue cornflower exploded across the grounds, the wildflowers transformed the hilly landscape.

The screen door pushed open and snapped shut. Harry came out to find Gen.

"It's nearly time," he told her. "Deb and Kelly are ready, how about you?"

"I'm ready." Gen turned and grabbed the arm Harry held out for her. "I heard they picked a new magistrate."

"They did indeed." Harry placed his hand over hers. "And I named my replacement."

"It's you, Harry!" Gen stopped. "Congratulations. I mean I'll miss you, we all will. Who's your replacement?"

"You are." Harry smiled. "There is no one else I trust more with my Charges."

"Oh Harry." Gen hugged the angel who had been by her side for nearly forty years. "I'm honored. I hope I make you proud."

"No doubt you will," Harry told her. "I have one more thing for you, for all of you."

Gen tilted her head. "What is it?"

Harry turned back and held his arm out, a cloudy white portal appeared and through it walked Xavier. He wore tan pants and a crisp white dress shirt. His hair was neatly cropped and combed. His hazel-colored eyes sparkled when they met hers.

Gen let out a crying gasp. The crowd's eyes turn in her direction. Smiling Xavier walked over and wrapped Gen in a warm embrace.

Stepping back Gen said, "I've missed you. I have so much to tell you."

"We have all night." Xavier spread his arms wide.

Their brothers came running over to reunite with Xavier while Harry took his position at the front of the aisle.

Gabriel slipped his arm around Gen's waist. "That's the best wedding present I think I've ever seen."

Leaning into her husband's shoulder she sighed. "Yes. Yes, it is."

"Shall we join them." Gabriel pulled his arm back and grabbed Gen's hand.

"You know, we're going to need a much bigger kitchen in our next house," Gen said.

"Why is that? Gabe asked.

Gen smiled. "To fit our growing family."

THANK YOU

I appreciate you reading my Heaven Sent trilogy. Your support means so much to me.

The idea for book one in the series came to me when I dreamt of the character Gabriel. I decided I would write his story through the lens of his wife who had been searching for him for forty years. Once I formulated that idea, I needed a large cast of characters to navigate what would become a vast and treacherous supernatural backdrop. The O'Mara family grew out of my desire to name the characters after my nine real-life nieces and nephews. Though that was challenging for many reasons, I am thankful to be able to honor family in this way.

Visit my website at www.JLROTHSTEIN.com and subscribe to my newsletter for information on upcoming events, new releases, and access to free content not available to the public. If you enjoyed the series, please consider leaving a review.

Happy reading,
JL Rothstein

ABOUT THE AUTHOR

JL Rothstein lives in western Massachusetts with her husband and their two cats Brady and Mr. Thumbs. Jennifer is a business professional pursuing her MFA in Creative Writing. Vengeance is book three in the Heaven Sent Series.

Visit her online at www.JLRothstein.com or via social media on facebook.com/authorjlrothstein. Follow her on Twitter & Instagram @jlrothstein1.

www.ingramcontent.com/pod-product-compliance
Lightning Source LLC
Chambersburg PA
CBHW050855210726
48290CB00004B/1236